Jove titles by Bridget Morrissey

LOVE SCENES

A THOUSAND MILES

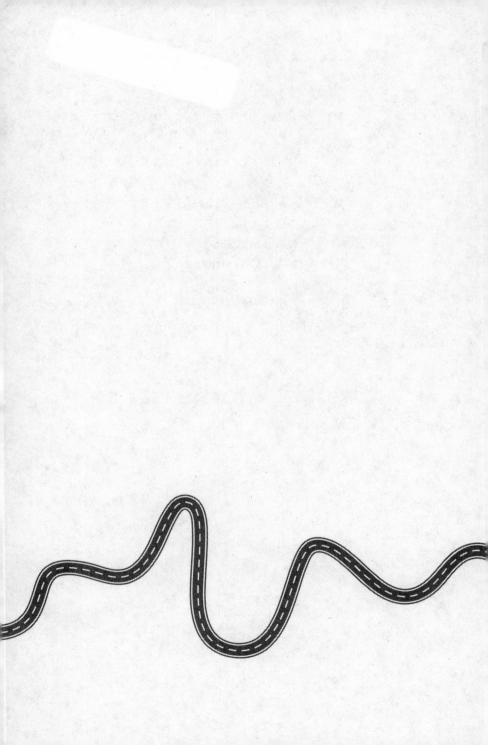

PRAIS[E]

LOVE SCENES

"An endearing and entertaining read, *Love Scenes* is the romance all lovers of Hollywood need."   —Shondaland

"Morrissey's sarcastically humorous voice shines in her debut contemporary romance and her characters (including Sloane's big, beautiful family) will absolutely charm the pants off you."
—BuzzFeed

"Real, raw, and immensely tender, *Love Scenes* is a book about second chances: in love, in work, in family. Bridget Morrissey writes with the kind of effortless warmth and complexity that elevates characters to real people you know and love, with quirks and flaws you understand."
—Emily Henry, #1 *New York Times* bestselling author of
People We Meet on Vacation

"*Love Scenes* is pure joy from start to finish. With Hollywood antics, a simmering slow-burn romance, and a tremendous amount of humor and heart, this book makes even its most famous characters feel like friends. A love letter to the messy, wild, wonderful families who make us who we are."
—Rachel Lynn Solomon, author of *The Ex Talk*

"*Love Scenes* is an enemies to lovers story set against a Hollywood backdrop, but it's so much more than that. It's the messy love of a complicated blended family. It's the ugly parts of Hollywood, not just the glitz and glamour. It's a heroine fighting to be her own person despite what the gossip sites and a songwriting ex-boyfriend say. It's an earnest, swoonworthy hero doing his best to be a good man, despite his past. Bridget Morrissey has a voice that leaps off the page and invites you to join her for a page-turning good time. Good luck putting this one down!"

—Jen DeLuca, author of *Well Played*

"A fascinating peek at the on-set lives of movie stars. Nuanced characterization and an endearing ensemble cast make this one a must-read!" —Michelle Hazen, author of *Breathe the Sky*

"Morrissey is at her best when she allows Sloane's musings to shed light on the caprices of the entertainment industry. Even as Sloane's bond with Joseph develops with charming ease, her evolving relationships with a diverse array of relatives illuminate the many peculiarities inherent to understanding, accepting, and loving family. A compelling and unique riff on the potential of second chances in love." —*Kirkus Reviews*

A THOUSAND MILES

Bridget Morrissey

JOVE
NEW YORK

A JOVE BOOK
Published by Berkley
An imprint of Penguin Random House LLC
penguinrandomhouse.com

Library of Congress Cataloging-in-Publication Data

Names: Morrissey, Bridget, author.
Title: A thousand miles / Bridget Morrissey.
Description: First Edition. | New York: Jove, 2022.
Identifiers: LCCN 2021061103 (print) | LCCN 2021061104 (ebook) |
ISBN 9780593201176 (trade paperback) | ISBN 9780593201183 (ebook)
Classification: LCC PS3613.O7769 T48 2022 (print) |
LCC PS3613.O7769 (ebook) | DDC 813/.6—dc23
LC record available at https://lccn.loc.gov/2021061103
LC ebook record available at https://lccn.loc.gov/2021061104

First Edition: June 2022

Printed in the United States of America
1st Printing

Book design by Tiffany Estreicher

To all the roads that led me here.
I remember every mile.

A THOUSAND MILES

ILLINOIS

1

DEE

It's very hard to break up with someone you were never really dating. Which is why a man named Garrett I met three weeks ago on an app is currently crying in my bathroom.

He doesn't know I saw the tears. It would probably embarrass him if I mention it, so I am sitting on my couch reading listener emails while I wait for him to finish up, wondering if I should put on a movie or put him out of his misery and suggest he leave.

My extremely nonchalant request that I "take a little more time for myself" was met with the classic "that makes sense" from him—a veteran move that made me entirely too comfortable with the whole process. I skipped right past the usual assurances: what a fun three weeks we've had, how great it's been to get to know someone new after a recent rough patch. We've been having sex in my apartment and sometimes ordering delivery. I've never even tagged him in an Instagram story. I truly thought he understood what was going on with us.

We have a similar dry humor. It's how we connected in the first place. But tonight, for the first time ever, we went out to dinner together. He was so rude to the server in the name of being snarky that I thought I might walk myself straight to Lake

Michigan and take up boat living. In the middle of a rainstorm, no less.

My choice to continue our breakup conversation by saying, "We clearly aren't the kind of people who should ever go out in public," did not land as I'd hoped. He let out a hollow, wounded kind of laugh that made me immediately backpedal, even though what I said was true. In front of an audience of restaurant patrons, our connection had dissolved like cotton candy in water. All that sweetness between us vanished into nothingness. But I dared to call attention to it, and next thing I know he's telling me he has to go to the bathroom, and tears are rimming his eyes.

He doesn't even have my number saved! Just three days ago, I texted him a meme while he was taking a shower, and from my nightstand I saw my full ten-digit phone number flash up on his screen. How could he not feel the straining awkwardness throughout our meal tonight? Is it really possible that my empty *yeah*s and colorless *wow*s came off as anything other than detached? It's all so absurd it makes me cackle. By the time he's back in my living room—tears dry and brow furrowed—I am laughing louder than the thunder that booms outside.

"What did I miss?" he asks.

Everything, Garrett. You missed everything.

"What's my last name?" I prompt.

"Um . . ."

"Do you know my job?"

"You record a podcast or something."

"How many siblings do I have?"

"I don't know."

"Your name is Garrett Matthew Robertson. You work in

finance, in an office near the Hancock building. Your little sister Hannah just graduated from college. Communications degree from DePaul. Send my congrats, by the way."

"Okay, so you're a stalker. Good for you."

There it is. The darkness that always comes out at the first sign of real trouble. A bruise that blooms from whisper-soft pressure. It's amazing how quickly it happens. How little effort it requires on my part.

"I'm a stalker?" I ask.

Predictably, he has no follow-up.

"We've been hooking up for weeks and I follow you online," I continue. "Your full name is in your bio. You post a skyline shot almost every day. I watched part of your sister's commencement ceremony when I accidentally clicked into your graduation livestream."

Garrett glances forlornly at my door. He pushes back the top part of his hair—a truly aspirational sandy blond, if I'm honest—then lets it fall again down his forehead. "Look, this clearly isn't working." He says it with such finality, you'd think it was his idea. If it gets him out of my apartment, he can keep thinking that for the rest of his life.

Still, it's hard to resist a comeback. "Good observation." I give him a thumbs-up.

"Dude, why are you so fucking mean? Like what the fuck?" At once, he gets teary again.

Now I recognize it for what it is: a manipulation tactic. No one gets the upper hand over a handsome man who is crying.

"I'm mean?" I ask, incredulous. "For asking if you know my name?"

"I don't have time for this shit."

He picks up his overnight bag and huffs to my door. He's still wearing his shoes, because no matter how often I ask, he never takes them off right when he enters. It's such an irritating little detail that I almost throw a pillow at him, but he exits too quickly for me to react, slamming my front door shut with an aggressive theatricality my nosy neighbors will certainly register. Add it to their long list of grievances against me.

It devastates me to realize my heart is racing—that Garrett Matthew Robertson the finance bro has gotten any kind of reaction out of me at all. In an effort to release every last ounce of residual adrenaline, I slip off my bra and lean back into my couch, letting the green velvet cushions hug the sides of my face. Not the most orthodox of calming methods, but it gets the job done.

I can't believe I put on nice clothes for this. What a waste of a powder-blue halter jumpsuit and teardrop earrings. I could feel myself overdoing it when I was getting ready. It's been months since I bothered to curl my hair into long copper waves. In spite of every piece of evidence to the contrary, there was a part of me that wanted to believe that Garrett and I had the potential to be something more than hookup buddies.

No choice but to incinerate that part of me to dust!

Three minutes later, he's knocking. He may not know my last name, but it's nice to see he remembers that my apartment door automatically locks and he can't just barge back in and yell, or whatever it is he thinks he needs to do to prove this was all a part of his plan, not mine.

"What do you want?" I call out.

He doesn't answer.

It infuriates me to imagine him waiting for me, ready to unleash a list of grievances he made up on his walk toward the train station. I gave him a chance to go quietly, and he's not taking it. Neighbors be damned. I want a fight.

With as much gusto as possible, I swing my front door open and bark out one loud, aggressive "What?"

It is not Garrett Matthew Robertson the finance bro waiting on the other side.

Instead it is the last person in the world I ever thought I'd see again.

Ben Porter stands in front of me.

It takes me a second to orient myself. Surely this is an alternate reality intersecting with my current one, and Garrett accidentally got swapped for Ben, and soon the ceiling will become the floor and I will learn that we all speak colors and smell numbers.

He has one battered duffel bag slung across his taut midsection and three dark beauty marks dotting his left cheek. Those moles are my very own Orion's Belt, because that's the only constellation I ever bothered to learn, on the only face I've ever cared to memorize.

His eyes are still brown and bashful. His hair is long enough to curl at the ends, soft brown waves ringleted by the rain, contrasting with the new sharpness in his cheeks. A stipple of scruff further accentuates the angles. No more worn-out Chucks and rumpled band shirt. No more baby face. He looks steady. And well aware of how good a drenched navy blue tee looks clinging to his skin.

"A promise is a promise," he whispers, soaking wet and breathless, dripping puddles onto the carpeted hallway of my apartment complex.

My hands lose feeling. My mind insists on running a highlight reel of memories for me, making sure I haven't forgotten that this is a person I've slept with, and dreamt of, and written intensely embarrassing Notes app poetry about that I've already asked my cohost, Javi, to read on our podcast in the event of my untimely demise. Just so Ben would really feel my absence.

Now I feel his presence, and my first instinct is to close the door, lock myself in my bathroom, and stare at myself in the mirror until the pores on my nose upset me for a week straight. But as impulsive as I can be, I am occasionally great at silencing my first instinct and waiting for a better one to emerge.

It turns out in the event of my high school best friend arriving unannounced in the middle of a thunderstorm—after an entire decade of complete silence between us—my second instinct is to intimidate. I fold my arms across my chest, mostly because I am furious at myself for daring to answer while not wearing a bra. Lucky for me, the gesture lends to the steely mood I'm hoping to strike.

"What does that mean? What are you doing here?" My foot taps against the floor as if my time could be better spent looking anywhere but at Ben Porter's face.

If he's expected a kinder greeting from me, he doesn't show it. Instead he smiles. A heartbreaking, earth-shifting, choir-of-angels-singing kind of smile.

"Hi, Dee." He pauses. "It's good to see you too."

At once I'm flooded with the same bone-deep nostalgic longing that makes me open YouTube at three in the morning and watch all the videos we posted together back in the day. I've made all of them private so my listeners don't stumble across them and uncover the one thing I refuse to directly discuss on my show. The first time Ben was ever mentioned while recording, I made Javi bleep out his name in post. Now Ben is known on the podcast as Name Redacted, an infamous, mysterious side character in my otherwise very open-book life.

One of our YouTube videos is ten minutes of us walking around our hometown. We spend the first half coming up with an elaborate undercover identity for our science teacher, Mr. Davis, all while navigating the aftermath of the previous night's snowfall. The video takes a turn when Ben steps into a snow pile that's not sturdily packed, and he ends up chest deep. Instantly, the two of us are nearly heaving we're laughing so hard. I can't grab onto him tight enough to pull him out because my arms are getting a tickle sensation. It's so cold his cheeks are flushed berry red. I set the camera down on another snow pile, and for the rest of the video, all you can see is his face and my back. And the way he's looking at me. It's like I created the universe with my own bare hands.

Here's that very same Ben Porter. And the way he's looking at me right now—it's really not that different from the old clip of us. Even though everything is different. Down to the shade of red in my hair and the city we're in and surely every single thing about our lives.

"Can I come in?" he asks, because I have been standing here waiting for the sky to fall through the roof. "I can explain everything once I'm inside."

"I don't know if I want you to," I accidentally admit.

Ben backs up until he's against the wall across from my door, a trail of rainwater marking his path. He slides down until he's sitting, all the while never breaking eye contact. "I understand. This is a lot."

"Yeah," I say weakly. Leave it to Ben to understate a thing.

"I'll wait here. And if you still feel the same way after an hour, I'll leave."

All those well-practiced talking points I've assured myself I'd launch into immediately if I ever saw him again? I can't remember a single one. In this moment, I truly cannot recall why we haven't spoken or why it is that I'm not supposed to be nice to him. It's a marvel I even know my own name.

Second instincts be damned.

I slam my door shut.

2

BEN

You can do anything for a minute.

That's what Darius says when I join him for his famous 4:30 a.m. running workouts. I should give him a call. Running has always been my least favorite form of exercise. But right now, 9:23 p.m. on a rainy Friday in Chicago, my body seems to think it's in my best interest to get up and do a 5K.

If Darius is right, and I can do anything for a minute, then I have thirty-seven more to go. Sitting and waiting. No matter what my body seems to want, my resolve has to be stronger. Even if she never comes back out. I need to know I stayed here as long as I said I would.

Gam once called me a loose nail. I stick myself out when no one is prepared, snagging things without trying. She meant it to sound like a surprise no one would pick up on when first meeting me. Most of the time, I make myself into whatever I need to be to keep everyone happy. It feels good to make people smile, and it's nice to keep things uncomplicated. Until suddenly I'm getting into my car and driving across state lines to see a girl I haven't spoken to since I was eighteen, and I'm standing in her doorway, sopping wet, saying, *A promise is a promise.*

Five words. After ten years. There's so much more that needs to be said beyond those seven syllables. But I took one look at her face, and the rest seemed unimportant.

Maybe it's better for the both of us if I leave. I only know that I did that once, and I ruined everything. So I have to stay. Minute by minute. I can't give up again.

A promise is a promise, and this time, I intend to follow through.

3

DEE

A little under two minutes left on the clock, I find Ben sitting exactly where I left him.

"I expected the full hour," he tells me, forcing out a laugh. He's still soaking wet. His teeth are chattering.

"Well? Are you going to get up?"

I make the brave decision to saunter out of his view, like it doesn't matter to me whether he follows me inside, though my thoughts are screaming, BEN PORTER IS IN MY HALLWAY AND NOW THAT I AM WEARING A BRA I ACTUALLY KNOW I LOOK GREAT AND THAT IS EXTREMELY SATISFYING AND ALSO DEEPLY OVERWHELMING.

By the time I turn around, Ben has placed his shoes beside the slippers I keep at the door. The gesture hurls me back through time, the brick walls of my lofted apartment morphing into the chipped paint of my mom's front room. I want this to feel awkward, but it feels more like home, seeing proof Ben Porter is inhabiting the same space as me again.

"I'm sorry. I'm still dripping all over," he says as a well-timed water droplet splashes onto the hardwood.

Wordlessly, I hurry down the hall to grab him a towel.

All of my arguments have come back to me within the last

hour. I'm just not sure I'm ready to initiate any of them. Even though I firmly believe we all have a right to stay mad about things that happened to us in high school—there's no such thing as growing out of it, only growing more resigned—it does feel a little juvenile to imagine myself yelling at Ben about how he ripped up the picture collage I made for him to hang in his locker.

I spent an entire week editing our faces onto all those Nickelback photos! I imagined myself screaming, teary-eyed, and it sobered me up enough to open my door again. Plus, I will admit—to no one but myself—I am *desperate* to know why he's here. If I start shouting about Nickelback this early into things, he might never give me the answer.

When I return with a towel, I hate the way I watch him run it through his hair, like I might be quizzed on all the differences between the past and the present Ben Porter. There's something so unnerving about how normal it feels to be around him. How all the adrenaline that first thrummed through me has completely stilled.

He's really here. In my apartment. At a time in my life when I feel good about who I am and what I've done for myself. And he's so much more assured than the last Ben I knew. It's in the way he moves. He knows I'm watching him, and he's letting me see. Maybe even indulging me. It could be that Ben Porter has always known how to twist his torso just so as he wrings water out of his perfectly flopped curls, and I am the one who never previously gave him the option.

When he looks up, he holds my gaze.

Part of me wants him to see the ways I've changed too. I'm no longer rimming my eyes with dark, smudgy liner or blunting the ends of my hair with kitchen scissors. I haven't put on ripped tights in at least five years. There are no canvas sneakers in my closet that I've decorated with permanent marker. Now the ink is on my skin, and it's not angry song lyrics, it's delicate flowers and whimsical butterflies tattooed onto my inner forearms.

Most of what I wore in high school was armor. I'm proud of the ways I've grown, but for him, I don't want to be completely defenseless. So I break the tension between us by looking away, reminding myself to harden.

"Please. Take a seat. And explain yourself," I tell him.

He drapes his towel over one of the bar stools pushed up against my kitchen island. "Your place is really great, by the way."

My apartment is nothing like the house I grew up in. Surely Ben must be thinking that, weighing this drafty, modern aesthetic against the cramped, decaying vibe of my mom's crumbling two-bedroom ranch. He must be wondering how it's possible I got myself here when all circumstances pointed to something entirely different for me.

"I'm moving next month," I say.

"Really? Why?"

I shouldn't explain—I owe him nothing, after all—but what else am I going to do? Not yell about the Nickelback thing, that's for sure. And I will slingshot myself into the sun before I'm the first to bring up what happened between us senior year. "Everyone in this apartment complex knows I record my podcast here." I pause in hopes of catching an expression that gives away whether or not he's ever listened.

Unfortunately, he reveals nothing.

"Apparently, most people in this building are on that app where you post about your neighbors," I continue. "Someone tipped me off to what they were saying on there. All kinds of people are always coming in and out of my apartment to record with me. So my neighbors think I'm a sex worker. If anyone in this building bothered to listen to a single episode, they'd know I'm not. They'd also know I obviously don't have a problem with sex work."

I let that sit in the air, watching for traces of judgment from Ben. He remains a portrait of stoicism. That's another thing I'd forgotten—he has an infuriatingly impressive poker face. It's rarely used, which is what makes it even more effective.

"Sounds like your neighbors suck," he says. Succinct but true. So very Ben.

Hearing his voice again is such a thrill it makes me shudder. The gentle timbre has deepened a little. Where he once sounded young and questioning, he sounds older and assured.

"Pretty much," I tell him. "They've been determined to make my life in this apartment hell. And they've won. Once my lease is up, I'll let them loathe another woman."

He grins. "That could be an album. *Loathe Another Woman.*"

"Indie folk," I answer quickly, urged forward by the heady rush I get from daring to joke with him. "Trying to be subversive but ultimately middling. You'd listen to it."

He shakes his head in dismay. "I probably would. At least once."

"What would Penjaminborter say about it?"

"Oh god." He rubs his mouth, soaking in the memory of his music-vlogging alter ego. Back in high school, he had a YouTube account full of unlisted videos that only I could access where he reviewed new albums and songs in incredible detail. "Probably 'subversive but ultimately middling. I only listened once.'"

"And I'd leave a comment that said, 'Hmm. Wasn't I the one to say that first?' And you'd reply, 'I'll delete this if you want to post it yourself,' and I'd respond, 'I do.'"

"But you don't," he says.

"Of course not. I'm no Penjaminborter."

It's a gigantic risk to be this familiar. We are dipping our toes into a very deep and irresistible pool of memories—some real, some imagined—without knowing how much either of us is willing to swim. But Ben is grinning so wide, and I'm feeling so strangely exhilarated, I decide to push forward.

"You'd remind me about it one more time," I add. "Like a month later."

"Very subtly," he notes.

"Oh yeah. You'd try to be extremely casual. Like you weren't thinking about it every single day since you deleted your video. And I'd tell you I already recorded my own, and that I'm gonna post it on my channel soon. But I'd never do it."

"*Shit*," Ben whispers, annoyed at the very idea of it.

"It's okay," I remind him. "Because the album wasn't even good."

We could go like this all night, talking circles around the point. I regret how much I'm already enjoying it. I can't lose track of the fact that it's been an *entire decade* since I've seen him. Suddenly, he's at my front door, and we're imagining past realities while making up fake reactions to fake albums, and the missing years somehow feel like only a few hours, and there's really only so long we should go on pretending this reunion isn't a monumental occurrence that hopefully has some kind of purpose beyond dismantling my Friday night.

"What's your podcast called?" he asks at the exact time I toss out another "What are you doing here?"

It's a good thing I've spent the last ten years developing my own poker face, because knowing Ben has never scoured the internet for traces of me makes me feel the most exposed I've been yet.

He's a seventh-grade science teacher in Indiana. I learned

that from his LinkedIn, which is his only known online presence. It has no photo attached. Neither does his school's website. Other than that, he's deleted all the accounts he had in high school. If he has new ones, he's not using any of his usual aliases. His brother, Richie, has a private Instagram and a Facebook page where I can only view a few public posts and his profile picture. A couple months ago, he changed it to a photo of him and Ben as kids. The first time I saw it, I panicked and thought Ben had *died*. Turns out, Richie's just sentimental.

Ben's name was mentioned twice on his town's local Patch. Once when they covered the school astronomy fair Ben voluntarily founded. He appeared in a group shot—too far away to really make out any details, but I know that face—and a student named Kyle Anderson said of the fair, "It was really fun. Mr. Porter makes the stars seem cool."

The second time the Patch featured Ben, it was in a post encouraging kids to sign up for Little League fall ball. The photo showed twelve prepubescent boys and three adult men, all dressed in the same black-and-yellow jersey, staring into the camera. Ben stood on the back right. He had his arms clasped together behind his back and a humble grin on his face. Sweet and serious in perfect measure.

I spent the rest of that night going through the old photos of us that I'd saved in various places on the internet: hidden Facebook albums and archived Instagram posts from the oldest days on the platform. Then I switched to the pictures I'd gotten printed out and stuffed into a repurposed cookie tin I keep beneath my bed.

"You go first," Ben says, right as I reply with *"Did I Forget to Tell You?"*

"Did you forget to tell me what?" It's the first time since he showed up that he looks genuinely startled, which is hilarious considering he's the one who arrived unannounced.

"That's the name of the podcast," I explain. *"Did I Forget to Tell You?"*

"Oh yeah. That's right."

When my face quirks in surprise, he looks to the ground, trying to wipe away traces of recognition. It doesn't matter, though. I already saw. Ben Porter *has* looked me up. The real question is: Has he listened? He would know how much I've talked about him, without ever saying anything directly.

"What are you doing here?" I nudge again.

"Gam died," he says at once.

His answer sucks the air out of the room. "Oh no. When?"

"In January."

It's strange to think I should've felt it. Like a rock dislodging from the mountain I've built to make my life. I met Ben's grandma Joan only once, but it was enough to feel like I always knew her. If there was ever a woman I thought had both the wherewithal and the connections to figure out how to live forever, it was Gam. Steely and kind, with a face full of faded freckles and a mouth full of vinegar, she had the kind of strong-spined conviction that perfumes your memories forever.

"I'm really sorry to hear that. She was special," I say.

It feels inappropriate to ask what Gam dying five months ago has to do with Ben being here now, so I don't. Though I want to. I suddenly want to ask Ben so many things I shouldn't—and there's a certain thrill in anticipating the discomfort that would come from doing it. Ripping off the bandage and revealing our wounds before we're ready to expose them. I've made a whole career out of getting addicted to that feeling.

Something tells me to pace myself. Hell, maybe that's Gam

herself, stopping me from being too forward. *Let this breathe, Dee. Give him a second.*

"She got really sick last year," Ben continues. "There was no one around her to help with appointments and meds and all that. And no one else in the family wanted to do it. So she left Colorado to move in with me in Indiana." He pauses to take a breath. "It got bad pretty fast. And then she was gone."

He's always had an unflappable sense of duty. He carried himself as if he was the person solely responsible for keeping his family glued together, and he was determined to do it all with the biggest, friendliest smile in the world, never giving away an ounce of the effort it required.

The urge to reach out and touch him is too irresistible to ignore. I lean across my kitchen island to rest a hand lightly on his forearm. "I'm so sorry."

He notes the pressure between us. My hand on him. Our space in this room. The impossibility of all of it.

"She never sold her house in Colorado," he says. "It's sitting there full of her stuff with no one living inside. I've been putting off getting up there and emptying it. I want to get it on the market before the school year starts again." He eyes me expectantly, waiting for me to make sense of the fragments he's laid out. "Do you remember our road trip?"

I pull my hand back.

If friendships came with highlight reels, that road trip would be the centerpiece of ours. The beginning of our ending. Spring break our senior year of high school. Driving Ben's Honda Civic to see Gam in Colorado. A thousand miles there. A million memories made. And one promise—to take the same trip ten years later.

A promise is a promise.

"Ben." I back up. "You're not serious."

His shoulders round forward as his chin dips down. He becomes the silent, sullen Ben no one but me was ever allowed to know.

Ninety-nine percent of the time, he was this astoundingly affable guy. If he played football, they'd have made him the quarterback, strictly on principle. He played baseball instead, and he probably had an equally important position on the team, but I never could get myself to remember what it was. The point is, he was *that* guy. The one everyone loudly worshipped across all social groups. He was nice to everyone. Sincerely. He'd do things like pull over and help someone with a flat tire or volunteer to bring baked goods to the local senior center. When he entered the cafeteria, people would legitimately cheer. Or they'd yell, "*Porteeeerrrrr!*" and he'd nod and wave as he walked until he found *me* sitting crisscross, eating a granola bar with my iPod turned up as loud as it would go.

In fact, he was so well-liked he got voted class president and he hadn't even run. He didn't want the responsibilities, so he graciously passed the title off to our friend Victoria, who had spent a better part of six months campaigning.

One percent of the time, there was a withdrawn Ben. Pensive to a dangerous degree, shutting down for hours—or sometimes days—processing whatever had gone wrong in his life by retreating inward until all that remained was a glossy, smiling shell of himself. You had to know him to know the difference. And only I did.

"Gam asked me to stop letting life pass me by," he says in explanation.

"Well, did Gam ask you to rip up the Nickelback photos of us in your locker too?"

The one thing I wanted to leave on the cutting room floor, and it's the first thing I mention. Suddenly, all my latent adrenaline reactivates tenfold.

"What the hell makes you think I can stop my life and hit the road with you?" I continue. "You don't know what I have going on. What if my partner is out getting us snacks and you're interrupting our date night? What if I have friends coming to town? What if I have work? How could you possibly think you can just arrive, tell me your lovely grandmother passed away, and expect me to get into the car with you for a week?"

My words start to melt together, coming out in such a rush I have to remind myself to breathe or I might do the most mortifying thing of all: cry. That's something I absolutely cannot do until Ben is at least one hundred yards away from the premises. Until then, I must survive without so much as a single welling tear.

"Dee," Ben says, quietly insistent. "We promised we would."

"We sure did! And in high school I also promised my guidance counselor I would apply to college. I swore to Mr. Delham I'd make a real effort in gym class. I pledged allegiance to the flag every single day."

"You always sat during the pledge."

I fold my arms across my chest.

"Look, I know a promise you made in high school isn't some kind of unbreakable oath," Ben continues. "But I . . . I can't do this alone."

I should feel outraged. Insulted. Put off by the very idea of his pitch. If someone else lived this situation and then explained it to me, that's how I'd react. It's not the truth, though, even if it makes the most sense. The truth is I actually feel something closer to relief. Like I've been waiting my entire adult life for

Ben Porter to show up at my door, needing me. But he can't know that.

"What about Richie?" I throw out to buy myself time.

Ben and Richie used to be what I'd call politely close. They have a five-year age difference between them and an impressive variation in their style of handling things. Richie believes in having opinions on only hockey, beer, and Dave Matthews Band. Ben could probably write a dissertation on spoon sizes. Only if you proved you really cared to read it.

Richie would be the perfect companion for packing up the life of a loved one who recently died. His relationship to the moment would be like his public Facebook captions: direct and uncomplicated. *Boxes packed. Gonna miss this house. RIP Grandma Joan. You were the realest of them.*

"I don't want to go with Richie," Ben says. "I want to go with you."

He's being more candid than I could possibly be prepared for, even if I'd known he would be here, on this day, in my shiny new world I've built entirely in his absence. Without any chance to set up a single emotional protection barrier, I am helpless.

"I'm on summer break," he explains. He sees me grabbing for an excuse, breaths inhaled and held. Words stopped right before release. "So I have as long as you need. Unless you need more than two months."

I don't want to fight him. I *have* to. Or I'll have lost the long-standing war between us before it's even had a chance to reignite. "You think that sounds very accommodating, but I cannot even begin to explain how stressful it is to know you are willing to wait for me for an *entire summer*." I stop and stare until he writhes in his seat. "You'll what? Sit in my hallway for the next few weeks? I don't even want to know how you got my address. This is a lot." I pause. "A *lot*."

Ben was never the impulsive one between us. Which is why I haven't rejected him. Because beneath the hurt and betrayal and unspoken words, I have always wanted Ben Porter to take a leap of faith. (That doesn't mean I won't have strong opinions about the way he's leapt. I have strong opinions about everything.)

"I wasn't really thinking about it that way," he admits. "You're right. This is inappropriate." He stands. "I'm really sorry, Dee. About all of it."

Before he can get out, I block the door. After all this pageantry, he doesn't get to walk away this quickly. Not again. "Now hold on. You can't throw out a blanket apology like that and then *leave*." I step toward him. "I never said I wasn't considering it. We're about to be on hiatus with the podcast, so it's entirely possible I have time. But I'm not sold."

We eye each other again.

"This is the part where I'm supposed to say that I don't know whether or not you've turned into a serial killer," I continue. "But I talk to people about their secrets all the time. There are a million ways to be sinister." I give myself permission to look him over slowly. "Have you ever tied up a partner without their consent?"

To Ben's credit, he remains unflinching under my critical gaze. "No."

"If a server brings you the wrong dish or forgets a side of ketchup, what do you do?"

"Politely tell her that I ordered something else. Or request the ketchup again."

"Why is the server a she? Do you unconsciously believe that incompetence would come from someone who uses she/her pronouns?" It's taken me years to learn how to make people feel safe when I ask them hard questions. It's so much easier to make them stressed.

"I hope I don't, but you're right, I should have used a neutral term."

"If at any point someone tells you no, in sex or in daily life, what do you do?"

He makes a gesture from him to me, noting the fact that we are both standing inches from my front door, which I have barricaded. "I think I've showed you that I'd stop. But you didn't say no."

"Correct. That means we're in a gray area. I know what you really want, but you have no idea what I want."

"What do you want?"

I close the space between us until it can be measured in eyelashes. His Adam's apple bobs up and down as I drop my voice into the throatiest whisper I can muster. *"For you to leave . . ."*

I reach behind me and push my door handle down. To open it, I have to press myself against him, feeling the cold shock of his damp clothes against my jumpsuit.

We are close enough to kiss. It's all I can think about, to total distraction. Those soft lips I once adored, and those sweet eyes that used to look at me with complete care—such a potent combination, designed solely to destroy me.

"So I can pack," I finish, still staring at his lips.

He shakes his head in disbelief. "Really?"

I don't give him the courtesy of answering his question. Instead I ask my own. "Is your number still the same?"

"No."

"Well, *my* number hasn't changed."

I grab him by the waist and spin us until he's in the hallway. If he remembers my number, he remembers enough to move on to the next round. When I release him, I pick up his shoes and his duffel bag and push them into his chest. "Good luck out there. I think it's raining," I say with a wicked smile. Then I close my door and slide down the back of it, staring up at my lofted ceilings until my eyes hurt and my thoughts dull to a static roar.

This can't be real.

This can't be real.

There's no way this is real.

My phone vibrates with a text from an unknown number.

Hey. It's Ben. I'll see you tomorrow. Is 10am good?

Let's make it noon, I respond, my fingers shaking. **I have something to do beforehand.**

Good god.

This *is* real.

And it will be my undoing.

Did I Forget to Tell You?

EPISODE 03: NATURAL DISASTERS

DEE MATTHEWS: Sometimes it's not about what you keep from your loved ones as much as what you agree to never mention again. Most of us have walked in on a family member using the bathroom in the middle of the night or opened a bedroom door without waiting for a response. But what happens when you factor in a natural disaster? Our very own Javi Hernandez answers that question for us today, with a tale that involves tornadoes, adult entertainment, and a very Catholic family who has never so much as breathed a word about this event since.

DEE: So, Javi, first of all, thank you for agreeing to air this out. I cannot believe I have never heard this before, and I'm honored you're sharing it with me now.

JAVI: You're welcome. I never thought this day would come, but it's time for me to break my silence. I'm ready to tell my tornado story.

DEE: Set the scene for us.

JAVI: Well, Dee, let's travel back in time together. I'm a teenager, and my older sister Victoria has recently given me her dying laptop because she's just gotten a MacBook for her birthday. It's raining outside, which isn't anything new for Illinois, as you know. When I go into my room for the night, I have one goal. By the time I get my setup ready, it seems like the weather's calmed down. So I get to business.

DEE: What was your setup?

JAVI: Under my covers with headphones on and pants off. Box of tissues. Door locked. Browser history immediately deleted afterward. Nobody was gonna catch young Javi slipping up.

DEE: Except Mother Nature herself.

JAVI: She said I am going to create an environment so toxic . . .

DEE: You will have to run pantsless through the halls of your home . . .

JAVI: Your family will never look at you the same . . .

DEE: You may briefly consider a new identity . . .

JAVI: If I'm being real with you, I might have to after this episode goes up. I know Victoria's listening.

DEE: She definitely is. Shout-out to our podcast's first—and as of now, *only*—fan, my dear childhood friend and Javi's older sister, Victoria Hernandez-Jay.

JAVI: Don't worry, Victoria. We can continue never speaking of this.

DEE: So it's raining, you're in the peace of your bedroom, enjoying a little private entertainment.

JAVI: Things are getting good. I love a strong backstory, and this was a classic tale of two gentlemen who've gotten off on the wrong foot. Neighbors fighting over a loud party. Finally, they've . . . come to an understanding, and my mother flings my bedroom door open, screaming that I have to get down to the basement with the rest of our family.

DEE: Talk me through the door situation. You said you locked it.

JAVI: I *know* I locked it. I've replayed this many times throughout the years. To this day I do not know how my mom opened it. But I was . . . a little distracted when it happened.

DEE: So she barges in. Does she see the laptop screen?

JAVI: Yes.

DEE: And you're not wearing any pants.

JAVI: Teenage me really thought all acts of pleasure had to be performed at least half-nude.

DEE: I love that for teenage you.

JAVI: He needs a hug.

DEE: He does.

JAVI: So my mom throws open the door. She registers what's happening but makes the choice to yank me out of bed. It's a tornado, I'm not wearing pants, and I'm trying to cover myself up and also close my laptop and it's all happening so fast I start screaming.

DEE: Oh my god. Why?

JAVI: My emergency backup plan was always to act like I didn't know what I was watching or something. Like *Oh no! How did this get on my screen? Help! Save me from the oily naked men!* It was pure survival instincts. Then my headphones fell out of my ears and I realized how scary it was outside. Our windows were rattling and the siren was blaring. So I immediately decided to rationalize my screaming as a reaction to the tornado. But it wasn't.

DEE: I remember this tornado very well, by the way. A tree in my backyard got pulled out of the ground.

JAVI: That's right! I remember that too.

DEE: Take me back to what was unfolding at your house, though. Much more interesting than mine.

JAVI: So my mother's dragging me to our basement, muttering prayers, saying nothing about what's just happened between us. We get down there, and I am still so very half-naked, cupping myself and fighting for my dignity. Victoria takes one look at me and closes her eyes to pray. My little sister, Julissa, who's about nine at the time, hasn't noticed me yet. She's got her head in her hands, crying. My dad's rummaging around looking for a flashlight. Then our power goes out, right when my dad finds it. Of course he shines the light directly onto me.

DEE: Of course he does.

JAVI: The "batteries die" immediately. Julissa cries out into the darkness, "Why doesn't Javi have on pants?" My mom yells for everyone to stay calm. And then I blacked out the rest. No exaggeration. I do not remember anything other than the fact that our power didn't come back on until the next day after school. And we had to get a new roof.

DEE: You know what's so wild about this? I distinctly remember that next day. *Everyone* had a tornado story. But when I told Victoria about the tree falling in my yard, she said nothing really happened at her house. And I remember saying, "Damn, you're lucky."

JAVI: I'm telling you, Dee, I changed the fabric of my family forever, and we have never said shit about this to each other. *Ever.* I never saw that laptop again.

DEE: And here you are, immortalizing this event for all time. I wonder what happened to the neighbors in the video.

JAVI: Oh, they put their differences aside and threw a party *together.*

DEE: That's beautiful.

JAVI: Always nice to see two people overcome their past.

DEE: It is.

JAVI: Wow. I'm actually shaking right now. I really thought I'd die with this memory.

DEE: I know how that feels.

JAVI: Well, now would be a great time to bare your soul with me! I'm out here all alone!

DEE: I mean, I can't think of anything on the spot!

JAVI: Oh stop. Yes, you can. What about whatever happened with you and [NAME REDACTED] at the end of your senior year?

DEE: Oh. No. That's not the same kind of thing at all.

JAVI: How do I know that? I've never heard the story! No one has!

DEE: And no one ever will!

4

BEN

Hold on, hold on. Lemme put my shit in my trunk," Darius tells me. "I just did plyo outside at Hillman Park. You should've come."

"Except I'm in Chicago," I remind him.

"I said lemme put my shit in my trunk, man. Hold on."

The line goes quiet as I stand in the middle of the snack aisle in a downtown Chicago Walgreens at eight forty-five in the morning. My head hurts. I haven't had a proper night's sleep in weeks.

Darius comes back on. "Okay. You drove to the city to do *what now?*" He sounds echoey and distant.

"To take a road trip with Dee."

"Who is Dee?"

Dee is my childhood best friend. Dee is the first person I ever lost.

"A girl from my past," I tell Darius.

"I don't need you to drop her social security number, but you gotta give me more than this."

"Sorry." I explain the whole situation to him while I stare out into a wide array of crackers and pretzels.

I should grab a bunch of snacks and let Dee choose what she wants from the pile. But her objections won't be something I imagine when I let my mind wander a little further than comfortable. The real Dee will not hesitate to point out that I didn't remember what she likes. Or that I tried too hard to remember what she does.

"I always thought you never did enough. Now you're doing too much," Darius tells me once I finish walking him through how I got Dee's address from an old mutual friend. "Hey, though, at least you're livin'."

It's one of his favorite sayings. He's never had a reason to use it on me, which feels less like an accomplishment and more like a warning. He usually reserves it for when one of our coworkers gets too drunk at a holiday party or we see someone at the gym doing something unorthodox on the treadmill.

Suddenly, Darius's wife, Jade, is on the line. "Ben, honey? Darius has you on his car speaker. I heard the whole thing."

Darius is eleven years older than me. He teaches eighth-grade science in the classroom right beside mine, and we became fast friends because he's genuine, he doesn't press unless he has to, and he answers only what you ask to know. Most mornings, we get to work early after the gym, and we sit in Darius's classroom drinking coffee in companionable silence. Being friends with him has taught me how much I appreciate being around someone who doesn't need anything from me other than my presence. It's not really a surprise that he's with his wife and didn't tell me. She works out with us once or twice a week, and they are a family of extremely early risers who love the morning.

"I think what you're doing is sweet," she tells me. "Don't let Darius make you feel like Bozo."

"I wasn't making him feel like Bozo," Darius challenges.

"Yes you were," Jade whispers. "It's too late for us to talk him out of it." Louder, she says, "You're a nice young man with a stable job. You show up on time and you keep your mouth shut when you should. If this Dee agreed to go with you, she must know all this."

Another voice chimes in. "Mr. Porter?" It's Rochelle, Darius's daughter, who was in my class this year.

I'm rethinking my fondness for Darius's sparse details. "Oh, hey, Rochelle." Instinctively I lean my head into my shoulder as if I can shield myself from any other unexpected bystander joining this conversation. The entire Carlson family on the line is enough.

"You should tell Dee you love her," Rochelle says.

I fumble the Cheez-Its box in my hand. An older man in the store, holding a pool noodle and a box of matches, makes a point to stop and stare at me. "That's not—this isn't that kind of trip. This is about apologizing for the past. And fulfilling a promise."

"So why did you call my dad?" Rochelle asks.

"I—I needed to tell someone where I was going." I can't believe I am explaining myself to a thirteen-year-old. Then again, it is my job. Which should make this moment a lot easier than it is.

Jade pops back on. "Oh. Do you need us to come check on your pets?"

"I don't have any pets," I say.

"Water your plants?" This is Rochelle.

"No plants."

"So it's like nine o'clock in the morning and you wanted to tell my dad you're going on a trip with a person you knew in high school because she said she would ten years ago? Not because you love her?" Rochelle is tough to motivate when she's not interested in something. But when she cares, she's a very astute student. And she, much like her father, has no passion for subtlety or empty conversation.

"It's a bad idea," I admit to her. "I think I called your dad because I know that, and I was hoping he'd confirm it for me."

"It's not a bad idea," she tells me kindly. "It kind of doesn't make sense, though. No offense." After a thoughtful beat, she adds, "You shouldn't show up places unannounced. That part *is* bad. Sorry. It's kind of stalkerish."

"Rochelle," Jade warns.

"What? It is! I'm not gonna lie about it!"

Darius is laughing his ass off.

"Thank you for not lying to me," I say.

"You're welcome," Rochelle responds. It's easy to picture her satisfied smile, much the same as her father's. She shares a lot of his features, but the most noticeable similarity between them is the sneaky, sly grin she gets when she's proud. "And I'm sorry, but aren't you the one who is always telling us science is about finding answers to questions you don't even realize you're asking?"

"He does not say that," Darius interjects.

"I actually do," I tell him. "Kind of a lot. Just assumed I was talking to myself most of the time."

"He pretty much said it every day," Rochelle informs her family. My phone is hurting my cheek I am squeezing it so hard between my head and shoulder. "So if you're not gonna tell her you love her, I guess keep looking for your answer? And maybe then you'll know the question? I don't know. You're the one being random."

Darius huffs. "I can't believe you've got my daughter telling you to find an answer to know the question."

"Hopefully she also knows the three types of rocks." The line goes quiet. "Sedimentary, igneous, and metamorphic," I mutter.

Still quiet.

Reaching, I ask, "So . . . how are all of you doing? Going to Wisconsin Dells next weekend, right?"

"C'mon, Ben. You don't have to do this," Darius says.

"Do what?"

"Check on us right now. This moment can be about only you. Sometimes that's how it goes."

"Unless you want to hear about how Darius bought the wrong kind of soil for my garden," Jade interjects.

Darius's voice gets smaller. "They all looked the same."

"I sent him a picture of the bag," Jade explains.

Their easy rhythm amplifies the ache in my chest. Jade tells him the truth, even when he doesn't want to hear it. She's honest with him, even when it's uncomfortable.

If only my family had been honest with me, then the past few months of my life wouldn't have been so confusing. But they weren't. And now my life has snowballed so completely that for the first time, I'm attempting to ask my only friend for help. I'm not even sure how to do it, because I've never tried before, and I don't like to do things I know I'm not good at. So I give up and end the call, thanking Darius and his family for chatting with me, knowing full well I didn't get what I needed out of our conversation. Asking for more doesn't come naturally to me. It makes me feel like I am letting Darius down by being less than my best for him.

Rochelle is right. What's the question I'm asking?

I already know I'm not ready to find the answer. So, quickly, I grab four things: Cheez-Its, peanut M&M's, Goldfish, and Takis.

Safe choices.

In my hometown, not many people understood my friendship with Dee. We stayed close from grade school, to middle school, all the way through high school. She had an uncanny knack for intimidating people. If someone stuck their foot out to trip her, she could make it look like she meant to fall. She laughed when she felt like it. She went where she wanted to go. She talked to only the people she liked. By some strange luck, one of those people was me. Even when I was a young kid who hardly knew anything, I knew better than to throw that away. She became my North Star—the constant that kept me centered as I wandered through my childhood, figuring out what I wanted my life to be. I held on to her as long as I could. Until the day I let go completely.

At the checkout, I see something else—Twizzlers.

In a moment of boldness, I grab those too.

Did I Forget to Tell You?

EPISODE 22: SNACK TIME

DEE: I have to say, food play has never interested me.

JAVI: You know I've tried it.

DEE: I mean, me too. I just didn't like it that much. Did you?

JAVI: It was fine!

DEE: You heard it here first! It was fine! Nothing more to say!

JAVI: Well, there is, but believe it or not, some things belong only to me and God.

DEE: Glad to know whipped cream makes that list.

JAVI: It was caramel sauce, actually.

DEE: Okay! Good for you.

JAVI: Dee's making a face at me.

DEE: No I'm not! I'm actively listening! This is my active listening face!

JAVI: I can't believe you want me to say more. You're the one who's made an entire character out of a person you won't talk about!

DEE: First of all, I've made many characters like that. Second, the one you are surely referring to is Name Redacted, and I have good reasons for not talking about him directly! Thirdly, the face was because I don't like caramel. I feel like it would be a sticky nightmare.

JAVI: I gotta ask. Too many people are on our case about it. Shouldn't the nickname just be Redacted?

DEE: People, it's way too late. We've already committed. His name is Name Redacted. And actually, I'll say this about food—the only time Name Redacted and I ever slept together, there was a Twizzlers package stuck to my back for part of it, because we forgot to take all our snacks off the hotel bed.

JAVI: Why were you putting your snacks on the bed in the first place? *Here I am at the Marriott! Gonna dump my Sour Patch Kids onto the sheets!*

DEE: Look. Some things belong to me, God, and Name Redacted.

5

DEE

"A re you staying over at that guy's house tonight?" Javi asks
as I roll my favorite sweatshirt up like a burrito and then
tuck it into the left corner of my luggage.

He's wearing a gray sweatshirt and matching joggers, sitting
in the center of my couch. Somehow he pulls off the exact kind
of comfortably chic athleisure look that makes strangers think
he is either a professional athlete or a famous musician. He can't
sing to save his life, but he *is* incredibly good at pickleball.

Right now he's staring at his laptop resting on my coffee table. There are three of my cups scattered around his MacBook:
one for his iced coffee, one for his orange juice, and one for his
water. I keep my fridge stocked with all of his favorite drinks for
this very reason. He's more like family than friend to me at this
point, and it makes me happy to see him inhabit my apartment
so comfortably. I never thought I'd have a place of my own that
other people would feel safe inside.

"Garrett? No," I respond.

Javi sips his orange juice. "Where are you going, then?"

It's not that he'd judge me if I told him. It's that talking about
it out loud makes it real, and the only reason I'm surviving in

the first place is because I've convinced myself this is an elaborate figment of my imagination.

Unfortunately, Javi misreads my apprehension as me being coy. "Oh my god. You're finally taking a real vacation, and you didn't invite me?" He looks me up and down. "I'm hurt."

"No, no. Well, not *exactly*."

I didn't want to have to pack while he was here, but I procrastinated so much that our final work meeting has now overlapped with my wild, impulsive decision to take this trip.

In classic Javi fashion, he snorts in excitement before I've even begun to explain. He has the best laugh of anyone I've ever known. It's infectious and inviting. In my mind, it's one of the biggest reasons our show has become as popular as it has. It's exciting to get Javi excited.

"What are you up to? About to go meet Name Redacted in Hawaii?" He presents this like a joke, because in his mind, it's something so outlandish and impossible that it works as a non sequitur to toss out before I give the real story.

Javi and I have put out an episode a week—with minimal interruption—for the last three and a half years. That's got us clocking in at 175 episodes full of secrets, sex talk, and everything in between. We've told each other so much personal shit over the years that almost nothing I could say right now would shock him.

Except for this.

"Ben and I aren't meeting in Hawaii. But we *are* driving to Colorado together. We leave at noon."

Javi slams his laptop shut. He unfolds his legs and sits up at attention. "Is this a joke?" His voice is already low, but this question sits at the very bottom of his register.

"No."

He is in such disbelief that it takes three run-throughs of the story for him to fully process not only what happened last night but also the fact that I agreed to go on this trip without much hesitation.

For as much as Javi knows about me, he doesn't actually know much about Ben. Javi's family moved to my hometown when he was ten. I was thirteen. His older sister, Victoria, was the one in my grade. She and I became fast friends. Javi and I didn't get close until a few years ago, when we ran into each other at a bar in Boystown. To Javi, Ben is a fun little character on our podcast. He isn't really a person.

In a way, that's what Ben has become to me too. He exists in carefully curated fragments. The good times that make me smile and the silly things that charm me. Though sometimes, in fits and shadows, the disappointments surface too.

They still don't feel real.

"This is exciting! Right?" Javi asks once he's assured that it's truly happening.

"It's something to do," I say noncommittally. "You and I are supposed to be planning . . ."

"You're the one taking a road trip with the guy who has an entire Reddit thread dedicated to his identity! But yeah, let's talk about how to incorporate our mattress-in-a-box sponsorship into our return episode!"

I glare at Javi, even though he's right. I can hardly think about the next hour of my life, much less what will happen with our show when we come back from our break. We're taking off the entire month of June. It's the first time we've ever gone this long without recording an episode, and we want to come back bigger and better than ever.

"I will know more once the trip happens," I say. "Until then, I'd actually like to talk about work. It will be a good distraction."

Javi opens his laptop as slowly as possible, giving me ample room to change my mind. It doesn't take long for him to surrender to my unyielding stare and start discussing what we're supposed to do with our time off.

Our podcast has shifted a lot since the start. We got the idea for the show when my mom came out drinking with us one night. "I used to have sex for money. Before you were born," she'd yelled over the music at the bar. When my jaw hit the floor, she added, "What? Did I forget to tell you?"

My mom is famous for tossing a conversational grenade, then being surprised when it goes off. I had a lot of questions for her that night. So did Javi, a naturally curious conversationalist who could probably get a stranger to tell him their bank pin if he wanted.

In a stroke of what turned out to be drunken genius, I thought it would be interesting if we recorded our conversation with my mom. At the time, I wanted to be sure I remembered everything. Looking back, it was another example in a long list of instances where I've failed to set proper boundaries for myself.

My mom, Javi, and I took a Lyft back to my shitty old apartment, and we recorded the conversation with my iPhone. We had no mics. No real vision. We were three drunk people navigating family secrets and surprise revelations, laughing and gasping in equal measure. Next thing I knew I was getting into podcasting full-time, like some white bro with a half-brained idea and an unwarranted well of confidence to pull from at any given moment.

Javi and I tried for a while to drink before each episode. That got old quick. As did hyperfocusing on our sex lives. We learned fast that gimmicks had a much shorter shelf life than open, honest conversation centered on simple prompts.

Eventually, we got an actual podcast publisher to produce our show. And sponsors. And a community of listeners who enjoy what we have to say. With a lot of work, and some serendipitous connections that have really expanded our reach, we've started booking bigger and bigger names. Nowadays famous guests come on and talk about their secrets with us, and the money we make from our various sponsorships, partnerships, and streams actually covers all my bills with some change to spare.

What started as Javi and me swimming side by side through the most confusing, hidden parts of our lives has given me everything I never had before. Not that it was very hard. I had close to nothing before this. Being able to buy a new outfit without worrying that I won't be able to pay my rent has yet to stop shocking me.

After we finish talking about work—artfully hedging what it is we actually want to do when we return from our break—Javi makes himself an egg sandwich in my kitchen while I go into my bathroom to gather my toiletries.

"What are you gonna do over our break?" I call out.

"I don't know. None of my exes have shown up at my doorstep yet," he yells back.

"It's still early!" I put three different face washes into a cosmetics bag that's already full of serums gifted to me that I've never once used. I have no idea what I should pack, and therefore have decided to pack everything. "And Ben isn't my ex!"

"Whatever! Do you want a sandwich?"

"No thank you!"

My stomach is too full of anxious butterflies to think about eating. This can't be real. This is all a joke. Ben will abandon me.

Maybe that's for the best.

After a while, Javi appears in the doorway. "I know we're not supposed to, but I'll probably sit around and worry about the podcast," he admits, biting into his sandwich.

Now that we are off the clock, the real talk comes out. We have this habit of cataloging our own experiences as Podcast Worthy or Not Podcast Worthy. Our anxieties about our job fall firmly in the Not Podcast Worthy category, so we only talk about them when we're not officially discussing work. It's odd, but it's our way.

"I know," I say. "I'm worried too."

"We need a big idea," he reminds me.

The beautiful thing about Javi and me is that usually, when one of us gets like this, the other one is always ready with assurances. Right now, everything is so strange that all I can offer is a half-hearted "We'll find one."

We don't know how to climb any higher with the show. I'm not sure there's anywhere left for us to go. I've spent so much of my life immersed in uncertainty it's almost comfortable to be back here, threatened by the idea that everything could end. I wonder when I'll stop expecting disaster.

There's another thought that's Not Podcast Worthy.

By the time I'm packed, Javi's sister Victoria has unexpectedly whooshed into my apartment with her usual flourish. Her dark ringlets are slicked back in a perfect bun, baby hairs neatly swooped at her temples.

"I wanted to see what you're wearing," she tells me as she kisses my cheeks.

She manages the makeup counter at the MAC store inside Bloomingdale's, which means her face never looks anything short of flawless. Today she's got a soft brown eye shadow perfectly blended above her usual winged eyeliner. There's a hint of cool-toned blush brushed atop her cheekbones, and a rich mauve lip that suits her perfectly.

"What did Javi tell you?" I ask, standing still to let her appraise me.

Javi knows what I share with him is free to go straight to Victoria. In a way, it's easier. I wanted her to know, but I didn't want to be the one to tell her.

"Just the basics." She spins me around and takes in my cropped tank top and jean shorts. "This is cute. Casual. Not forced. I like it. But I think we can do better."

I let out a sigh that sounds like I'm annoyed, even though I'm actually relieved. There is nothing quite as satisfying as Victoria's ability to enter a room and take charge without any prompting.

She lays my suitcase on its side and starts combing through my belongings with no reservations. "What have we packed?"

"I have no idea," I admit.

She immediately discards a pair of hiking boots I'd convinced myself might be necessary.

As she works through my luggage, she asks surprisingly few questions about how this could be happening. Unlike Javi, she knew Ben well, so the idea of this trip must make more sense to her than it would to anyone else. She was around for the first one. She remembers the promise. Plus she's a person who lives and dies by her word. When I was eighteen, I pinkie pledged Ben that in ten years' time, I'd once again drive halfway across the country with him. To me, that was a sweet thing to say after the best week of my life. To Victoria, that was a blood oath.

When she's pleased with her modifications, she zips my suitcase shut and stands it upright for me.

"Before we get you changed, I need a favor," she says matter-of-factly, wheeling my luggage to the door.

"Here I was thinking you rushed over because I'm in crisis," I say.

She waves her manicured finger at me. "I'm in crisis too, Deandra."

No one, and I mean *no one*, is allowed to use my full first name aside from her. It's no longer clear how she even gained the rights to use it, other than the fact that her voice is the only one I can handle saying it. There's a gentle firmness to her tone that comforts me. My therapist once said it might be because it reminds me of the maternal structure that I've always craved, because I never received it from my actual mother. Personally, I think it's because Victoria has always been cooler than me, and I have a limitless amount of respect for that.

"I need you to RSVP to the ten-year reunion," she explains.

"Oh my god. Invoking my full name for this!"

"Yes. And I'll do it for the twenty year if I have to." She plucks a lip stain from her purse and comes toward me. Cupping my face in her hand, she coats my lips in a sheer rosy pink. "You know how much this means to me."

Even up close, her makeup looks poreless and fresh. She always smells phenomenal, and today she's used a bright, full floral that reminds me of summers at the lake with her family. The two of us would walk to the outlet mall and try on the samples we liked best, perfuming everything within five miles of us. It was the peak of luxury to me. To this day, I still wear more perfume than I should because of it.

"Why do you need me to go? We see each other all the time," I say to Victoria.

"You should go," Javi chimes in. "I need to know if Derek Blake is still hot."

"Your sister can tell you that."

He gives that throaty laugh I love, weaponizing it against me. "Vicky's boring! She's not gonna tell me what I want to know. She's *married*!"

"Happily," Victoria adds, pinching my cheeks to pull the color forward. "Just look Derek up on Instagram. He's doing fine."

"You know that's not the same," Javi tells her.

The reunion is in a month. As our senior class president, Victoria always knew she'd be the one to plan it. She has looked forward to that responsibility since the day we moved our tassels across our caps and graduated.

When she started actually planning for it last year, I started avoiding purchasing a ticket.

There's no real reason for me to resist. With Ben and Victoria using their separate but important social status to protect me, my high school classmates left me alone, for the most part. They didn't understand me, and certainly not my friendship with Ben, but they were all so used to it that they stopped questioning how it was possible. Not that I could answer even if they did ask. It just was.

Of course, I still had my issues with certain people. Mostly teachers and some select assholes I'd dated that tried and failed to make me a pariah. Generally speaking, high school was a place for me to be. A place that wasn't home. Somewhere where the air didn't smell like cigarette smoke and the corners weren't packed with boxes of junk that should be thrown away. At the time, I liked school for giving me somewhere else to go. Now that I'm an adult, I have no need to return. I got everything out of it that I could possibly need. I got Victoria and, by extension, Javi. It's hard to explain that I don't really want all of our old classmates to tell me how much I've changed. Because who I was then wasn't wrong. That was exactly who I needed to be to survive.

"I may have turned in the final guest list today. And you may already be on it," Victoria finally admits, looking far less guilty than she should.

"You bought me a ticket to this?"

"Ben has one too. So you need to make sure he attends as well."

The silence hangs in the air for so long that Javi coughs out a laugh. "You have to admit," he says. "She's good."

Shaking my head in dismay, I look straight at Victoria, who levels me with her all-knowing gaze. "There is nothing you won't do to have a good party, is there?" I ask her.

"Nothing." She blows me a kiss.

"We'll see," I say to her.

"Oh, I bet we will," she says back, smirking. "Now let's get you into a better outfit and out the door. I don't want you to be late."

6

BEN

Ever since Gam told me the truth about my family, it's become a habit of mine to wonder whose life is about to change the most. In the lobby of the Congress hotel, is it the two teenagers filming themselves dancing while they wait for their parents to finish up at the front desk? Is it the old man reading the newspaper? Or is it me, again?

For Gam's final real meal, she wanted to go to Cracker Barrel. After we finished eating, she asked to sit in the rocking chairs outside the restaurant. It was December. Way too cold outside. But I loved her too much to deny her. So we sat looking at the snow piles in the parking lot, digesting our meat loaf and mashed potatoes, when she said she had something to tell me. I leaned forward, expecting to hear a precious gem of wisdom she'd gained from a life well lived. But she put her hand atop mine and said, "My son isn't your biological father."

Words stopped making sense. The weather no longer seemed very cold. My brain kept trying to rearrange what she'd told me, working very hard to make her words fit with the story of my whole entire life.

My dad wasn't my biological dad? She wasn't my biological grandmother?

I wasn't the me I thought I was?

"I've been asking myself, 'Why do we lie to protect each other from the reality *we* created?'" she continued. "We chose comfort over truth, Benny. We all did. Promise me you won't do that." She squeezed my hand so tight her rings made an imprint on my skin. "I want you to go after what you really want. Look me in the eyes and tell me you're gonna do that. I'm tired of watching you do what you think is safest."

This new truth buried everything I once knew. I had so many questions I wasn't ready to ask. It was all too shocking to speak about. By the time I wanted answers, Gam was gone. Now I'm still here, holding on to everything she left behind. Carrying secrets I didn't ask to know. The problem with her request is I no longer have any idea what safe is. My entire life, everyone has lied to me. The worst part is I was so busy trying to keep everyone smiling that I never stopped to consider what I was preventing them from feeling.

One of the dancing teenagers clears her throat. "Um. Your phone?"

I've been so in my head I assumed the incessant ringing sound was coming from the old man with the newspaper, even though I turned on my ringer specifically so I wouldn't miss any calls or texts from Dee.

When I put the receiver to my ear, she's already talking. "I was gonna drop-kick you if you didn't answer. You didn't tell me where I'm supposed to meet you."

"I thought I did," I admit. "I got a room at the Congress last night."

To my surprise, she laughs. "*Ben.*"

It pings through me, hearing her say my name like that. She's asking why I'd choose somewhere as random and upscale as here.

She knows I don't have an answer. She's *also* making fun of me for showing up sopping wet to book a room here at eleven at night. She can say all of that with one word.

"It was close to you," I explain.

"I know," she whispers through laughter. "I'll be there at noon. Meet me in the lobby." Before she hangs up, she adds, "Of the fucking Congress Plaza Hotel," with another quick bark of joy.

She doesn't wait to hear my goodbye.

7

DEE

It will be nice to get a change of scenery. Summer means adventure. Regrets are risks you fail to take. Or, as my last therapist, Linda, once said to me, rather famously, "Perhaps you need closure, Dee."

These are all the things I keep reminding myself as I walk up Michigan Avenue toward the Congress Plaza Hotel. To take an impromptu road trip with Ben Porter, of course.

Just another day in the life!

Before humidity can swallow up the afternoon, everything in downtown Chicago is lovely. It smells like exhaust fumes and new life after rainfall. Traffic hums in fits and starts beside me. The mid-June sun peeks out behind clouds, warming the concrete. Despite it all, I'm wearing my most impressive scowl, pretending this city doesn't charm me and this trip doesn't excite me.

Even after both Victoria and Javi assured me my final outfit was good, I changed. Two more times. In the end, I dressed myself in a striped crop tee and black overall shorts. A very specific, regressive nostalgia dared me to also put on ripped tights and a denim jacket covered in band pins, but thanks to the strength of my friends, I resisted.

(They forced me to change.)

I've never been nostalgic for high school before. As I walk toward this impossible trip—toward *Ben*—it's oddly nice to imagine jotting my class schedule into my planner and packing an almost-expired peach yogurt for lunch, taking small bites while I write Paramore song lyrics on my wrist with black pen. I could weave a line from "Misguided Ghosts" through the small azaleas that are now permanently inked onto my left forearm.

From a full block away, I spot Ben. There have been way too many times over the last ten years where I've caught a glimpse of a curly brown-haired white man in fitted jeans and a plain shirt and felt my stomach threaten to rehome itself in my lungs. Now he's in a loose gray tee and a backward baseball cap, and I know for certain it's him. Instead of my intestines somersaulting, I'm walking faster, almost skipping.

He stands under one of the many red awnings that line the side of the Congress hotel. He's holding a plastic Walgreens bag open, and he's counting, nodding his head along with each whispered number, observing whatever's inside with an almost hilarious level of gravitas.

The stopped traffic beside me speeds up again. A bus makes a wheezing screech as it roars back to life. It's a familiar noise, so commonplace in this city that I could fall asleep to a soundtrack of it. Ben startles. He looks first at the street, then somehow immediately finds me among the people on the sidewalk.

His smile bursts wide, showcasing all the sweet crinkles in his cheeks.

What am I *doing*? What good can come from constant forced proximity to a person whose entire existence shattered my teenage soul into a million pieces? How will this possibly bring me closure, Linda? There's a reason you're not my therapist anymore!

Ben showing up really is the most impossibly bizarre surprise of my entire life, and that's counting the time my mom's neighbor revealed that she'd taxidermied what she thought was our pet rabbit. It turned out to be a wild animal that frequented our backyard, and when she found him dead on the street, she wanted to help us grieve.

Ben jogs across the street to meet me. "There you are," he says, still smiling at me like I've never once hurt him.

"Here I am," I answer, because this is indeed where I am, standing at Michigan and Harrison with my right hand glued to my suitcase and my left tucked into the pocket of my overall shorts. This is perhaps where I will always be. I live here now. "I thought we were meeting in the lobby."

"I know. I just got excited." He hesitates, second-guessing the words that have already left his mouth.

It's so sweet it makes me want to pass away. I die here now. "What did you buy?"

"Some snacks for us for the road."

"You got our road trip snacks without me?"

"I wasn't sure you'd want to come to the store."

"You felt confident enough that I'd drive a thousand miles with you, but you weren't sure I could handle a Walgreens run?"

"Let's go back and get more," he offers.

Watching him squirm revives my recently dead heart. I grab his arm to lead him across the intersection. My legs are jelly. My heart's a hummingbird. "No, no. Please. We will drive forward on the strength of your snacks alone."

"Don't you want to see what I got? To make sure?"

"I like to be surprised."

By the time we make it to the front of the hotel, I'm still holding on to him. In the time since I last saw him, I have put myself in countless different places, trying on new, exciting versions of

my life. Why hasn't any of it come close to the thrill of Ben Porter's pulse beneath my fingertips?

"I have to get my luggage from upstairs and my car from the
parking garage." He looks right at my hand on his arm.

I release him quickly. "Oh yeah. Totally. I'll just—"

"Wait here," he finishes. It sounds more like a request than a
completion of my thought. He hands me the snacks and jogs
inside.

Once he's out of sight, I open up the bag to inspect what
he's gotten. Right at the top, I see Twizzlers. "Oh my god," I say
aloud, reacting like my audience of podcast listeners can hear
me now.

All of my stories, the funny Name Redacted anecdotes I
sprinkle throughout episodes like bread crumbs? They are Ben's
stories too. In fact, they are ours. Together. Every single thing
I've branded as my own little secret belongs to Ben as well. And
none of it is very funny or very little anymore.

He pulls his car around to the front of the hotel. He has one
arm casually stretched across the back of the passenger seat as
he dips his head down to peer at me. He's still smiling his infinite, inviting smile. And still driving his safe, steady car, I notice, looking at his gray Honda Civic. It's not the exact same car
he had in high school, but it's the same make and model. Leave
it to Ben to be reliable as ever. As he always was.

Until the day he decided he wasn't.

When the trunk pops open, I walk around to put my suitcase
inside. There's an intimacy to this that could startle me if I let
it—my bag beside Ben's, miniature versions of our lives packed
up and placed side by side, expected to carry us through whatever the next few days are about to bring. If I stop to really analyze what I am doing, some of my carefully locked floodgates

will open up, and I will be drowned by all Ben used to mean to me and what it felt like to lose him. So I slam his trunk shut and close all my luggage and worries in there with it.

When I open his passenger door and slide into my seat, it's like sliding into an old life with a brand-new body. There's so much I didn't know about myself the last time we took this trip. How to hold my space without backing down. What it means to really listen to someone else without trying to project my own shit onto their life. Without the extra baggage, so to speak, this is the kind of second chance I've dreamt about.

If only I could go back and do things differently, knowing everything I do now. I'd be less insecure. More curious. I wouldn't let little things seem massive, or be too cynical. I'd be better at sex and better at making it mean less to me when it involves Ben.

This is my chance to do all of that. Past the nerves and the pressure and the weighty drama of our past, this has the potential to be something really fun. In a lot of ways. This isn't closure, Linda. This is *redemption*.

"You made some interesting snack choices," I bait. For every ounce of charm Ben sends my way without even trying, I'll send it back twice as strong, with concentrated effort.

His eyes flicker over. "I did good, didn't I?"

"Let's not get too confident. You got peanut M&M's. Not peanut *butter* M&M's."

"Not everything in there was just for you."

"Oh yeah? So you like Takis now? And you've moved past your bizarre stance on Goldfish?"

"It's not bizarre to think that they should have either a deeper relationship to fish or less connection to a common household pet," he says.

"Yes it is."

We are exchanging casual warm-up quips with ease, daring each other to be as interesting and funny and exciting as possible, trying to see how much we can level up before we plateau. It feels a bit like my podcast does in its best moments, when Javi and I have hit our groove. No matter how deep we dig or how much of ourselves we reveal, Javi and I always know it's for the entertainment of strangers. Here, in this Honda Civic, Ben and I are each other's only audience.

"You haven't changed a bit," he says fondly.

Of course I have. So has he.

But I know what he really means.

We haven't changed a bit. Not at our core—the place that lives beneath the hurt and the silence. Past all of that pain, we're still the same Dee and Ben. It's an easy space to reinhabit. It's an open window blowing air through my fingers. It's the midday sun shining through the front windshield, warming the tops of my bare thighs. It's cruise control.

Ben steals a look at me. "I've missed you."

My heart tries to pump the brakes. "I've missed you too," I answer, accelerating faster instead.

I will do it all right this time.

And it won't hurt me at all.

8

BEN

Dee has already adjusted the air-conditioning vents on her side and fixed her seat so that she has more legroom. Beneath her overalls, a striped shirt hugs her body, revealing a small patch of pale white skin below her left rib. Sunlight catches the strawberry in her hair as the air blows the finer pieces across her cheeks. The rest is pulled up into a high ponytail, exposing her long, graceful neck. There are tattoos on the insides of both of her arms. Tiny flowers and little butterflies and short phrases, too small for me to read without staring.

I have no right to want her. So I don't.

I *won't*.

"We should eat," I say. Without a response, she plugs her phone into my car's USB port and cues up directions to a nearby breakfast place. "Oh, is that where we're going?"

"If you don't bring me to pick out snacks, I don't consult you on our first meal."

"Fair enough."

The place she's selected isn't far from my hotel. I turned the opposite direction on our way out, so I have to circle back around.

The last time I ventured anywhere near this part of Chicago

was last November. Richie asked me to come to a Bears game with him. Gam insisted I leave her side and attend. Richie—never one to miss a chance for community hang time—had us tailgate outside Soldier Field beforehand. We sat in the freezing cold with strangers, talking about nothing with the kind of dogged sincerity only midwesterners possess. During a lull, nursing a beer and shivering, I found myself intentionally wondering about Dee for the first time in a very long while.

She'd always wanted to move to Chicago. That was her plan after high school. She couldn't afford college, not that she wanted to go in the first place. The only reason I knew she'd made it into the city after all was because Richie saw her once. Bartending. From that point forward, I decided the entire Windy City belonged to Dee. Which meant I rarely visited. I couldn't risk accidentally stumbling upon her. I hardly ever went to our hometown to see my parents either, on the off chance Dee was in to see her mom. When I got forced into Chicago, I'd only go to places I was positive she wouldn't be. Like a football game.

That day at Soldier Field, she came into my head without warning. It was the cold that made me powerless. I was too focused on staying warm to stop myself from picturing who Dee had become. I imagined her bundled up in a huge parka, scowling as she walked against the bitter wind. The image was so simple it seemed real. It was easy to insert myself into it.

"It's a little cold, isn't it?" I pictured myself joking.

"Don't even fucking start, Ben," she muttered in reply.

Even in my own imagination, I knew I'd asked her to join me for something, and she'd begrudgingly agreed. That was the way we always operated. I used to text her, **Do you want to get pizza with me after baseball?** And she'd answer, **No,** then follow up ten seconds later with **What time do I need to be ready?**

Dee gave me a hard time, but she always, *always* showed up. Only after she was gone did I understand how much that meant to me.

Out there in the parking lot of Soldier Field, Richie tapped me on the shoulder and whispered, "Dude, everything good?"

"Yeah, yeah," I assured him, shaking away the false memory I'd created. "Sorry."

All through the game—and long into the night—I worked like hell to stop revisiting the thought of Dee. She always pressed against my thoughts like a headache. Even something as small as tying my shoes could bring her to mind. She never learned how to lace with a real knot. She only did bunny ears. Picturing her hurt me, which is why I did my best to ignore all the places she popped up. It was better to forget her. Or easier, at least.

Now she's here, sitting shotgun in the new car I leased from the Honda dealership last month, and she's somehow exactly how I expected her to be while also being so much more than I could have ever prepared for. Being around her turns the volume of the world up to full blast. Every color becomes noteworthy. Every sound is something worth mentioning. When we are together, we are surrounded by opportunities. No amount of imagination could ever account for this—the way her sheer presence cuts through all the static in my brain.

"Why are people like this!" she screams as a jaywalker sprints across the street. "I do shit like that all the time, but it's way scarier when we're the drivers!"

"Operating a two-ton vehicle does have a way of putting things in perspective." I steal a quick glance at her. She's got her hands squeezed between her legs. "Do you have a car?"

"Nope. I take the train or walk."

"That's for the best."

"Oh, get over yourself. I'm a *visionary* behind the wheel."

Dee loved to drive. She was very, very bad at it. She didn't have a car then, either, so she'd beg to drive mine. Every so often, worn down by her pleading, I'd agree. She'd brake too early, in a way that was guaranteed to send your head toward the glove box. She accelerated like a getaway driver. Her lane changes seemed to surprise even her. Sometimes she'd say things like, "Guess we're in the left lane now!" and laugh as she turned up the volume on the music.

"You know, I haven't gotten a speeding ticket in a whole year," I offer in return. Teenage Dee was a bad driver. I was a fast driver. They may seem like the same thing, but they are not.

After a genuine gasp, Dee rolls her window down even further. "Everybody, look out! We've got a Former Bad Boy coming through! A Reformed Rebel of the Road! Beware! He may redevelop a need for speed at any moment! Please! I am begging you! Stay vigilant!"

I hold back a grin. "Thanks. I'd hate if anyone wasn't ready for my arrival."

"Should I call the diner ahead of time? So they know who they're dealing with?"

"That would be great."

She reaches into my snack bag and makes a point to pull out the Twizzlers and press the package to her ear. "Hi, I've got seventh-grade science teacher Ben Porter arriving in about five minutes. With the curly hair and the dopey grin? Yes. That's the one. He's driving about fifteen below the limit right now, but we're in traffic. Things could change at any moment. I just want to make sure your staff is aware." She pauses, nodding. "Right. Yes. Thank you so much!"

I don't remember telling her the details of my job. Then again, this entire twenty-four hours has felt like a fever dream. The entire last year of my life has, if I'm honest.

"What did they say?" I ask after she pretends to hang up.

She places a hand on my bicep. "It's better if you don't know."

The touch is unexpected. But not unwelcome.

It should be, though. It *has* to be.

A decade ago, we promised we would take this same trip again in ten years. Even if my entire life has been a lie, I want that one thing to be true. Sleeping together broke us apart. Keeping my distance is the only way I can make sure nothing goes wrong between us this time.

We arrive at Dee's restaurant of choice, which is so close I did not need to get my car out of the hotel spot yet. We end up parking in a garage that can't be more than a block away from where we started. It's my fault for not suggesting food sooner. At the same time, every extra moment with Dee is worth it. I'd circle the block a hundred times if we got to keep laughing together.

We get seated near a window, and a server takes our drink order immediately. Two coffees. As soon as she leaves, Dee puts both of her elbows on the table and leans her face into her hands. Across the street at Grant Park, there's a distant but notable view of several large sculptures.

Squinting, I make out a series of giant legs walking in all different directions. "What exactly am I looking at?"

"*Art,*" Dee explains.

"Right. Of course."

"I love how weird it is." The thoughtfulness in her expression is familiar. Wherever we went, she always found something to appreciate. Her face sinks deeper into her hands. "I don't really get it. Which makes me feel like I *do* get it. Because maybe that's the point?"

"That's how I feel when I try to explain cell regeneration to my students."

Her gaze leaves the statues and lands on me, making no secret of how she inventories every inch of my face. "Yeah, what's up with teaching?"

Our waitress drops off our coffees. Dee takes a large gulp, not even waiting for the liquid to cool.

"Remember when you wanted to be an endodontist?" she continues. "You were *obsessed* with root canals. It was like, your *thing*." She still has this unforgettable way of placing heavy, bolded emphasis on certain words.

"That was weird," I admit, mixing sugar and cream into my cup.

"It was *extremely* weird. But I liked how much you loved it."

"What can I say? Dental trauma really changes a person. Didn't I give that up around . . . sophomore year, though?"

"Yeah. You did." She confirms it with so much assuredness that I believe her more than I believe myself. "But you were completely serious about it for at *least* a year. Then you wanted to be a physical therapist. *After* your professional baseball career ended, of course."

"Right." A trail of steam curls up toward my face. It smells so nice. *This* is so nice. Being with someone who grew up alongside me. Who knows my life for more than just the highlight reel.

"How did we land on seventh-grade science? That *never* came up." Anyone else and I'd assume they find this boring. Dee used to read my mom's grocery receipts and ask me questions about each purchase.

"Well, I always liked science," I remind her. I helped her with her chemistry and physics homework more than a few times. "And teaching was way lower stakes than saving people's infected teeth every day. Plus I started coaching Little League in college, and I learned that kids are really cool."

It's been so long since those sleepless nights in my Indiana University dorm, staring at the ceiling, wondering if it was okay to do something different than I'd planned. It's almost funny to think about how much I agonized over not making it as a walk-on for the IU baseball team. I was so upset, I wouldn't even go to their games my freshman year. None of that feels important enough to mention. Everyone in my life rolled with the changes. As long as I was happy, they were happy. No further discussion required.

Except Dee picks up on the oversimplification right away. "I don't know." She lets her doubt linger in the air, watching how the pause affects me. "You liked science a normal amount. Not a make-it-your-career amount."

My hands get sweaty. It's been ten years since someone challenged me like this. "It was a surprise to me too. A good one."

She makes a point to scrunch her nose and scrutinize me, showcasing the fact that her doubt has not been fully erased. I hold her gaze. This isn't something I'm uncertain about. The fastest way to prove that is to look her dead in the eye.

With one swift nod, she accepts my answer. "Cheers to good surprises," she says, breaking into a winning smile as she holds up her mug for me to clink mine against.

After we toast, I take my first sip of coffee. It's hot enough to scald my tongue. Did Dee get a different brew than me? There's no way she's downing this.

Suddenly, she takes hold of my forearm. Her hand is warm

against my skin. Steady. "Wait." She puts down her drink to stare up at the light fixture overhead. Her face is tense with concentration. "What was that phrase you'd always sing in middle school? *The malacharia is the produce of the cell* or something."

I can't contain my laughter. Of course she'd have one more question for me. One final test to pass. "The mitochondria is the powerhouse of the cell."

"Right! Yes! Oh my god. You *did* love that. Not as much as root canals, but I'll say it was in your top ten. Is that what you teach?"

"That's exactly what I teach. I even teach the song."

"No you don't. Oh my god. *Ben.*" There it is again. My name from her lips has a dozen meanings, all better than the real one. "I bet your students like you."

"You never really know with seventh graders."

"Of *course* you do. They're just guarded. They're learning the world is shit, and they're trying to figure out if you're worth their trust or you're another lying adult."

"That's true. Working with twelve- and thirteen-year-olds has definitely taught me that the fastest way to earn their respect is to be yourself. While also laughing at yourself. They hate when you try too hard. And they can smell a liar from a mile away. So I do my best not to lie to them."

I could be wrong, but it feels like Dee is asking if *I'm* worth her trust.

When I showed up last night, she looked ready to kill me. Which is about what I expected. But then she looked . . . well, she looked for a moment like she *wanted* me. That's got to be me being my own loose nail. Dee Matthews is way too evolved to still care about a high school love affair gone wrong. Which confirms that when it comes to us—no matter how much it lights me up inside to see her face or hear her laugh—this trip is about repairing our friendship. Nothing more.

Gam asked me to go after what I want. I want Dee back in my life. That doesn't need to be complicated by the fact that we slept together once, ten years ago. Back then, I thought I should be an endodontist who also played professional baseball and then retired into a life as a physical therapist. I used to eat cafeteria cookies for breakfast. I went to bed at three in the morning and made it to class by eight with a smile on my face. As far as I knew, my family was still biologically mine. Things were different.

Our waitress comes back to take our food order. Neither of us has looked over the options, but if there is one thing I am good at, it's spending five seconds glancing at a menu and picking the first thing that appeals to me. In this case, it's a frittata.

Dee—the one who has actually been to this restaurant before—gets flustered by the prospect of ordering. If she's still the same Dee I used to know, she'll end up getting something sweet, like French toast.

She asks if I'm ready. When I tell her I am, she sighs at the waitress.

"Okay, let him go. I'll be fast," she says.

My order goes by so quickly that Dee reacts with another exasperated sigh. To buy more time, I grin at the waitress, a gruff older woman with the kind of face that scolds.

"Is this busy for you?" I ask her.

She answers by deepening her frown, then tapping her pen across her order pad. "Nah. This is the lightest Monday afternoon we've had in a while. You from out of town?"

"Yeah. I live in Indiana."

"That's hardly outta town," she tells me matter-of-factly.

Dee flails her arms, reacting to the menu like she's fighting with it.

"True. But I don't come to Illinois much anymore. So"—I read the waitress's name tag—"Marge, where are you from?"

"Do ya want me to come back?" she asks.

Dee looks up at me with stern intention. A clear no.

"She's almost ready," I assure Marge. "Until then, maybe you could tell me about all the pins on your apron? Since it's not busy? I see you're an Eagles fan. How the hell did we get an Eagles fan all the way out in Chicago?"

This cracks right through Marge's hard exterior. She grins at me with a warm, weathered smile as she explains the origin of each of her apron decorations.

Just as she's gotten to telling me about a sunflower pin from her granddaughter, Dee signals that she's ready to place her order. She flashes me a deep, apologetic smile, and it hits the center of my chest like a wild pitch—quickly and with uncontrolled force. Then she orders cinnamon French toast. Exactly like I predicted.

"I could've guessed that," I say once Marge leaves.

"But then we'd never know that Marge's second husband is from Philly and her granddaughter June owns a beautiful sunflower farm in Idaho."

Dee smiles at me again. If she were in fact a pitcher, she'd have to be pulled from the game for how she's behaving. She's right on the edge of being dangerous, holding my eye a little too long, then letting her gaze wander to my lips.

As if she knows it, she lets out a quick laugh and looks away, amused with either me or herself. It's impossible to tell. Still smiling, she reaches for her purse, rooting around in there until she pulls out several things: a notebook, three hair ties, a bottle of lotion, two loose gum sticks, and a blue pen.

Without saying a word, she opens her notebook and scrawls DEE AND BEN'S REUNION ROAD TRIP across the first clean page she finds. It's an unexpected shock to see our names together. We used to be a pairing everyone knew. Like salt and pepper. You could have one without the other, but you always remembered them side by side.

Now I'm Ben or Mr. Porter. Coach B to my Little League kids. Even when I've dated people, we haven't become synonymous with each other. My last girlfriend, Melissa, had a friend who called me Bran, because she insisted that's how I introduced myself. The more I asked her to stop calling me that, the more she committed, until eventually Melissa's entire friend group had taken to the nickname.

On the next line, Dee scribbles ILLINOIS TO COLORADO. Her handwriting hasn't changed. Still messy and hard to read, scribbled out in dense scratches.

"Mr. Compass, what's the plan?" she asks in a singsong tone as she writes the words DAY ONE. *That* was a nickname she made up for me in sixth grade, when I tried for exactly three hours to be a guy who kept a compass in his pocket. It was a gift from my uncle who lives on a boat. Dee never, and I mean *never*, let me live it down.

"Thanks for asking, Captain Business," I respond in my best re-creation of her playful melody. My nickname for her came a while later, for reasons I can no longer remember. Ever since, it's existed in tandem with mine. "If we were to drive straight through, it would take about sixteen hours. But we've got places to go. Things to see."

She pretends to write down what I'm saying, her marker hovering right above the page. "Yes, yes. Of course. Places to go. Things to see. Exactly." Without so much as a waver, still using her sing-speak voice, she transitions to a real question. "Will we be going to Wally's Fishbowl Aquarium again?"

"Why not? Des Moines is about five and a half hours away from here. We can do dinner there."

She writes it down for real.

This is how we are. We're joking, but we're serious. It's a communication style I haven't practiced in years. I settle back in with little effort. The danger is that it's almost impossible to tell what's true and what's make-believe.

Our food comes. Between bites, we continue putting together a loose outline of the trip ahead. There are nights when the only way I can get to sleep is to get up and tinker with my lesson plans for the next morning's classes. Things make a lot more sense to me when I can see them laid out. Dee doing this feels like an even bigger olive branch than agreeing to come on this trip in the first place. She's agreeing to let it have a little structure.

When we get to planning what we will do in Colorado, and I ask if we can actually go to a baseball game this time, she says, "Oh god, Ben. Not the *baseball* game. Are they even *playing* right now?"

"I'm sorry to tell you they are," I respond. "Actually, the Rockies happen to be playing the Cubs when we're there. We can't miss it."

"Benjamin, you know I'm a White Sox fan."

I squeeze my eyes closed. "Please don't say things like that."

She starts singing "Don't Stop Believin'" by Journey, a song that has plagued me ever since the White Sox made it their anthem when they won the World Series in 2005.

When my wince turns into resignation, Dee relents, only to recite her favorite sports take. "Baseball would be a lot more fun for everyone if people could like more than one team! It's just a name! All of your little players could get traded to another team tomorrow, and suddenly you're not rooting for them anymore? Why? They're all the same people! Just wearing different colors!"

She used to make this argument so much that, truthfully, I *did* internalize it. Richie sometimes insults complete strangers for wearing a Packers jersey or a Cardinals hat, and it's another place where I've found myself accidentally thinking of Dee. Because she's right. It doesn't make sense. When my Little League kids quit or change teams, I don't stop caring about them as people or as players.

"True," I offer up. "Rooting for a team is about more than the players, though. It's about the place too." If she's going to use her favorite take, it's only right I return with mine.

"But the Cubs and the Sox both play in Chicago. You're making it north side versus south side, which seems a little elitist to me!" There's a soul-deep satisfaction in her smirk. She's always loved to call me on my bullshit, and she's very good at it. "When we go to our game, we're cheering for *both* teams."

Our game.

She called it *our* game.

"I'll try my best," I say.

"Very good." She doodles a star next to the prospective baseball game. Then she writes, *Go Rockies! I love them so much! It means a lot to me to see them play! They're all great guys with big hearts!—Benjamin N. Porter.* She looks up, waiting for the laugh I am eager to give. She knows just how funny I find her.

When it's all written out, sprawled across the pages of her notebook, our plans look to be an inarguable guide to reviving our friendship.

We will do it all right this time.

And it won't hurt us at all.

Did I Forget to Tell You?

EPISODE 171: ETIQUETTE LESSONS

(ft. Sloane Ford, star of the upcoming film *Horizons*)

DEE: So you paid for the whole meal?

SLOANE: Yes. Before I even got seated.

JAVI: You're legendary.

DEE: What did your boyfriend think of that?

JAVI: Not you calling Joseph Donovan "your boyfriend."

DEE: What else am I supposed to say?

JAVI: Maybe "Emmy-nominated actor Joseph Donovan."

DEE: Okay, Sloane, what did your boyfriend—Joseph Donovan, Emmy-nominated actor for a miniseries I'm sorry to say I did not watch—think of you paying the bill?

SLOANE: He was shocked, actually. In a good way.

DEE: This is legitimately thrilling to hear. Javi can tell you that this is a move right out of my playbook.

JAVI: Dee is obsessed with paying for people's meals. Sometimes I say, "Please, it's okay. We're at Starbucks. I've got it."

DEE: Look. For most of my life, I could barely pay for myself. Now that I can, it's something I want to do as often as possible! And Sloane Ford—two-time People's Choice Award nominee for her work on my favorite show, *The Seeker*—agrees!

SLOANE: I do. It's a good move.

JAVI: At no point did I say it wasn't. I just think too much worrying about who has paid for what, and you're going to get yourself into a whole new headache.

DEE: Yeah, but I'd have to imagine that's a whole different world for two people born into money like Sloane and Joseph. Right?

JAVI: Dee!

DEE: What? It would be weirder if I acted like they weren't! Stars, they're *not* just like us!

SLOANE: I'm not going to lie to you. Money has never been a concern of mine. I'm conscious of it. But I've never worried about what people owe me. My dad, on the other hand. He's obsessed with knowing what people owe him.

DEE: Oh my god.

SLOANE: Shit. I shouldn't have said that. Sorry, Dad!

DEE: That's the point of the show. We're airing it all out! And, Mr. Ford, if you're listening, quit being so stingy! We know you don't need to chase down your friends for their half of the dinner bill!

JAVI: You forgot to list her dad's credits.

SLOANE: No. Please don't. My dad knows them.

DEE: He has at least two Oscars. That's all I've got.

JAVI: Sloane, I'm sorry that Dee is putting you through it today.

SLOANE: I don't mind at all. I like her grit.

DEE: Thank you. If we are going to have a literal celebrity on our show, the least I can do is prod a little bit about the financial aspect of her relationship! And we all know money is a very sensitive topic for me!

JAVI: We certainly do.

9

DEE

As soon as Marge comes over with the bill, Ben hands his card to her.

"Why'd you do that?" I ask. Marge quirks her eyebrows in surprise, then skirts off as fast as she can.

"Oh. I was—" Ben pats his pockets like he's feeling the missing weight of the credit card he just passed off. "I figured—"

"You figured what?"

"That I should pay," he finishes weakly.

"Why?" This single syllable is a warning shot, made doubly dangerous by the scowl on my face. My whole body leans forward.

Ben stiffens. "I don't know."

"Me either. I can contribute."

"Right. Yes. Of course. I just—I don't know."

"I don't know either." This is my best attempt at resisting the powerful urge to mention aloud that I've put entirely too much stock into why he's done this. I was only a little offended before. Now my cheeks are on fire as my fingernails dig into the cushioned seat beneath me. There's a certain song and dance to this that he shouldn't have skipped.

I'll pay—

Come on. Let me chip in.—

No, no, Dee. You're coming all this way with me—
But I owe you—

That's the real truth. I owe Ben hundreds of dollars in meals and activities. Maybe thousands. It's a financial backlog I tried my best to keep up with when we were young. At some point it became so immense I started praying I'd win the lottery so I could give him half. When you don't have any money, you're very aware of how often someone covers for you. Ben may as well have been my personal roof.

Things are about to go south. We may not leave Chicago. In fact, I might need to abandon a quarter of my wardrobe and the entirety of my skincare products in the trunk of Ben's car, all over a breakfast that costs $42.47.

"I thought I should," Ben tries.

This is, once again, the wrong response. It's the wrong response and we're not even on the road yet. Now I'll have to spend endless hours trapped in a car with a guy who still thinks I'm a broke teenager who can't afford to purchase a bag of Doritos. It doesn't matter that I've managed to claw my way out of the sinkhole that is poverty. Ben only sees what I used to be.

My newest therapist recently asked me to write out all my buttons—the fun little things that make my temper flare. The first button I wrote down was money. Because until you've stolen untouched dinner scraps from the restaurant you work at to take the edge off hunger you can never fully satiate, you don't really understand what someone can do with ten dollars when they're desperate. So any kind of flippancy about money—any casual inconsideration, even with the best of intentions—makes me feel like my throat's been wrung out.

It's taken me a lot of conscious effort to identify when a button of mine has been pushed. This one blares red throughout me, setting my every nerve alight. My therapist reminded me of something I hate to admit might be true right now: my buttons will get pushed even when the other person hasn't actually done anything. I can be a better person than I am. Sometimes I don't want to be.

Maybe Ben really did mean to pay as a thank-you. If we'd just done the song and dance. Or he'd said as much after any of the several chances I gave him to explain. But he didn't. Talk about people who haven't changed. How much between us would have been solved by Ben saying things outright? Probably everything.

"Dee," he says, like there's anyone else in the restaurant he could be talking to.

"What?" The statues across the street provide me a satisfactory visual distraction. *Let me join you, legs. I am ready to become inanimate.*

"I shouldn't have done that. I'm really sorry."

This gets my attention. Ben readjusts his baseball cap, pushing down his unruly curls. He does it twice, with his lips squeezed between his teeth in clear anticipation of my response. I want to have a rebuttal. Or a quick, cutting dismissal. But he's apologized without pretense, and it's such a shock that all I can do at first is say thank you. The relief floods his face, softening me further.

"I'm sorry too," I say back, meaning it. "I knew what you meant."

"But I didn't say it."

"You didn't say it," I echo.

Our last fight is so clearly on both of our minds. My unanswered questions roar forward. *Where did you go? Why didn't you ever turn back? How could you leave?*

"Where'd you learn to apologize like that?" is the one I ask aloud.

It's not like me to be a coward. It's kind of my whole deal, actually. Blazing forward through uncomfortable moments. Asking the questions other people avoid. With any other person, I'd hold their feet to the fire and ask the hard thing. But when it comes to Ben, there are already too many shards of fear in my heart from the last time we fought. If I came here to do everything better, then I can't be accusatory and harsh. The old Dee couldn't manage her pain. This Dee can.

In silent communion, Ben accepts that the window of opportunity has been shut. "Teaching," he says.

We are back to safe again. Back to a place where neither of us will be hurt.

"*The students were the teachers all along*," I joke. "Never would have learned that in endodontics."

"Not a chance."

Marge returns with Ben's card. It's a little awkward when he signs the receipt. Marge tries valiantly to make it even more uncomfortable by thanking *only* Ben for coming in, not me. Little does she know, it doesn't even faze me. Ben's always captivated people with so little effort on his part.

"Hope you can make it out of Indiana to come and see me again soon," she tells him. "It's not that far away."

"Absolutely," he assures her. Once she's out of earshot, he leans forward and whispers, "*Guess she fucking hates when people order French toast.*"

I lean forward too. Both of our elbows are on the table. "*If only I wanted a frittata . . .* "

"*You could've avoided so much pain . . .*"

Our shared laughter breaks us apart. My laugh mixing with

Ben's makes the sweetest sound, distracting all the other patrons in the diner.

Because of Ben I understand laughing more for the company than the content. His willingness to commit to the random shit I throw his way makes things ten times funnier. The words don't matter. It's the intention. Our joy follows us all the way out onto the street, where we hit a comfortable stride on our way back to the car.

Abruptly, Ben turns his head.

"What's that?" he calls out.

I look around. There's no one near us. Still, he nods as if he's listening to someone.

Handsome.

The word intrudes upon my confusion. He used to be cute. Now he is handsome.

If we'd known each other all this time, I'm not sure I'd be able to notice this change. Now I'm here watching him commune with the wind or whatever, and all I can ask myself is *Why would they make a person that looks like this?* It should be illegal. As if this is a face I'm just meant to witness! The sharp cut of his jaw? The fine shadow beneath his cheekbone, with the lightest layer of facial hair? The constellation on his cheek and his honey rich eyes, deep set and thoughtful? No one can withstand this!

"Sorry," he says. "That was Marge. She told me she knows who you are. And she wants to know if she could come on your podcast."

It's another joke. An unexpected one. Bizarre and nonsensical. Exactly the way I prefer my humor. But the mention of my job flusters me. On my podcast Ben is nothing but a funny, mysterious character I mention teasingly in passing, not a six-foot-tall Libra sun with a Pisces moon and a Virgo rising who squeezes his lips together when he's nervous and used to categorize his music playlists by their ability to capture the essence of certain days of the week.

A shadow thought emerges.

This conversation is Podcast Worthy.

"I don't think she'd tell me her deepest secrets," I say, pushing the thought of my show far, far away.

This isn't Name Redacted. This is Ben. Somehow they are different. And things that happen with Ben are not for the podcast.

"There's still time for you to get a frittata before we go," he tells me.

"It's okay. I don't wanna look in the rearview."

Ben gazes at me with his illegally handsome face. "Onward?"

Wordlessly, I charge ahead, warm with the knowledge that Ben plans to follow me the whole way.

10

BEN

Every time I've made this drive alone, I've had to chug an energy drink and plow forward. The ground stays flat almost the whole way, until suddenly, when you least expect it, the Rocky Mountains appear, carving jagged outlines into the crystal-blue Colorado sky. That's a thousand miles from where we are.

Right now there's not much to see beyond the Chicago traffic bleeding back to the suburbs. Concrete barricades run on either side of the freeway, bisected by the train. It should be boring. But with Dee in my car, every mile brings a new opportunity. Maybe we will make up jokes about the other drivers we pass? Maybe we will count how many hats we see or guess what kinds of couches everyone has?

Dee can make the world bend for her. When she wants things to be light, they are. When you've crossed her, everything becomes heavy. Money has always been a sensitive thing with her. Something to tiptoe around. It's never been something I've had to think about. Not in a matter of stray tens or twenties, at least.

It was wrong of me to assume I'd have to carry the entire financial burden of this trip. We've just never known each other in any other way. There's so much we have to relearn, and it's hard to know what needs to be said versus what's understood.

Out of nowhere, she flicks a Cheez-It at my face.

"What was that for?" I ask.

"Guess."

If she wants me to bring up the check again, it's not written on her face. I'm not putting myself in hot water when I don't need to. So I say, "For not taking you to get the snacks?"

"Hmm. Strong guess. But no." She turns down the music. "For all the times you still lied."

My heart rate increases. "Lied about what?" To the best of my knowledge, everything I've said to her so far has been true. Maybe some of it has been vague, but nothing's been a lie.

"Earlier, you said you tried your best not to lie to your students," she explains. "But I know you have!"

Leave it to Dee to pick back up a conversation that ended almost two hours ago. "Sometimes you have to lie," I concede.

"I knew it!" She flicks another Cheez-It my way. "Give me one example where lying was better."

There are so many stories she would enjoy. I hadn't consciously kept track of them. Now that she's asked, they seem to be right within reach, like there's a drawer in my brain labeled DEE that's stuffed with everything I've ever wanted to tell her over the last decade. It's so overflowing I'm desperate to give her as much as I can, as if all these funny memories and charming anecdotes will ensure she sticks around after we're done with this trip.

"When I was a student teacher, I worked with third graders for a quarter," I start. "Their teacher put me in charge of the classroom bulletin board, and one month the theme was Be the Change You Wish to See. So I had all of them do an assignment where they wrote down what they planned to change about the world. And this one girl wrote, 'I wish to cure genital herpes.'"

The laugh that erupts out of Dee is bigger than I anticipated, and I knew she'd find it funny. Her generous spirit has always drawn me to her. Even as a grade schooler, she was never afraid to be the person who clapped first in a crowd or cheered into silence.

"The girl drew all these hearts around it and stuff," I continue. "I could tell she really thought she was onto something big. When she turned it in and asked me what I thought, I lied to her about how excited I was, and I said, 'That's great! I hope you find that cure!'"

Dee's near tears she's so amused. "*Ben, no!* Did you send it home to her parents?"

"I couldn't bring myself to," I admit for the first time ever. "One of them probably *has* genital herpes, and I do really hope they get that cure. Something told me they wouldn't want to discuss that with me, though."

"Wasn't it up on the bulletin board for the month?"

"I hid hers behind a plant. Not even her actual teacher could see it."

"*Ben!* Maybe this was an opportunity to talk to the class about sexual health."

"A class of third graders? No. That was not my job."

"Okay, okay. Fair. It's really never too early to talk about sexual health, but I get it." She reaches across the gearshift to pick up the Cheez-Its beside my leg.

"Thank you for cleaning up your litter," I say.

"I'm not making any promises. You know I'm a messy eater."

"I've accepted that Taki dust will soon live in the cracks of my seat."

"You're the one who made yourself the king of snacks. I would've gotten pretzels or something." She pauses. "And probably left the Twizzlers off the list."

She's daring me to travel back in time. Not that it's hard. I can imagine the sticky heat of her bare skin on mine. I can hear the air conditioner wheezing beside us. And I can see that damn Twizzlers package stuck to the space between her shoulder blades.

"We forgot to put away the snacks," she'd whispered into my ear. Her laugh melted away all of my nerves. "Do you want one?"

"A Twizzler?" I'd asked, distracted.

She twisted her arm to pull the package off her back. "You sure?" She smiled down at me, naked and beautiful and happy, then ripped the package open.

We each ate a Twizzler. In the middle of having sex. Which was weird. But it was also perfect, and somehow exactly us, never really thrown by anything getting in our way. Except each other. When we got in each other's way, we did not recover.

No.

This is all me being my own loose nail again.

We are adults who haven't seen each other since we were teens. We are two people in a car, driving across the country. We used to know each other well, and that familiarity makes this seem more significant than it is. That's all. There's no use in trying to make anything more out of what's happening. We are fulfilling a promise. Completing an assignment we gave ourselves ten years ago. Drive to Colorado. Dig up the time capsule in Gam's backyard. Share some laughs. Then pack it all up and move on. Friends again.

"I like Twizzlers," I say to her.

"I know you like them," she counters, indignant. "I remember."

Dee's fond of a warning shot. Sometimes it's with words. Sometimes it's a glare. Sometimes it's a firm hand on the wrist. In this case, it's all of the above. She's reminding me that one wrong move from me and this falls apart. But I don't want to ruin this. Not now. If I can help it, not ever again.

I swallow back the itch that would turn this into a fight and go for playful instead. "Hey, you haven't picked out a road trip game for us to play."

The pressure of her stare burns into me. She is well aware she makes a mark. In the end, she seems to make the same decision I have—this fight isn't worth it.

She hums out a soft sigh and says, "Good point," then turns to peer out her window. "Two Truths and a Lie. Alphabetical. Winner of each round controls the music for an hour."

"So all of our truths and a lie have to start with the same letter of the alphabet?"

"Yes."

"What if we both correctly choose the lie?"

"Split the hour. Thirty minutes to each of us."

"What if neither of us gets it right?"

"We listen to the radio."

Keeping my eyes on the road, I extend my hand for a shake. "Deal."

Dee takes hold. "Deal."

It's so nice to feel her palm in mine. It reminds me of the moment right before a movie starts. That heady, eager plunge into darkness, leaving the familiar world behind to go somewhere unknown. She lets go, then tears the Twizzlers bag open, grabbing one for herself and one for me.

After a long bout of silence—the two of us chewing, my tires treading the pavement, and my mind fighting the urge to replay that same old memory of us and the Twizzlers over and over—Dee begins the game. "My favorite animal is an anteater. I have astigmatism. My first boyfriend was named Adam."

It's not like her to start this easy. She must think I'm out of practice.

Infamously, I came home from kindergarten one day and told my mom I had a girlfriend named Dee. Unfortunately, I hadn't yet told Dee she was my girlfriend. I was pining from afar. She wasn't even in my class. I only saw her at recess. We'd never spoken. I did not expect my mom to *find Dee at the end of the next school day and ask her about it.*

In the first of countless times Dee backed me up without any context, she proudly told my mom she was in fact my girlfriend. Then she told me. Which made for the first four words Dee ever spoke to me. *Hi. I'm your girlfriend.*

"This is obvious," I say. "Your first boyfriend was me."

Dee places a hand on my cheek. I almost swerve into the next lane.

"I'm sorry, but that's incorrect," she says. "I don't have astigmatism. In fact, there are no issues with my eyes. They are perfect. Like me."

I swat her hand away. Pretending to want to touch my face is a powerful move, but I can't be fooled. "There's a picture of you kissing my cheek from kindergarten graduation."

"First of all, adults who encourage romance in their six-year-olds are fucking weirdos, and I very much include our parents in that. Second of all, my first love affair was with Adam in day care. Which was also encouraged by my weirdo mother. It was also *way* before you and I met, Benjamin."

"You've never mentioned him before."

It sounds ridiculous considering she's talking about someone she knew when she was four, and we haven't spoken in a decade. There's an undercurrent to everything that says we are choosing to treat the ten-year gap between us like nothing more than a single missed stair step in the long path of our interconnected lives.

"I don't like to talk about how Adam and I drifted apart," she explains with pretend regret. "We eloped inside the playhouse. My mom pulled me out of day care because she couldn't afford it anymore, so Adam and I didn't stay in touch. If I believed in the sanctity of marriage, I'd ask you to call me Mrs. Gonzalez."

Hot on the heels of her trick, I come up with my own. "Well, Mrs. Gonzalez, good luck choosing my lie. I can spell 'antidisestablishmentarianism' in under five seconds. My dad's name is Andrew. I have no allergies."

"Come on! Are you kidding me? Your dad's name is Garth." She clears her throat and drops her voice an octave. *"Porter residence, this is Garth speaking."* It's a pitch-perfect impression of my dad answering the landline back in middle school. She nails his stiff inflections and oddly heavy vowel sounds.

"You're wrong," I tell her.

"No I'm not."

"Yes you are."

"You can't win by cheating!" She grabs my ear and twists. "You know how I feel when people cheat during games!"

It tickles more than it hurts, but I still play it up. "Let go of me! I'm driving!"

"I don't care! I demand justice!"

"I have a mild allergy to pineapples," I squeak out. "Figured it out in college. I'd eat them, and my throat would get scratchy and tight."

Dee sits back, confused. She tucks her hands underneath the bare part of her legs. "Then you told two lies. I *know* your dad's name is Garth. No one forgets a name like that."

"Turns out, he's not my biological dad." I try to say it lightly, like it's not a big deal, but it lands with all the grace of dropped bricks.

"How can that be?"

The strain in my voice won't let up. "I haven't really gotten around to asking my mom the details, but I'm pretty sure it happened the old-fashioned way. With her former boss. Andrew."

"That's fucking wild," Dee says, her mouth agape.

She's the first person I've told since finding out from Gam, and still I know she's the only one brave enough to give me a real reaction. She's not trying to soften her response to please me. It's strangely the first thing to make me feel better. To hear from someone else how unbelievable it all sounds.

"How do you know his name is Andrew?" she asks.

"My mom worked as a receptionist at this doctor's office before I was born. Then she became a stay-at-home mom, so if Gam says it was her old boss, it has to be that guy. Dr. Andrew Ward."

It's odd to say it aloud. I've only ever read it. His name sounds so unassuming. He could be anyone. To me, he's apparently my father.

"He sent us a Christmas card once," I continue. "Maybe he sent them every year and this was the only time I ever saw it, but I happened to be in the room with my mom when she opened it. I was probably eight or nine. She took one look at the picture, then immediately threw the card away. I asked her why she did that. She said, 'It's a bad picture.' I vividly remember taking it out of the trash after she left the room and seeing this smiling guy standing on the beach with his wife and three kids. At the bottom it said 'From our loving family to yours. Wishing you nothing but health and happiness this holiday season.' I thought to myself, 'They look nice. What's wrong with them? Why can't we hang them up with the rest of our cards?'"

An unexpected surge of emotion rises in me. If I try to say more, I'll lose it. So I call the round a wash and tell Dee she can pick the radio station.

She looks at me for a long while. Long enough to make my mind race. She wants to ask more questions. How could she not? My whole life has been fundamentally changed by this.

Instead she picks 90s on 9 and turns the radio up, screaming along to the Spice Girls.

This is what I hate about myself. I clam up when shit gets hard. I've gotten better at lifting my chin and pushing through, but it's not natural to me. It's even harder seeing how well Dee remembers this about me. Like it's obvious. Ben Porter—can't be pushed too hard too soon.

Holding in everything that really matters.

11

DEE

All the things Ben thought he knew about his life have been rearranged without his permission. Even after I've made us sing at the top of our lungs and tossed M&M's into my mouth with horrible aim and started pointing at cars and pretending to know the people inside when we drive past, he still can't talk about the hurt he's carrying right on the surface.

I used to be the one who couldn't laugh anything off. I still can't. Not really. But when we were teens, there would be moments my struggles would unexpectedly bubble to the surface, and Ben would be waiting with concert tickets to see our favorite band or a reminder that we said we wanted to play mini golf and we *had to go right that very second.* He could always pull me back. Save me without showing me the life raft.

I want to keep myself from getting in too deep. It's hard when we're two feet apart and our conversation has picked up like the pause was merely hours instead of years and Ben is a wobbly chair, and for once, I'm the one who can provide the stability.

I turn down the radio. "Birdhouse," I say, soft and unsure.

Birdhouse was a place we used to live inside our heads—we never really said if it's a home or a bigger living space—but only we inhabit it. Its features are always expanding, with one constant: the birdhouse out front.

Almost instantly, Ben's shoulders relax. "Fireplace."

"Private pool."

He leans back into the driver's seat. "Waterfall."

"Waffle maker."

"Espresso machine."

"Rocking chairs."

"Two-story porch." His desperate clutch on the steering wheel softens.

I close my eyes and envision it. "Library that spans both stories, with a really tall ladder to reach the top shelves."

"Oh. That's good." He lets it sit, then adds, "Outdoor movie theater. With beanbag chair seats."

"And a popcorn machine," I throw in.

"Definitely. And a candy bar full of the staples." He smiles, genuine and full. "Okay, hear me out. A car wash."

"Wow. What kind? Park and wait, or a drive-through?"

"Definitely a drive-through. It's elaborate. Colors and lights. Lots of different soaps. Maybe it's themed." He pauses to think it over. "Yes. There are animatronic dinosaurs."

"I'm sold," I tell him, grinning. "T. rex at the end. His roar is what dries the car."

"Inspired."

Before I can get out my next feature, building on the chaotic greatness of a dinosaur car wash, Ben says "Birdhouse" again. To say it is to end the game without another word. It's a hello and a goodbye, and when we finish, I always picture us waving as we reverse out of a long, winding driveway, heading back to our regular lives again. We don't usually end this early. Sometimes we can go for hours.

Ben makes a sudden show of looking at his car's touch screen. "We're making good time," he says in an oddly formal voice.

I bet this is how he sounds when he teaches. The only image I have is of him at that science fair in the red tie with the blue chambray tucked into black slacks. The messy curls done just so. I picture him leaning over a projector, because I don't know how schools work anymore and I'm not ready to imagine everyone on iPads. He's really into the mitochondria or whatever, but he can tell that he doesn't have the attention of his class, so he's talking in a false, elevated tone, trying to pretend he's not affected by losing them.

"Are we?" I ask.

I've never had a good sense of time. Up until pretty recently, it's always moved wrong for me. Rent's always come up a little too soon. The next paycheck has always been a little further out than it should be for all the long, listless nights of work, serving and bartending at three different spots to keep my head above water, recording podcast episodes on three hours of sleep.

Even still, we haven't been driving long enough to really decide how quickly we will get to Colorado from here. It's *at least* fourteen hours away. And I've got an entire journal's worth of activities we have to complete before we get there.

Ben stares intently at the road. "I just said it to have something to say," he admits. "Thank you." His voice wavers. "I haven't thought of Birdhouse in so long."

We don't ever mention Birdhouse once we're done. We arrive unannounced and we leave without a trace. Since Ben's already broken an unspoken rule, I take this chance to ask him about something I've always wondered. "Where is it for you?"

"In your backyard," he answers without hesitation. "Well, the backyard where you grew up."

My mom's house is comically small with a bizarrely large, completely unkempt backyard. Football teams could hold a practice out there, if they weren't worried about stepping on shards of glass. Trees canopy overhead. Their trunks rot into the earth, knotting over cracked dirt. The one that fell during the tornado is still there, waiting to be removed. The grass grows so unwieldy that Mom no longer tries to mow it.

"Wow. Why? I would never think to place Birdhouse out there," I say.

"It always felt like magic. At least when we were kids."

Ben and I spent most of our grade school summers playing games in my backyard with some of the neighborhood kids. It was the one place where I wasn't lesser for my lack of money. My yard was an invaluable resource. A wide-open space with no one around to judge. Everyone had to look out for broken bits, and I couldn't give anyone snacks when they got hungry. We always walked to Ben's for that stuff. I was the wild. He was the shelter.

"Where is Birdhouse for you?" Ben asks me.

When I zoom out and look down the road to see where I've placed our little utopia, it's clear we're at Ben's grandma's house in the mountains. The very place we're traveling toward now.

"I think—"

I pause. It's hard to make it sound like a coincidence. As if the location happened to me as opposed to something I created. *Oh, how odd! Didn't even notice we were here!* When given the choice, I would rather discuss sexual positions on the internet than admit I've built a secret world somewhere deeply meaningful to me.

"It's at Gam's? Or something?" Saying it puts me a little closer to my emotional core than I planned to be, but this thing with Ben and me is a seesaw. When Ben goes skyward, I won't leave him suspended in the air.

"That's really nice," Ben answers. "I don't think the pool will fit."

I scoff. "You added a themed car wash."

"I'm working with a larger plot of land than you."

"The dimensions of Birdhouse are fluid."

"You're right."

"Of course I am."

We turn our heads in unison, stolen glances met in the middle. Over and over, we're proving that we can let go of what happened ten years ago without ever needing to mention it.

Maybe it *is* true. Old hurt can be buried, and something new can grow atop it.

IOWA

12

BEN

Four hours into this whirlwind trip, out of Illinois and into Iowa, Dee doesn't even get excited for animals grazing in the distance anymore. She still says, "Cow," and points, but we both know her heart isn't in it. In her journal, we've started keeping track of the different license plates we see. Our goal is to spot all fifty states. We are stuck at four: Illinois, Indiana, Iowa, and Michigan.

It would all be very boring if it weren't for the fact that Dee keeps finding ways to touch me.

She won the second round of Two Truths and a Lie, so she plugged in her phone and put on a playlist that's almost exactly the same as the mix CD she burnt for us the first time we took this trip. Every time a song comes on that we both used to love—which is every song—she grabs my arm or rests her hand on my leg. At first I thought it was . . . not an accident, but something she didn't mean to do to me *specifically*. Now it's happened so much I can't focus on the road. My mind is moving faster than my car ever could, though more than once I've looked at the speedometer and found myself closing in on ninety miles per hour.

"I need food," I say. What I really need is space. And something other than pavement to look at.

Dee fakes a gasp as she puts two hands over the Walgreens bag that lives between her shoes. *"Don't listen to him. He doesn't mean it."* Then she sits up straight and squeezes my bicep. "Should we stop and get better snacks?"

"I could eat," I tell her.

"Like, a meal? It hasn't been that long since Marge hand grew every ingredient in your frittata, then lovingly prepared it to your taste."

"It's almost dinnertime."

She looks at the clock on the dashboard. "You eat dinner at five fifteen p.m.?"

"Sometimes."

She throws a Cheez-It at me.

"I'm not lying!" I protest.

"Well, stop eating dinner before the sun sets! You are twenty-eight years old! Live a little!"

"I *am* living a little!" I make a gesture between her and me. Which is another one of those things I do without thinking. It's true that asking her to go on this trip again might be the most impulsive thing I've ever done. Admitting that takes it to another level. She's about to say something more when a call for her comes through on the CarPlay screen. The name Garrett appears with two pink heart emojis beside it.

My hands tense around the steering wheel. "You should get that."

"Oh, I don't think that's a good idea," she tells me.

She hasn't mentioned seeing anyone. I also haven't asked. I've been so desperate to say the right things that I haven't said much at all.

The shrill ringtone amplifies my frustration with myself. "Garrett Two Hearts is waiting."

She's about to press decline when suddenly her finger hovers over the green instead. "You're my boyfriend," she whispers to me as she presses down to accept the call.

"I'm your wha—" She puts a hand over my mouth and pulls a *shh* finger to her lips.

"What do you want?" She barks out to Garrett. "I'm with my boyfriend."

"Cut it out and answer your door," Garrett responds.

It's so harsh it makes me concerned. Maybe she's in the middle of something bad with this guy, and she came on this trip because she's in danger. She looks over at me with such candid amusement it doesn't seem that I'm right, but she's always been good at hiding her real pain.

"I'm not home," she tells Garrett. "I'm with my boyfriend. Like I said." She snaps her fingers to get my attention, then mouths, *Say something.*

What? I mouth back. *I'm not saying anything. I don't know what's going on.*

Dee giggles. "Sorry," she says to Garrett. "He was just . . . fingering me."

The sentence makes me gasp loud enough for Garrett to hear.

"See?" Dee says. "That's him."

Garrett's voice lowers. "Does he know about me? That I was just with you last night?"

"Yeah. He said that he had to show me all the ways he's so much better than you ever were."

"I doubt it," Garrett says.

They're flirting, which is not particularly fun for me.

"Keep doubting yourself, buddy," Dee says. "But I have to go. His fingers are still inside me and I'm about to finish. Something you don't know anything about!"

The idea of my fingers inside Dee is so overwhelming that it becomes hard to breathe. The Dee I knew in high school was like this too. Solely for the sake of being shocking, she was usually the crudest person in any room. Even the guys in the locker room never really talked like her. They could be gross too, don't get me wrong, but most of the time they were softer than anybody ever guessed. Craig Diedrich—ultraserious college prospect pitcher—cried before almost every game he pitched because his mom wrote him nice messages on pieces of scrap paper and tucked them into his game bag. My good friend Bobby Ramos—decent third baseman—used to make all of us belt out power ballads on the bus when we had road games. If anyone didn't fully commit, he made us start over.

A few years ago, Richie jokingly asked me to rank all the women I've ever slept with, and I got so upset by the proposition I had to take a walk around the neighborhood. It was two in the morning.

When Dee ends the call with Garrett Two Hearts, she falls into hysterics. "That was perfect."

"Was it?" Barely three minutes ago, I thought Dee might want me. Now it seems she's in some twisted thing with this Garrett guy, and I'm a pawn in their chess game.

I need to get out of this car.

"Oh, it was incredible," she tells me. "He was so pissed. You know, I broke it off with him like five seconds before you showed up last night."

"I'm sorry." This explains her willingness to join me and her insistence on touching me. She's grieving the fresh loss of this love, and I'm an easy distraction.

"Trust me, there's *nothing* to be sorry about."

She's trying to be brave, but she's hurt. This gives me a perfect opportunity to be her friend. Friends ask about relationships.

I tap my thumb against the steering wheel. "How long were you two together?"

"Not long enough for him to be calling me like that, that's for sure."

"Do you think you'll get back together?" I am so bad at this. Every question comes out sounding like a wince. Then again, she told this man I had my fingers inside her.

"If I ever get with Garrett again, it's only because I'm drunk and lonely."

"Why?"

"Because while he's a good time when we're alone, he's an asshole to other people for no reason. And look, I can be a bitch. I own that. But I try pretty hard to make sure I'm only a bitch when it counts." She lets it sit for a bit, then turns to me, placing a hand on my forearm once again. "Tell me. Would you ever call someone a stalker for learning your last name?"

No seems like the right answer, so that's what I say.

"*Exactly*," she responds.

"Did he do that?"

"Yes!" she yells. "And he *cried* when I said we should stop seeing each other. But he didn't even have my number saved in his phone!"

"*No*. How could he not have you in there? Don't you have two hearts beside his name?" The questions come easier after she's painted a clearer picture of this guy. He sounds like a loser, but I might be biased.

"That's what I'm saying! I was really feeling charitable when I did that. And he couldn't even put me in as Dee with a little smiley beside my name? A flower? A fucking peach or something?"

"It's the least he could do."

"I agree."

"You're saved as Captain Business in my phone." The words fall off my lips before I realize what it means to say them.

She sits up straighter. "No I'm not."

"Yes you are. Look at my phone. I promise. I added you back in last night."

The airflow has changed in the car. Not only have I admitted to using her nickname before we started using them in person, I've confirmed there was a stretch of time when I'd deleted her from my contacts completely. Hopefully our current reality matters more. The second she told me I had to text her old phone number to be able to reach her again, I was able to recall those ten digits faster than I can remember my own. And it felt natural to give her a more personal title in a contact list full of first and last names. Because even if she didn't come along with me on this trip, at least she'd be preserved in there as someone who stands out from the rest.

She grabs my phone from where it's resting on the dashboard. "Are you sure? You have to unlock it . . ."

"Bring it up to my face," I say.

She holds it out in front of me as I keep my hands on the steering wheel and my focus on the highway. Once the facial recognition unlocks it, she pulls the device into her lap, daring me to look between her legs.

I keep my eyes on the road.

"I could do anything I wanted on this right now," she notes.

"I know," I confirm, feeling the weight of her stare burning into me.

Eyes on the road.

When she finds herself in the contact list, she lets out a small hum of surprised satisfaction. "You put a CD emoji next to my name?" Before I can even explain, she's off on her own riff. "You swiped through the entire catalog of choices and landed on a blank CD? And you say you did this last night? Walking through the Loop in the rain, on your way to book a late-night room in the fucking Congress Plaza Hotel, you were typing out Captain Business, then scrolling for the CD emoji to keep there for all of time?"

"You used to love a mix CD," I explain.

This has the potential to be embarrassing. Not with Dee, though. Never with Dee.

"I *know* why you did it," she chides. "It's just funny." She places her hand on my arm again. "You know what I've learned, Mr. Compass? Life is full of disasters, and I should have as much fun as I can between them. Garrett—before he turned into a weirdo—was fun. And *this* is fun." She squeezes my arm in a very specific way, pressing into my bicep with insistent fingers, almost to the point of pain.

She's just explained that her time with Garrett Two Hearts was fun. And she's told me that I'm fun too. Which means that I'm not going out of my mind.

Dee Matthews is propositioning me right now.

Can I really sleep with her again? I wonder. I'd say it won't kill me to find out, but more than once my car's lane assist has had to guide me back to my place on the road, and that was before she confirmed she's making a pass at me.

"I'm getting gas," I announce. Several cars honk at me as I cut across three lanes of traffic to pull off at the next exit. I peel into the first gas station we see. When we get beside a pump, I fly out of my seat, yank my wallet out of my pocket, and grab twenty bucks.

"Here," I say. "I'll fill up. You go get what you want."

At once, Dee's hazel eyes lose their playfulness as her expression darkens. She glares at the money in my outstretched hand. "I can handle buying us some snacks."

She storms off before I can even begin to try to scrape together an apology.

Shit.

I did it again.

If I really am a loose nail, would someone please take a hammer and level me?

Distracted, I fumble through the process of filling up my tank, trying to come up with the best way to apologize without apologizing. In high school, finding ways to pay for the both of us without upsetting Dee was always a chess game. The best solution was to never acknowledge what I'd done. Otherwise Dee felt like she owed me, and she didn't. I'd have spent my life savings twice over to make sure we got to grow up together the exact way we did.

A large red truck pulls up to the pump on the other side of me. An older white man in reflective sunglasses steps out, looking in my direction. "Any reason you decided to cut me off?" He has a very distinct scowl fixed to his face.

"I . . . don't recall . . . doing that."

"Don't make it a habit."

"I don't plan to."

He walks around the pumps to get closer to me. "What's that?"

I let go of the gas pump to hold up my hands. "I apologize for cutting you off. I won't do it again."

"I don't like your tone," the man tells me.

This has all the makings of a very bad situation, and I don't even know how I got here. That's becoming a theme.

"I'm not trying to have a tone." Silence would have been the better move from me, because the man lunges forward, preparing for physical combat.

Back in my baseball days, when I'd stand beside the bag talking to the guys on the opposing team who'd made it to first base, I got

really good at small talk. There's an art to finding the right question to ask to keep the energy good, even during a tense game. I
had one of the most interactive positions, so it was important to me
to be a good representative of our team. It's a tough skill, to be both
friendly to my competition and attentive to the action. I could
keep the rhythm of the game flowing well and keep the energy
from souring.

Somehow I've lost this about myself. I don't know when.
But it's never been more clear than right now, as this complete
stranger puffs his chest, waiting for me to kick off our apparent
fistfight in front of a nondescript Iowa gas station.

Dee reappears. She wedges herself between the man and
me, her hands on her hips and her back pressed into my chest.
"This guy bothering you?" she asks me.

She's so close I can rest my chin on her ponytail. Her hair
smells like eucalyptus.

It turns out her question was rhetorical, because she stretches
out her arm to poke the man in the chest. "I might not look like
much, but I'll tell you straight up, I don't fight fair, and I don't
give a shit. I'll punch you in all the places it hurts the worst, and
I won't feel bad about it for a single second."

The man's copper sunglasses reflect Dee's face. She has
her chin up and one eyebrow arched, daring the man to try
something. I make a move to protect her. She senses my plans
immediately and puts up an arm to stop me.

"You really got your fucking lady out here handling things
for you?" The man makes a point to look over Dee.

"I am not his *fucking* lady," Dee snaps back. She might be on
her way to getting us murdered. If I try to stop her, she might kill
me herself.

"You're a coward," the man informs me.

Dee laughs in his face. "Oh, *please*. The only coward here is the big tough guy in his vroom-vroom truck who wants to punch a stranger for needing to fill up his gas tank. Go kiss your American flags good night, you shit-eating jackass."

The man appears both confused and enraged. His leathery cheeks have purpled, and there's spit at both corners of his mouth. He looks around the gas station at all the people watching, and the people on the street who have stopped to see this fight unfold.

He should be shoving my face into the concrete right now, but there's something about Dee. She could bite a diamond and crack it. He scowls at her for a bizarrely long time, until unbelievably, he backs up. His truck is still running, so he climbs in and speeds off without another word.

"That's what I thought!" Dee calls out.

Suddenly, I can feel my heartbeat in my ears. My hands are shaking from the adrenaline. I want to wrap my arms around Dee. Hold her. Thank her. Yell at her. All at once.

The other people at the gas station start clapping. Dee tosses them a laugh and one small wave of acknowledgment, then gets back into my car. Without a single new snack in sight.

I fumble to remove the gas nozzle from my tank. The last five minutes cram up all the available thinking space in my head. Dee propositioning me. The twenty in my hand. The spit at the corner of that man's mouth. Dee defending me. Everything keeps happening so fast. I can barely process one problem before another appears. Part of me wishes that man had knocked me out so I could have a minute to think.

You can do anything for a minute.

I'd like to use that time to lie down.

Dee says nothing to me as I get us back onto the highway.

She's even turned off the music. If battles could be won in angry silence, she would be a five-star general.

"I'm sorry," I find the courage to say outright.

"That guy was gonna drag you across the pavement," she responds. She knows I meant about the twenty, but in classic Dee form, she won't talk about it.

"What if he did that to you?"

"Please. I would have had him on his knees."

"What if he had a gun?"

"Oh my god, Ben. We don't have to think about what could have happened, because it didn't. The whole thing's already over."

"It's my job to live in hypotheticals," I remind her.

"Okay, Mr. Porter. You go ahead and keep doing that."

This has become a disaster, and there's nowhere to go and nothing to do but be around each other. Even if we turned around, it's still four hours to get back. I don't know a lot of things, but I know I didn't miss ten years to get only a few hours with Dee Matthews.

The quiet continues, just highway traffic whirring past us, and my tires putting more distance away from our starting point. Barely ten minutes ago, I was sure Dee wanted me. Now I know with certainty I am a person she's tolerating out of obligation. I'd be lying if I said that didn't crush me.

"Do you still want to go to Wally's?" I ask.

Dee's angled herself away from me, pressed up against the seat belt holder. "Of *course* I want to go to Wally's."

It sucks that she's mad, but it's a small relief that she's not touching me. Because the Dee who has her hands on me is dangerous. That Dee makes me forget what I know. The farther away she sits, the more my head clears.

"You have to pay," I tell her.

At first she glares, skeptical. Her arms are still tightly folded across her chest.

"That's right," I continue. "I am not spending a single cent in that establishment. Not a penny. Every American goddamn dollar needs to come from your bank account."

Her posture loosens.

"And I'm *hungry* too. This will not be me stopping in quickly and ordering a side of french fries. No, no. It's time I paid my respects to the theme of this fine establishment. I have to get seafood from Wally's Fishbowl Aquarium."

She lets me sit in my discomfort as long as she can. Right when I think I have her, she opens her mouth to say, "You *know* you can't get the fish there. It'll kill you."

"I'm sorry, but I have to," I tell her. "It's what Wally would want."

Her cheeks pucker. This is good. She's fighting off a smile.

"I think I'll get a drink too," I add. "And obviously I will be bowling. Several games." She has me standing out here on a ledge, but she hasn't tossed me overboard yet. Might as well keep going. "If they still have that arcade? It's over. I'm at the *Pac-Man* machine until I set a new record. And you're funding every single activity."

Dee puts her hand atop my leg.

My words stop instantly.

"You better floor it, Porter," she says. "I've got a feast to pay for."

13

DEE

I feel like a teenager again, fighting against emotions that crash into me like tidal waves. There is no reason for me to be so upset over the things Ben does. This is him at his absolute best, and instead of matching that, I've started swinging back and forth between euphoria and despair in the exact way I used to when I was a minor. It's honestly humbling. You really think you've got your shit figured out, and then your high school best friend shows up, and you realize you're still an absolute mess. At least my hair looks better these days.

I've had so much time to grow up, but I haven't done any of that *with* Ben. Evidently, we're starting where we left off. Which means emotionally, we are still eighteen. Hopefully I can expedite our progression by sleeping with him. Then getting an explanation for the Nickelback thing. And generally not being so sensitive about every choice he makes.

Yeah.

That should solve it all.

Wally's Fishbowl Aquarium was one of our favorite stops the last time we took this trip. We stumbled there by chance then, following a recommendation from a complete stranger Ben talked to at a gas station outside Des Moines. Thirty minutes later Ben and I were inside the most decoratively chaotic restaurant I've ever seen. On the ceiling, tucked into corners, and lurking over most tables, there were animatronic sea animals that appeared to be Rainforest Cafe rejects. The floor was carpeted in a glow-in-the-dark aquatic pattern. But the best part was the small bowling alley they'd built into the middle of the place. It had shark-head statues as the ball returns and blue lights projecting waves onto the walls.

When we step inside again, the maximalist whimsy has been so well-preserved that we both gasp.

"It looks the same," I whisper in wonderment.

"It really does." Ben's hand cups my wrist as he points at the gigantic dolphin figurine overhead. This is the first time he's been the one to reach for me. "Didn't you name that one?"

"Yes. Paul."

Ben waves. "Hi, Paul."

His grin is so wide and sincere it makes my chest ache. He's one of the only people who has ever indulged my kid side. It's even rarer for me now as an adult than it was as a teenager, finding someone who hears the words *fake aquarium–restaurant–bowling alley* and drives almost ninety miles an hour to get there.

"Thanks," I say.

"For what?"

"Putting up with me. I'm really sorry. I'm a lot."

"No thanks necessary. I'm a lot too. And you're the one who came on this trip with me with no notice. *And* you're going to let me bowl. I am definitely the one who needs to be saying thank you."

He's so good at smoothing things over. That's the gentle Pisces moon in him, soft and careful with my sharp Scorpio moon heart.

Podcast Worthy.

On the show, I love to talk about my love interests' astrological charts. It's something Javi always makes me prepare. I can practically hear his response.

"Phew. You two are intense and emotional. But compatible . . ."

To which I'd say, "Shut up. He's just a hookup."

And Javi would whisper, "If you say so . . ."

Ben has always been my only boundary. The one person I won't directly discuss on the show. No one knows his name or his job, because no one is allowed to find him. Saying his pronoun in episode 22 has already plagued me.

Ben can't be someone real to my listeners. They will love him. And they will want me to love him too. Ben cannot be Podcast Worthy.

We opt for the bowl-and-dine experience, which I pay for gladly. We get our rental shoes, pick out our bowling balls, and settle down at our lane. When the server comes over to take our order, Ben bravely requests the fish sticks, exactly like he told me he would.

"The last time I was here, I only ordered french fries," he explains. "I've always regretted this."

The server laughs. Charmed, as usual.

Personally, I hate fish. It's only out of deep respect for the theme of the establishment that I decide to order the tofu version they now offer.

"You're the first person to get those since we put it on the menu," the server tells me.

"Oh really? Did you just add it?" I ask.

"No."

Ben's eyes go wide. "That'll be interesting," he quips. "Can we get two beers while we have you? Do you have any IPAs? Something to wash down the pain?"

The server smiles wide, and Ben mirrors her, laughing at himself. When we get carded, he laughs even harder.

Oddly, the idea of us legally drinking together makes me want to cry. Freshman year of high school, we used to take warm rum from the liquor cabinet in Ben's parents' kitchen and mix it with Coke, choking down sips while maintaining that we loved it and we felt *so* drunk after a few sips. As the years went on, we went to parties together, nursing some Natty Lights Richie got us or drinking watered-down vodka someone brought from their family's stash. It was always a little warm, a little gross. Never about the taste.

Now we're twenty-eight-year-olds about to share a craft beer that's been shipped in from a brewery in Asheville, North Carolina. It's a simple, sweet pleasure that feels a little bigger than it should. Maybe that's the progression I wanted. Out of our teen years and into adulthood. We are adults who share beers now. And it's not any special event. Except despite my best efforts, everything with Ben feels like a special event.

Unfortunately for Ben, no amount of legally purchased beer can make him any better at bowling. While he has power in his release, his aim leads him straight to the gutter each time. It's funnier than it should be. Every time, he approaches the pins with hope and determination. And every time, he fails. When we bowled last time, he was this bad too. Clearly we both expected him to have grown out of that by now.

Between turns, he pulls up YouTube videos to learn about the proper approach, biting his fish sticks and studying the tutorials with complete focus, pausing only to cheer for me. Meanwhile I walk up, pull the ball between my legs, and throw. I get a nine or a strike almost every turn. I just can't pick up spares.

"Why does that work?" Ben asks as he high-fives me after my

third consecutive strike (or what we bowling pros know as a tur-key). It's been a real show of his resolve that it's taken him this long to wonder this aloud.

Last time we came, I wasn't this good. I cared too much about being cool to commit to throwing the ball how I wanted.

"It's about intention," I tell him as I chase another terrible tofu fish stick with beer. My stomach lurches a little. "I go up there believing I'll do well, and I do."

"But bowling is not a law of attraction sport!" he argues. "Bowling is standing in the correct place and releasing the ball with the proper speed, velocity, and rotation. And you need the right ball for the lane condition, drilled in such a way that the reaction to the oil is predictable."

I put a hand on his shoulder and pat. "It's okay, Mr. Porter. I bet you're a great bowler at heart." I look up at the scores. "Your thirty-six after eight frames does not tell the whole story. And I know that."

"I don't understand how you're getting it right while doing everything wrong!"

"Life isn't technical." An edge of warning creeps into my tone. "There are always going to be a million ways to get some-thing right."

"I know," he says immediately. "I want to find at least one of them."

He's so frustrated it's almost adorable. I'm glad I don't have to be pissed at him for being a jackass, because he looks so cute that I'm struggling to muster up the proper amount of anger. "No one who bowls at Wally's is here to master the discipline."

"But you have," he points out.

"I am the exception to every rule."

He bows his head. "Will you show me your ways, wise one?"

Fighting off a mighty blush, I take a big sip of beer. "All right Porter, shape up. You're about to learn from a master." I pick up the lightest ball we have, a lime-green eight-pounder that has the name RITA etched atop it.

"My fingers won't fit," he says when I hand it to him.

"No need to worry about hole size right now." Now he's the one blushing, and all is right in the world.

Side by side, we stand on the approach.

"First, you hold the ball with both hands, and you walk it up to the foul line with purpose." I post up behind him with my hands on his shoulders. I'm so high on my tiptoes that my heels have popped out of my ill-fitting rental shoes. "You are an apex predator, Benjamin, and those pins are your prey."

He turns back to look at me. The sweetest trace of trepidation is etched between his eyebrows.

"You asked for my ways. It's all or nothing," I remind him.

His eyes shift from me to the lane, and I release my hold on his shoulders. With a single nod, probably for courage, he walks Rita's eight-pounder to the foul line with impassioned commitment. "What now?" he asks.

"I need you to granny toss that fucker down the lane like you're trying to break the world in half."

He laughs, waiting for me to say I'm joking. When he realizes I'm not, he pulls the ball back between his legs and chucks it down the lane with the exact force I requested. It rolls just right of dead center.

Crash!

The pins fall down in a triumphant clatter, all ten collapsing under the force of Ben's throw.

"You did it!" I scream.

"I did it!" He echoes as he turns around, pure-hearted disbelief and pride all over his sweet face as he runs down the lane to meet me at the ball return. He picks me up off the floor and squeezes tight.

In an instant, our embrace shifts from celebratory to intimate. We haven't been this close in years. God, he feels so good to hold. Sturdy. He's a little warm, and it's the kind of heat that makes a lazy cat out of me. I could stay here forever, tangled up in him.

Slowly, he lowers me to the ground until he lets go. Then he backs up only a step, creating a strange distance between us.

"That was really good," I say, lacking all of my usual composure.

"Thanks for your help."

"Oh yeah. Anytime."

We are what I'd classify as standing awkwardly. Ben has now pinned his arms to his sides, and my hands have, regrettably, found their way to my hips, which I've decided to shimmy. It's quite unfortunate how this happens. If I were a weaker person, I might do the robot next in an attempt to move through this awkwardness. Thank god I was forged in the fires of the internet. I've been trained to withstand this kind of discomfort without resorting to anything too ridiculous.

The shimmy was a moment of weakness. It won't happen again.

In fact, this awkwardness is actually a gift. It proves that Ben felt the heat between us too. He may be the science teacher, but even I know this is all static electricity. One good, charged touch and we can break this sexual tension.

It would be nice if he made the first real move, but I'm also okay with being the mover. I always play for whatever team needs me. In whatever way applies. So I lift up again onto the tiptoes of these rented bowling shoes. I move my hands to Ben's chest, feeling the way he sucks in a breath of disbelief.

"Hey," I whisper. "I like the way you bowl."

The line is just random enough to be great. There's an art to disorientation. He can never know what will come next, because then the fun is gone. And that's exactly what this is. Fun. Nothing more.

I could kiss him quickly. His lips are right there. But there's something so delicious about the slow, sweet burn of waiting. The kind of *almost* that could set fire to this building. My mouth will touch his when the hunger expands to his pupils and tenses the muscles in his neck. He should be so desperate he can hardly stand.

He studies my face with a feverish intensity, watching for signs I give through touch alone. With each breath we take, drinking each other in, he grows more focused.

It's almost time.

I am about to kiss Ben Porter.

14

BEN

D ee Matthews is about to kiss me.

Her lips hover above mine. Wanting. Waiting.

I should kiss her first. She's right here, with her mouth open just a bit. Just enough. Her soft, full lips sigh toward me, daring me to move. My whole body leans forward in response. The feel of her body against my chest is enough to make me forget every boundary I've ever given myself. All that's left to do is place my hand under her chin to bring her mouth to mine.

But this isn't what I came to do.

Right? I told myself I shouldn't.

Why?

I can't remember. All I can see is her face. Her mouth. Teasing. The insistent press of her fingers into my pecs. Once won't be so bad.

Just once.

Suddenly, she staggers back a step. Her hands clutch around her waist as she shifts her gaze to the middle distance.

"Dee? Are you okay?" My desire is quickly replaced with concern. I've worked in enough classrooms to recognize her body language.

"What are you do—" she starts to ask as I wrap my arm

around her. The question leaves her once she realizes what I already know. She's about to be sick.

We make it into the stall right in time. Even the bathrooms at Wally's are aquatic themed. A school of rainbow fish swim the walls as Dee empties the contents of her stomach into the toilet bowl. Music pumps in through an overhead speaker, treating us to a very unfortunate heavy metal cover of "Under the Sea." I have one hand holding Dee's ponytail, making sure it doesn't wrap around and hit her face, and the other rubbing circles on her back.

Barely a moment ago, she was about to kiss me. Now she's slumped into my arms, crying. She buries her head into my chest, and her tears seep so quickly through my shirt that I feel them like rain.

"Fucking tofu fish sticks," she mutters.

I wrap my hand around her head to cradle her closer. "Now we know why no one's ordered them."

"This is gross. I am gross. I am so sorry."

She's correct. This is disgusting. I might have to throw out these clothes. But I won't stop holding her. "Don't apologize," I whisper into her hair. "I'm glad you're okay."

As soon as I say it, she's back at the toilet, decidedly not okay.

We need to get out of here. If we stay at Wally's Aquatic Fishbowl any longer, it will destroy this place's reputation between us. So I leave the bathroom to quickly settle our food tab and gather our things, then I escort Dee outside as she mutters apologies through snotty sniffles.

"I was supposed to pay for everything," she says, clutching her stomach.

"You'll get me back," I assure her.

"I better," she hurriedly replies, right before she makes good use of a trash can right outside the restaurant.

We can't keep driving with her in this condition. The plan was to go through as much of the night as we could stand, pull over at a rest stop and sleep for a few hours, and then get right back on the road. There's no way that's happening now. We have to stay somewhere with a private bathroom. A quick search tells me the closest place to us is a modest, two-story hotel called the Starfax Inn. Google shows me an expectedly perfunctory place. Hopefully cleaner than the bathroom floor at Wally's, but lacking all the personality.

The entire drive there, neither of us speaks. My phone is disconnected from CarPlay. There's only static on the radio. My eyes are strained from the day of travel, blurring lanes and moving guard rails. There is such little light on some parts of the highway that I'm hunched over the steering wheel, forcing myself to focus. It's not as late as it feels, but this yawning darkness swallows up all sense of time and space. Dee has the passenger seat laid out flat. When she lets out a long groan, it's enough to keep me focused.

By the time we arrive at the Starfax Inn, she can almost stand upright again. We make it all the way through check-in and up to our room without incident. It's as dull as the photos promised. There are two full-sized beds covered in dated floral bedding. A couch in the same pattern. A desk. A faded painting of white lilies in a vase. A confusing relationship to power outlets throughout. Dee puts her suitcase beside one bed, and I move to the other, quietly unpacking what I need for a proper night's rest.

"Oh no," she says at once. Her first words since we left Wally's. She hurries around the corner into the bathroom.

I Postmate us some Gatorade and Saltines, then get out the cleaning products I packed and wipe down a few surfaces. It's impossible to know how much Dee has left in her, but we could be in for a very long night. When she stops this latest round, I suggest we move to the beds so she doesn't have to sit on the hard bathroom floor.

She looks up at me with a face full of worry. "I don't want to ruin anything."

"In the hotel?" I ask.

She hesitates. Then, as she looks down at her nails, she says, "Or any of your stuff."

"I don't care about any of my stuff."

"Yes you do. Your car," she informs me, still examining her fingers. "I would've let myself die before I threw up in it."

"Dee, I don't care about my car."

"Yes you do," she echoes. "You keep it so clean. You love your car."

I almost say something back. Something way too big. I can feel the words sitting on my tongue. But Dee gets sick again, and the moment passes as quickly as it came.

By the time the crackers and Gatorade arrive, Dee still won't leave the bathroom floor. I explain to her that I can set up a trash can beside her bed and put hotel towels atop the sheets. She refuses to budge.

If I were forced to rank every activity I've ever done in life, sitting on two separate bathroom floors in one night would be very low on the list. Possibly right at the bottom. But I'm not going to leave Dee struggling alone. I can't sit on my bed knowing she's in agony in here. So we compromise. Dee stands and brushes her teeth as I strip the pillows and comforter from my mattress and bring it all into the bathroom, as well as my iPad, setting everything up against the back of the bathtub. I pat the space beside me so Dee can sit back.

"This is a nightmare for you," she observes.

"Yes," I confirm.

"But you're still doing it."

"Yes."

"I'm so sorry."

She puts her toothbrush away and studies herself in the mirror. For as sick as she's been, she still looks like Dee to me. Lovely. Tenacious. Impossibly stubborn. The only difference is she's currently several shades paler than normal, and some of her copper hair has escaped her ponytail, sweat slicked and stuck to the back of her neck.

"I am a disaster of a road trip companion," she tells me. "You really should've brought Richie. He never would've ordered tofu fish sticks."

"Dee." I wait until she looks at me. "I asked you because I wanted to go with you. There is nowhere else I'd rather be right now. I promise."

She leaves the bathroom, then comes back in with the Cheez-Its. The open box hits me square in the chest. Cheese crackers explode like confetti all around me. "That's for lying again. To me, and to that third grader who's gonna cure genital herpes."

"Please sit," I say, laughing. "It's worse if you leave me here by myself."

Reluctantly, she does, lowering to the ground with her face permanently winced in embarrassment. Our heads are both propped against the back of the tub. She keeps her torso positioned toward the toilet.

"This is really gross," she makes a point to say again.

"It's great."

"I might get sick again."

"I know."

"*On* you."

"Dee, I know." We look at each other for a while. And I wonder again how I could have spent ten years without her. When did I become a person who was capable of doing that? Because even here, when she is at her sickest, I am stressed at the idea of being more than ten feet away from her.

My legs are bent so my iPad can rest atop my knees. I comb through Netflix, waiting for her to tell me what she'd like to watch. She says nothing, letting me scroll without direction. I try to remember her taste in movies. She's surprisingly sentimental for someone who likes to be tough, but she thinks most dramas are more comedic than the comedies. Horror movies make her frustrated. Action movies make her shout.

"Maybe a documentary?" I ask out loud.

She says nothing. I've never known her to be this quiet.

Scroll by scroll, she creeps closer to me. Then she lays her head across my chest.

My breath hitches at the unexpected pressure of her touch. It should stress me out, but it works more like an anxiety blanket, calming me down. She rises and falls with my slow, deliberate breaths. I could live forever inside this moment, lying on the bathroom floor of a run-down hotel somewhere in Iowa, Dee Matthews resting on me.

She's sick, I remind myself. She's running hot. She's not in her normal state of mind. That's the only reason she's now draped an arm across my stomach, holding me like we fit together.

That almost kiss between us wasn't real. I'm sleep deprived. I made it up.

My eyelids grow heavy as I keep scrolling, no longer capable of deciding what we should watch.

At some point—minutes or hours later—I wake to hear Dee's gentle snore.

Delicately, I wiggle free to prepare her bed, setting up everything she might need if she gets sick again. Then I come back into the bathroom. She's laid out in the exact position I left her, holding a pillow version of my body. I lift her up and carry her out, relishing this chance to have her this close to me. Her face looks stormy even in sleep, brows furrowed like she's working through a problem that doesn't want to be solved.

Wanting her to have a layer of protection from her street clothes, I get a robe to put over what she's wearing. She's always been a heavy sleeper. She doesn't even flinch as I take her arms through the sleeves and gently tie a knot at her waist.

I shouldn't, but after she's settled under the covers, I rest one quick peck on her forehead. Featherlight and meaningless. More of a wish for her health than anything else.

Then I go into the bathroom to enjoy the longest shower of my life, washing and rewashing my body until I feel confident no trace of bathroom floor remains.

Did I Forget to Tell You?

EPISODE 64: UH-OHS AND NO-NOS

JAVI: We got a submission this week that I have to read. Samantha writes, "Javi and Dee, I am deathly afraid of candles."

DEE: Hold on. Is this real?

JAVI: You have to let me finish first. Then we can discuss. "Javi and Dee, I am deathly afraid of candles. I really think it might be how I died in a past life or something. I don't even care if they're lit or not. It's the actual candle that scares me. The problem is, my partner loves them. She buys really expensive brands. Like those gigantic Jo Malone ones that are the size of your head and cost the same amount as a laptop. We recently moved in together, and I wanted to get over this fear. So I asked her if we could use one of her candles in the bedroom. Long story short, I have a nearly second-degree burn on my thigh and a further-solidified fear of candles. Do either of you have anything you're scared of this much?"

DEE: Wow. That's *quite* a story.

JAVI: I can't say I relate.

DEE: Okay, but tell me, do you think it's real?

JAVI: Maybe! But maybe not. We definitely get some questionable submissions. I like the possibility of this one being real. Because it's like, you really never know with someone. What they've lived through.

DEE: Right. And I do believe that anyone can be afraid of anything. Even unlit candles. I will not invalidate you, Samantha! I am very sorry about the burn and the bad bedroom experience!

JAVI: We love you. We hope you find a solution that works for everyone. And to answer your question, I'm afraid of bees. But I'm allergic. So that's not the same as being scared of candles. I guess sometimes I worry my oven is going to blow up when I'm cooking?

DEE: I've had that thought before. When it makes a little ticking sound?

JAVI: That's when I start signing the cross.

DEE: Okay. I am also afraid of that. And I guess I'm afraid of crying?

JAVI: Dee!

DEE: I know. That sounds very punk of me to say. But when I was a kid my mom told me if I didn't stop crying my face was going to get stuck that way, so now I will do absolutely anything in my power not to cry.

JAVI: What happens when you do cry?

DEE: I get upset.

JAVI: Well, yeah. You're already crying.

DEE: Right. And I let myself see it through until it's over. Then I just get weird.

JAVI: Define weird.

DEE: It can't be defined. Only experienced.

15

DEE

The force of my own embarrassment pulls me out of a deep sleep. The worst part is, I don't even remember what I'm embarrassed about. There's just a gnawing sense of dread nestled in the pit of my stomach telling me it is time to immediately assume a new identity. I bolt upright in a bed—a bed?—and for a moment, not a single thing makes sense. The shower is running. It smells like disinfectant wipes in here. My head hurts and my mouth is dry. I feel gross.

Because I was sick, I remember with a start.

And crying.

To *Ben Porter.*

Aha. There's the source of the embarrassment. I could genuinely be tossed into a running washing machine right now, and it would be a welcome escape from this hell.

At some point I must have fallen asleep, and Ben carried my snoring, trash raccoon body here, leaving me a very thoughtful setup. There are towels around my head and a garbage can beside me. On the nightstand, he's left a glass of water, Clorox wipes with Mr. Porter written in permanent marker atop them, and a bottle of his private ibuprofen, labeled BEN across the lid, along with the crackers and Gatorade he ordered earlier. Is he in many scenarios where people are trying to steal his over-the-counter pills, forcing him to label his supply? What's going on here?

When I rip the bedding off me, I discover he's also very kindly put a robe on over my clothes. Ben is a shower-twice-a-day guy, and I made him sit on the bathroom floor of Wally's Fishbowl Aquarium with me. And then again at the Starfax Inn.

God. I was about to *kiss* him.

It's all coming back now. All hope of releasing the tension between us has been shattered by tofu fish sticks. There is nothing less sexy than getting food poisoning, which is bad enough as is, but I can feel myself needing to tap-dance over all the crying and holding him like a teddy bear I did afterward.

It's bothering me so much it's almost making me itch, knowing that I couldn't keep it together enough to stop myself from sobbing. He's seen me like that only once before, when my mom sold my iPod without telling me. I've convinced myself he's forgotten that ever happened. This is decidedly harder to forget.

Panicking, I tiptoe to my purse and get out my phone to FaceTime Victoria. Javi would laugh at me, which is normally what I'd want—someone to point out how comical this is. Not this time. I need someone to take me seriously. That's Victoria. She's never one to undersell the gravity of a situation.

She answers from bed. The light in her room is so low I can barely see her. I turn down my volume so that I can barely hear her too, in case Ben somehow catches any of this over the shower stream.

"Are you up?" I whisper.

Victoria scrunches her nose in distaste. This is her favorite face to make—pure disgust. It's the Taurus in her. "Am I talking to you right now?"

"Sorry, I'm kind of panicking."

She rolls over to turn on her bedside lamp. Her husband lets out a little groan of surprise, but she shushes him. "What's up? Where's Ben? Where are *you*?"

"We're in Iowa. Ben's in the shower." Victoria squints, trying to read my expression. "No, no. Nothing happened. Well, lots of things happened. But nothing sex related."

"Vicky, can you put in headphones or something?" her husband asks off camera.

Victoria reaches for the AirPods on her nightstand and puts them in, her shaky camerawork showing me every step. "Why are you panicking? Did you tell him you're both going to the reunion?"

"No. I forgot all about that."

She makes the face again.

"I'm sorry. I will do it tomorrow. If I make it there. I'm considering finding a boat and sailing out to open waters. Living the rest of my life at sea."

"Oh shut up," she says, laughing at me. "You are so dramatic."

"So are you."

"That's true. And you love me for it."

"I do. But, Vic, listen. I got sick earlier. And I started crying." This makes Victoria's eyes widen. She knows how I feel about tears. Especially for men. "Exactly. And now he's in the shower, and I don't know. What am I doing here?"

"You forgot, but you're there making sure my ten-year reunion party is well attended because you know how hard I've worked on it and how much it means to me. And you know the people want to see Ben Porter. And you."

"No they don't."

"They do. Our classmates listen to your podcast."

Hearing that sentence is like pouring a baking soda slurry

into the little volcano of dread in my stomach. I could legitimately be sick again. "Don't say that."

"Ben probably listens too."

"Oh my god, what are you doing?" I whisper urgently. "You
are making this worse."

"I'm just saying. I bet he has." She looks to her side. "Baby,
would you listen to a podcast if I made one?"

"No," her husband answers groggily.

"Yes he would," she tells me. "So you're stressed that you got
sick and Ben saw you cry, and while you wait to tell him about
his reunion ticket, you need to know you're gonna be okay?"

"I guess so."

"Deandra Linnette Matthews, you're gonna be fine. And you
are going to have a great time with Ben. Don't stress. It's all going to be perfect. Trust me."

The shower stops running.

"I gotta go," I whisper in a panic.

"Please secure my invites. I didn't run for class president to
be silenced."

I put my phone down and make the split-second decision
to pretend to be asleep. Ben comes back into the living area.
Through squinted eyes, I see a white cotton towel tied around
his waist, looped over his left hipbone. He treads lightly, glancing at me to make sure I'm not disturbed by his movements. It's
a disturbance all right. Not in the way he's worried about.

As he softly rummages through his travel bag, it occurs to
me to wonder how many people have had the privilege of this
view. Is this what they think of when they hear the name Ben
Porter? Beyond the obvious pleasure of seeing his well-formed
body, do they think of the soft line of hair between his pecs? Or

the way his front curls tendril up into a single ringlet after a shower? Do they make sure to notice the way his chin puckers when he's thinking?

Do any of them know him like I do?

He takes out a shirt and pulls it over his head. It's a white cotton tee with CREST RIDGE, his middle school's name, emblazoned across the chest in red and yellow. This is a sleepwear choice that's so free of pretense it almost makes me wince. It's the kind of thing you put on when you want to feel cozy and content. He's certainly not trying to impress me.

His travel bag obstructs the lower half of his body. That does little to prepare me for the fact that he *removes his towel*. He is half-naked. Bottom half. Standing ten feet away from me.

By complete accident, I gasp. Instantly, Ben's eyes dart straight to mine. And we stare bewildered, him half-naked from the waist down, clean and handsome and red in the cheeks, and me wrapped in a robe, surrounded by towels with a puke bucket in arm's reach. My embarrassment is an ocean with depths he could never begin to fathom.

"I—" He ducks down until he's out of view, crouched behind the other bed. "I thought you were asleep."

"I was," I lie. "I just heard you and opened my eyes. I didn't see anything." Which is true. "Sorry."

"No, no. I'm sorry. I should've been quieter. I forgot to bring clothes into the bathroom."

"You were very quiet."

"Not if you heard me." He's still in a duck squat beside his stripped bed.

"My eyes are closed now," I announce. "I'm rolling over! Please continue getting dressed."

Let this comforter be a cocoon. Make me reborn.

"Do you feel better?" he asks me hastily. The elastic of his underwear claps against his skin.

"Yeah." It's hard to speak through the vulnerability. We are in a war of embarrassment. My crimes are objectively far worse than his, but he is a more skittish kind than me. The fact that he was half-undressed when he "woke me up" has probably killed a small portion of his people-pleasing soul. "I should shower too."

With little grace and much flourish, I logroll off my bed. Because that's a very normal, not at all bizarre thing to do. My body thumps down onto the floor.

Ben gasps. "Are you okay?"

"Great!" I flash him a thumbs-up as I power walk straight to the bathroom without looking back.

What am I *doing*?

Why am I being so bizarre?

All of the bedsheets that were strewn across the floor are now folded up into a corner near the shower, with the pillows stacked on top. Ben's toiletries are laid out across the counter in a photo-perfect tableau. The bathroom mirror remains steamed from his shower, which is good. It would wound me further to know how terrible I look at the moment.

I have absolutely nothing with me in here except my toothbrush, which Ben graciously grabbed for me earlier, in between bouts of sickness. It's too late to go out there and get the rest of my stuff. My redemption must start now. It's important that I erase every trace of what happened today from both my memory and Ben's.

I start by stripping off all my clothes and climbing into the shower. Ben has brought his own shampoo and conditioner. The products are made for curly hair, which I do not have. He also has an expensive body wash. When I sniff it, I smell an ex-girlfriend's suggestion. Same with the high-end facial cleanser. The Ben I knew had Old Spice deodorant and a three-in-one bath product carrying the weight of the world on its $4.99 shoulders. This has to be a self-care routine built for him by someone else. Who has Ben known in the years between knowing me? Who has he loved?

If he were on my podcast, these would be some of the first questions I'd ask him. I can hear myself, in my most playful voice, gently prodding. *So, Name Redacted, how's your love life been since the Twizzlers incident?* Reducing our relationship to one quick joke in our storied history together.

I want to use his fancy body wash, but smelling like his ex's idea of him nauseates me as much as the fish sticks did. I opt to use the hotel's products instead. I will smell like repurposed Pantene products, and that will be enough.

Once I'm clean, and my teeth are brushed and my mouth has been drowned in enough of Ben's mouthwash to nearly dissolve my taste buds, I wrap myself in a towel and exhale. Considering how sick I was earlier, I don't feel as terrible as I'd expect. My mom used to tell me I inherited her stomach of steel. She'd say this when we'd subsist on oatmeal and peanut butter sandwiches for weeks on end. It always made me mad. I wanted a more sensitive stomach. Or a lower tolerance for repetition. Something, *anything*, that made the world want to do better by me. Right now, I don't think I've ever been more grateful. Things earlier were very bad. They could've been far, far worse. The fact that I feel mostly fine now is not something I take for granted.

I find Ben stretched out on his stripped bed, lying on his back.

He's got on black joggers, with his legs crossed and his hands stitched together atop his chest. His eyes are closed.

"Sorry," I say loudly, needing him to drop the pretense. There is no way he's already sleeping. "Just getting some clothes."

It would be nice if he viewed me in my towel. It could possibly redeem me in his eyes a little. Wet and clean? I don't know. It has to be an improvement from hunched over the community toilet at Wally's.

He keeps his eyes shut.

As loudly and destructively as possible, I dig a white camisole and cotton short-shorts out of my luggage. Unlike Ben and his middle school T-shirt, I thought I'd try to be subtly impressive with my sleepwear. Javi and Victoria agreed that this is the kind of nighttime outfit that's casual yet potentially flirtatious, depending on my goals. It's not as flashy as lingerie, but not as comfort forward as a middle school tee or a matching pajama set. Now it's all I have. Literally and figuratively.

Ben doesn't open his eyes to react to the volume of my efforts, refusing to grant me the pleasure of seeing me in a towel. I go into the bathroom and get changed. He is *still* pretending to sleep when I come back out.

"Hey," I whisper, frustrated. "Are you up?"

He says nothing.

I take one of my pillows and throw it at him, forcing his eyes open. "You need to sleep in the other bed." He cocks his head in confusion. "You sacrificed all of your bedding for me. You get the reward."

In protest, he closes his eyes again. "No, no. I'm perfectly fine over here. You're not feeling well. You can have all of that."

"I feel great now." I walk forward until I'm looming over him. "And you're on my bed."

He doesn't budge.

"I'll stand here all night."

His eyelashes are unfairly long. Those three beauty marks on his cheek still look like Orion's Belt to me. How funny that to his students, Ben made the stars seem cool. To me, the stars are scattered across his face.

God. Please let me get on that boat to nowhere.

"Dee, you need to rest," he whispers.

I make the decision to climb over him.

This finally gets his attention. His hands accidentally graze my chest as I work my way to the other side of his stripped bed. When he looks at me, he's shocked and confused and—if I'm guessing right—a little bit excited. "What are you doing?"

"Getting into my bed!" I say cheerily. "Would you mind hitting the light? I can't reach from this side. And make sure my phone's plugged in, if you could. Thanks!"

He leaps up, staring at me splayed across the white fitted sheet. He's so flustered he just stands there in indignation. "Why are you like this?"

I smirk at him so hard it hurts my cheeks. "Pure luck."

Without warning, he scoops one arm behind my knees and the other right below my shoulder blades.

"Put me down!" I shout as he pulls me to his chest.

"Gladly." He deposits me onto the other bed.

Before he can move away, I wrap my hand around the fabric of his shirt, grabbing so tight it swirls under my fist. I pull until we're nearly nose to nose. Taking advantage of his confusion, I wrap my other arm around his back and draw him down to the bed, wiggling out from underneath so that he lands where he placed me seconds ago.

"There," I say with a smile. "Much better. Enjoy your sleep!"

He manages to get a hand on my wrist. His touch is so delicate, I could easily break away.

"You know I can't let you win this," he says, low and serious.

My heart beats so fast it burns. I fight to keep my voice calm. "It's not a competition."

"Of course it is." His fingers press against my pulse.

"Then we should both win."

"How?" He looks so focused, determined to understand the solution and execute it competently.

"You scoot over so I'm not on the side closest to the door."

When he understands what I'm insinuating, he makes a horrified expression.

Great. Skip the boat. Put me on the next rocket into outer space instead. Nothing could be worse than Ben being *this* disgusted at the idea of sharing a bed with me.

Not one to back down—even when the mere idea of my presence makes someone look as sick as I was a few hours ago—I push Ben until he's forced to move over.

"We . . . we can't do this. There are two beds," he tells me.

"And we're only using one of them." I make a big, loud show of getting under the sheets to prepare myself for sleep. "Should I turn out the light?"

Ben has scooted himself to the far edge of the mattress. He hates every minute of this, but this is the only solution we will both accept, and he knows it. "Yes."

"Need anything?"

"Nope."

"You sure?"

"Dee, please."

"Okay. Good night, Ben! Be well!"

I turn out the light. The darkness amplifies the unfamiliar

sounds around us. Footsteps in the hall and voices from other televisions come into our room like taunting ghosts, daring us to speak over them. I roll to my side and attempt to sleep.

My eyes are closed but my body is so painfully awake that I might as well get up and do parkour in the hotel room. I am agonizingly aware of every single inch that separates me from Ben. I was so sick earlier that I didn't bookmark any of our closer moments to mentally revisit later. Now all I have are hazily remembered approximations, clouded by regret and embarrassment. If I'd known I would get the chance to hold Ben Porter, I'd have avoided the tofu fish sticks altogether.

For once, I will be the one with restraint. Because I want to hold Ben again. I want to fall asleep with my head on his chest, hearing the beat of his heart, secretly hoping it's racing as fast for me as mine is for him. This no longer feels like the kind of want that gets solved by one fun night together. This is the kind of want that makes me believe in good things. This is the kind of want that could fix the fractured bits of my heart. And I only trust myself when I'm a little broken. So I will myself to stay still. Barely twenty-four hours ago, all of this would have sounded absolutely impossible. This is enough.

Then Ben's hand presses against the small of my back.

My breath catches. He must have fallen asleep. It's an accident. A coincidence. There's no way he'd reach for me after all we've been through tonight.

The mattress lets out the smallest groan, telling me he's rolled closer. I can feel the nearness of him through the heat of his body, hovering behind mine. It's now *imperative* that I do not move any further. When it's all said and done, I know I'll somehow convince myself I orchestrated this. The only way to be sure I haven't is to fight as hard as I can against the urge to burrow into him.

Minutes—or years, or lifetimes—later, he moves again. This time it's to drape an arm over me. Even if he is asleep, and he thinks I'm someone else, it doesn't change the thrill that comes with being someone Ben Porter wants to hold in the dark.

I can't help myself. I turn so he can pull me closer. His breath blows against the top of my head.

"Good night, Dee," he whispers, erasing all doubt.

He knows it's me.

He's *choosing* to hold me.

And if words could kill, oh how I'd be dead.

16

BEN

There is only one person I can call at five in the morning.

"Don't tell me you need me to pick you up," Darius says in greeting. "I'm at the gym. Please don't make me leave."

"I don't need you to pick me up." I'm leaning against a vending machine in the lobby of the Starfax Inn. The whole place smells like stale coffee. Down here this early, there's only me and one very bored front desk attendant staring at her phone. "I appreciate that you would've come, though. Because I'm pretty far past Des Moines already."

Darius lets out a heavy sigh. "I'd have to. I can't even get a single ounce of respect in my own household anymore. Rochelle's telling me that all the kids from your class are in a group chat talking about how Mr. Porter's the coolest teacher at Crest Ridge. Jade's asking me if I would do the same thing for her. I keep saying to her, 'How could I know? We've never broken up, much less spent ten whole-ass years apart.'"

"How are you doing?" I ask, cutting him off. He told me last time that it's okay for this to be about me, but it's still hard to have this much attention on my actions. Which should, in theory, be enough to stop me from behaving like this. I'm the one who called him, and now the last thing I want to do is say why.

"I'm grumpy," Darius answers. "I hate the summer. It's too hot. Even in the morning."

"I'm sorry."

"Nothing you can do about it. And I need a new lawn mower, so that pisses me off too. But you know what? My family's safe, we've got a roof over our heads and food on the table, and we've got our health. That's all there is, at the end of the day." His voice drops into the same easy, comfortable softness that makes him everyone's *actual* favorite teacher, no matter what Rochelle tells him. "What's going on?"

"It's a long story."

"I've got time."

Darius and I are really good friends—not long after Gam died, I started telling him how much I love him, and he's taken to saying it back to me too—but he's also my coworker. There's a distinction there that matters to me, even if I keep calling him when things are hard. Which makes me realize the obvious. This is the kind of situation I used to handle with Richie. He can be pretty sage for someone so committed to acting like a doorknob. But ever since Gam told me the truth, opening up to him makes me feel guilty. There's so much he doesn't know. Life-changing information. It's easier to keep him distant. Then I don't have to feel how much power I carry, the ability to change his entire reality with one single sentence—*our family is built on a lie.*

"Dee and I had to get a hotel," I tell Darius. "And we slept together." I hear how it sounds. "Actual sleeping. But together. In the same bed."

"That's what most people do when it's nighttime, yeah."

"I want to be her friend."

"And you can't be friends if you fall asleep in the same bed?"

"I held her," I explain.

"Sure."

I take a deep breath. "She's the first person I ever had sex with." The front desk attendant sits up straight, peering over the counter to see me. Darius goes quiet. "In high school," I add, hearing once again how it sounds.

"I was gonna say, 'You know what? At least you're livin'!'"

The both of us laugh.

"You were with that Melissa girl for a while," Darius continues. "And I was thinking, 'Well, it's not my business unless you make it. You can do whatever you wanna do behind your closed doors.'"

"Melissa and I definitely had sex."

"Good for you, man."

We laugh again.

When my relationship with Melissa ended, she told me I wasn't available enough. I never really knew what that meant. But she wasn't the first to say it to me. It came up every time. So I doubled down. With every new girl I dated, I planned as many fun dates as I could. I listened to all of their problems. I made note of their favorite foods and activities. I see now I was checking off their criteria, trying to be the best version of myself at all times. It was never about who we were to each other.

When the amusement dies down, I say to Darius, "You must think I'm losing it."

"Nah. I think you've been going through it for a while, and it's finally catching up to you. Lucky for me, I am not going through it. Not right now, at least. So I don't mind. Unless you make me pick you up. Then it's gonna be a problem for sure."

"Consider this a promise. I will not make you pick me up."

"Sounds good. And I'm not gonna think you're out of your mind, even if the next thing you tell me is that you're celibate, or whatever it is that's got you hitting me up at five in the morning. Judgment is for God and Judy."

"Like Judge Judy?"

"I like her."

It's nice to smile. Darius is a good person. He is not Richie, and he would never try to be. I don't let many people help me, and it's taking some practice. Darius seems to understand this without me having to say it.

"Dee and I had kind of a serious thing back in the day," I explain. "Then we got into a big fight right before we graduated, and we haven't spoken since I showed up at her door. I'm here because I want us to be friends again. Sleeping with her kind of changes that. Because when I get close to her, I remember what I used to feel for her when I was a kid, and I'm not sure I can keep that kind of distance up if we keep touch—"

The elevator doors slide open. It's so quiet in the lobby that both the front desk attendant and I startle at the sound. We turn our heads to see Dee. Her hair is flopped across the top of her head, and her tight tank top sits crooked, exposing the skin around her navel. Her presence always sucks the air out of every room. You can't help but notice her. Can't help but hold your breath, hoping you're the person she's come to see.

Her eyes land on me. "There you are!"

I *am* the person she's come to see, but judging by the hellfire look on her face, that's not a good thing.

"I have to go," I hurry out to Darius.

"Love you, man. You got this."

"Love you too."

I smile as I hang up. He said it first.

"What are you doing down here? I thought you left me!"

Dee yells. She has a surprising amount of energy for five in the morning.

"I would never leave you." As soon as the words leave my mouth, Dee gapes at me. I've given us both an unexpected invitation to remember ten years ago. "I had to call my coworker," I say next.

Darius is my friend first, and we're on summer break, but if I tell her I'm calling a friend, I tell her I'm scared. And the problem with never talking about anything that happened between us is that we have countless things we haven't said. It becomes a game in and of itself—who can do the best job of saying the least about our past.

"Why? You're out of school," she challenges, forever capable of finding my weak spots and pressing as hard as she can.

"A teacher never rests," I say.

"If I had a Cheez-It, I'd throw it at you."

As we get into the elevator together, Dee makes a point to stare at the numbered buttons. My eyes wander to her face. Her body. The very body I held all night. Curving into me. Fitting just right.

Not now, Benjamin.

"Of course I didn't leave," I say. "My keys are still in the room. And all of my belongings."

"Whatever," she mutters.

When we exit the elevator and get to our hotel door—her stomping, me treading lightly—she folds her arms across her chest.

"Did you not bring a key card?" I ask as she stares at me.

"I don't know where the key cards are! I was a little incapacitated when we got here."

I have mine in my pocket. There was no reason for me to

ask, except that I never would have left the room without one. What would she have done if I wasn't downstairs? She must have rolled over and noticed my absence, then immediately left to look for me. My eyes dart to her feet, which are bare, confirming my theory.

"I didn't think you'd wake up," I offer as I open our door.

"Well, I did." Her words are as clipped as her tone. She storms into the room ahead of me and plops down on her bed. "I'm going back to sleep." She pulls the covers over her head as she rolls onto her side.

As much as I want to, I can't bring myself to join her there.

I go to the other bare bed, lie down on my back, and stare up at the popcorn ceiling. Dee thinks I might leave her without saying goodbye. Which makes me sad, because she has a whole decade of proof that I am capable of disappearing. It's not enough to just show up again. I have to prove to her that no matter what, I plan to stay.

17

DEE

To say I've made things weird is an understatement.

It's also my specialty.

There was a brief time when I was dating a really nice girl I met in line at Starbucks. When she finally came over to my apartment for the first time, after a few drinks I tried to very slyly ask if she wanted to look through my toy drawer. She had such a serene face as she said, "Oh, you have a kid?"

If the shock of that question wasn't enough to dislodge the vibe, I had to then explain what I actually meant. And she had to explain how she thought I was just her friend.

Two gal pals!

And *then*, because I'm truly the president of my own planet of destruction, I asked if she would come on my show and talk about what had happened between us. It turned out to be *quite* Podcast Worthy. It's our third most-streamed episode of all time.

This situation with Ben has escalated to these same levels of awkward. What makes this worse than Starbucks Girl—who is now genuinely a good friend of mine, a true gal pal after all—is that Ben won't talk about it. Not that I know what to say either. To admit, "I was really sad when I woke up alone," is to say, "You abandoned me when I needed you," and we would both know I didn't mean last night. Even though I've already brought up the Nickelback poster, I'll still march across the entire country naked before I'm revealing something like that unprompted.

We make our way onto I-80 again. Neither of us actually went back to sleep, so we checked out of the hotel and got into the car without saying anything beyond what was necessary. We have to get through the entire state of Nebraska today. It's an action-packed agenda, finishing with Ben's beloved baseball game in Colorado. There's no way we can sustain the energy I've forced us to establish. It's up to me to fix what I've done.

"Mr. Compass?" I ask. The nickname is an instant equalizer.

Ben relaxes his death grip on ten and two and reaches for one of the stale croissants he grabbed for us from the continental breakfast.

"Yes, Captain Business?"

"How many people have you slept with?"

He fumbles the croissant. "Pardon me?"

"Oh, I was just wondering how many people you've had sex with." Before he can speak through his own bewilderment, I decide to offer up my answer. "Mine is eleven."

Why let this be something good? Maybe it should be something even worse! Something so painfully awkward all we can do is laugh and be friendly about it. It worked with Starbucks Girl. It can work with Name Redacted. Because I'm not Dee right now. I'm the character of me I've created to survive my own life. She's bold. She's direct. She falls on her ass on purpose, just to get people smiling.

"Oh. Okay," Ben says. "Right on." It's such a perfectly funny response that my laugh comes out as a snort. Ben breaks into a quick, satisfied smile. "Do I have to answer?"

"Not at all. I'm only making conversation."

"Hell of a conversation starter for six thirty in the morning."

I asked because I want to make sure that I scorch every last bit of earth before the day is over, I think to myself. *If we're not going to sleep together again, I would like to be as chaotically unappealing to you as possible.*

"Sorry," I say quickly. "That was a bad boundary moment. My therapist would want me to acknowledge that. She'd be pleased to know I can identify it. Didn't stop me from saying it, though."

"No, no. It's cool." Ben's eyes remain on the road, but the speedometer is creeping up. "Are you happy about it?"

"My therapist or the amount of people I've slept with?"

"The, uh, people you've slept with."

"Sure," I say. "It's nice."

What am I saying? *Sure. It's nice.*

"It's always a surprise to people," I continue, accepting the bed I've made for myself. "They think that number is either way too high or way too low. The people who think it's high are puritanical and annoying. The people who think it's low assume because I talk about sex on my podcast that I am constantly having it with any willing participant. If they listened, they'd know me well enough to know that my gorgeous little brain would never allow me to be quite that carefree. It's proof you can never please everyone. I can only please eleven people, apparently. Which is—"

Ben cuts off my admittedly weak attempt at humor by declaring, "Four. I've had sex with four people."

I let the number sit with me, unexpectedly jarred. The silence that stretches between us might be strong enough to shift tectonic plates. Do I think that's high or low? Am I about to pass the same judgment on Ben that I just maligned for myself?

Ben Porter has slept with four people. What's his definition of sex? Probably intercourse. I can't ask any of this. Or maybe I can. But should I? What does it matter, really? The only thing I really have to know is, "Does that number include me?"

"Yes," Ben answers evenly.

I am one of four. Number one, in fact.

"Excellent," I say. Normally I'd want to hear all about the three other people. Women? Whoever they are. I'd want to know what the experiences were like. Was Ben satisfied? Were his partners?

For the first time since I can remember, I don't want to create images of these people in my mind, because then I'd have to contend with who I am in relation to them. Teenage Dee and one night in a hotel room with a bag of Twizzlers stuck to her back surely doesn't hold up against the experiences Ben has had since. Not that sex is a contest. Sex is whatever the participants want it to be. But I think it would break me a bit to hear that it didn't matter to him, or he thinks of it as less than perfect. Because to me, it was.

"Does your count include me?" he asks, much to my pleasant surprise.

"For sure," I say carefully.

"It's always nice to make the official scoreboard."

"Don't worry. You are forever locked into the three spot," I tell him.

"As you know, you're number one."

"I do know that."

"Pretty hard to forget the girl I lost my virginity to."

"Now, now," I scold. "You didn't *lose* anything to me, except for something that would've ended up in a sock if I wasn't around. No need to glorify my role in your sexual journey. Besides, what does virginity even mean, really? Not everyone is straight. The definition of sex is different in every relationship."

When I sneak a peek at Ben, he is smirking. "You've told me this before. And I stopped saying it." The idea of Ben holding on to me in this small way makes me flush. "I guess when I think of you and me, it doesn't feel right to not give the event its own title, though."

Oh.

Now that's new.

"Maybe we should workshop a new name for it, then," I joke. "How about *the reckoning?*"

He smiles. "Perfect. I'll start using it right away. 'Oh yeah, Dee? I had my reckoning with her back in high school. We reckoned in a hotel room. It was great. Unforgettable.'"

In my attempt to make things worse, I've only made this more dangerous. Ben has become the best version of himself. Honest and a little daring. It's like we're building a fire word by word, trying to find a sentence that sparks the flame.

If we keep talking like this, there will be no way for me to stop picturing him in that towel. One of four. The first. Unforgettable. Someone he wants to have a title. It will drive me to complete madness. There's already a rush of heat spreading through me. I turn up the air conditioning, pointing the vents at my face, hoping for relief.

We have to change the subject.

I use his stale croissant as a weak segue into remembering the shitty breakfasts we used to eat on the way to school. Then that turns into us reflecting on teenage Ben's near religious commitment to Panera Bread. Which somehow brings us to the light blue iPod Nano that I bought at a pawn shop with all the loose change I'd saved up since childhood—the one my mom sold—and all the times Ben and I would sit side by side sharing headphones, listening to the songs I illegally downloaded off websites that gave my mom's old PC too many viruses to count.

These are safe memories. Harmless. Enjoyable. They make us as close as ever while also keeping us as far as possible from me lifting his shirt over his head and running my fingers across his bare chest. No reckonings here.

Eventually Ben brings up the baseball game we're going to tonight. I got out of it once, and he's obviously waited ten whole years to make this chance happen again. He's chattering almost nonstop about the players I need to know. Despite my best efforts, I keep interpreting all of it as double entendres. For what other reason would he insist I understand the importance of getting to second base? Because second base is where he'd like to go with me? Are we the runners in scoring position? Should I ask about home runs?

It's the most juvenile, petulant way of thinking. I could genuinely shake myself for being this immature. Ben has moved on. He held me last night because I am a dear old friend. A fond memory. If he wanted more, he would've tried for it.

So for the nearly one hundred miles of driving it takes to get to the Iowa-Nebraska border, we run through our repertoire of good times. We have distracted ourselves so thoroughly that we both seem to have forgotten the significance of our next destination. It only occurs to me when the Bob Kerrey Pedestrian Bridge comes into view.

It curves fifty feet above the Missouri River, linking Council Bluffs, Iowa, to Omaha, Nebraska. Maybe I'm a simple person, but I still find the sight impressive. The water is beautiful, and the bridge looks so stately. My awe makes me glad to be who I am, because it's nice to remain amazed by what I don't understand. Such as how bridges work.

"Let's go get our picture," I say excitedly.

The foot traffic on the walkway is light. There's a skip in my step as we head to where Iowa ends and Nebraska begins.

"If you think about it, it's kind of funny," I say as Ben and I stroll across the bridge side by side. We arrive at the edge of the two states. "This border means nothing. We made it up. But it also means a lot."

"That's how it is for a lot of things, isn't it?" he notes.

I leap over into Nebraska.

NEBRASKA

18

DEE

Ben stays planted in Iowa.

Beneath our feet are the names of each state. In order to get them both in view of my camera, Ben has to squat to fit his head in the frame. He gives a thumbs-up and a closed-mouth smile. I tilt my head to the side and smirk. The sun of the new day washes us in a soft, hopeful light. With one press of a button, I capture us like this forever.

Without even looking at the picture, I know I'll hold on to it like I've done all the ones we took before, hidden in that tin under my bed. I'm supposed to be older and wiser now, but I think I'm actually worse off than I was at eighteen. Back then, I didn't know that Ben could hurt me. It never even occurred to me that we would ever stop speaking. For all the ways life had let me down, Ben had not. Every new memory we make becomes something I will undoubtedly keep too close. Something I will lie about to anyone who asks.

I scuff my shoe over the words on the ground. "Do you remember what we did here last time?"

Ben is still in Iowa, leaning over the railing to take in the view. He bites back a smile as he gazes out at the water. "You kissed me."

"I kissed *you?*"

"Yeah. At the border?" His expression shifts quickly, caught between genuine curiosity and something like fear.

A jogger runs by, pushing a breeze past us. The rush of air helps cool the anger rising to my cheeks. "No, no. I know where. But *you* kissed *me.*"

"What do you mean? You took the picture of us, then you turned your head, and you kissed me."

"Are you out of your mind? *You* took the picture! I couldn't figure out how to fit us into the frame and still get the states in there. It was your little red digital camera. The Nikon. You got it for Christmas from your aunt? We couldn't see the picture we were taking, so it was harder to make it work."

I am grabbing for every single detail I can recall and laying it all out like evidence to a jury of one. He has to remember this the way it actually happened. There isn't another option.

"You took it from me," I continue. "Your arm is longer, so you could hold it higher. When you pulled it back down so we could check the shot, we looked at each other instead. Then *you* kissed me."

"There's no way I'd ever kiss you first," he says matter-of-factly.

"What does *that* mean?"

He shakes his head, at war with the words he never seems to want to say. "Never mind."

"You cannot just never mind that!"

In the seconds it takes him to reflect, my anger floats away. This isn't a button he's pushed. It's a curiosity he's scratched. Which in the long run always ends up being worse for me. "Please. I have to know what that means. I will stay up for nights and nights wondering."

It's embarrassing to say this aloud, but it's so much the truth that there is no point in hiding it. If he doesn't explain himself, this is the kind of thing that will wake me up from a dead sleep in five years. It will interrupt my thoughts when I'm looking at cereal in the grocery store. It will stop me up in the shower until the hot water has run cold. Why wouldn't Ben Porter ever kiss me first?

Maybe he knows this. Because he crosses the made-up border into Nebraska to tell me, "I thought kissing you would be a mistake."

I do my best to swallow back the mortification of being labeled a mistake. My nod is strained, every muscle in my neck pulling tight. "Got it."

"No." He shakes his head. "See? I'm already screwing it up. I shouldn't have said it."

"You are truly making it worse."

"I know I am." Tension hardens the line of his jaw as he clenches his teeth together. "Dee, I guess it wasn't obvious, but you were like my whole entire world in high school. I figured if I kissed you, you'd hate it. You always went right after the things you wanted. And you never went after me."

Countless protestations die on my tongue. How could he ever think that? Why would I leave all my dates early to hang out with him? Attend every party with him? Find him whenever the night was dying down and it was time to go home, because he was always the one I wanted to leave with, no matter what? Lean my head on his shoulder while we sat on the couch watching movies? I did everything short of renting a skywriter and asking for the message BEN, PLEASE TOUCH YOUR LIPS TO MINE —DEE to fly over his house. At some point I figured I'd stop embarrassing myself and accept that he'd friend zoned me.

"I thought that must be because you didn't want me," he continues. "I knew it wasn't something I could just improve. Or make happen. That's why I know *you* kissed me. Because I would never, in all my life, go against that. No matter how much I wanted to. And trust me, Dee, I wanted to."

It's so much to take in I am almost light-headed. This cannot be what he thinks happened between us. He clearly experienced an alternate reality from mine. We are witnessing the Mandela effect firsthand.

"I wanted to kiss you too," I say with a surprising amount of insistence. It's not often I feel shy. Here on the bridge, rewriting Ben's history for him, coloring it in with my emotions, it's all I can do not to blush. "Probably since the moment our moms made me kiss your cheek in that kindergarten photo." I wag my finger. "Please don't read that as me condoning those actions. I still think it's incredibly gross. But yeah."

Ben gives me his best, most perfect smile. "Do you still?"

"Want to kiss you?"

He nods.

And somehow, my hands are on his chest. His are around my waist. And I see now how it is that we can't agree on who kissed who. Because if someone told me my life depended on explaining how we've ended up holding each other, I'd have to die. We just are.

"Of course I do," I whisper.

Ben tilts his head down. This is the same game we played last night. Inches between us. Breaths held. Pulses racing.

"Prove it," he baits.

Never one to resist a dare, my lips crash into his. Urgent and certain. He meets my energy immediately. This is not the Ben I used to know. He kisses me like he could flip me over and wring me out. The pressure makes me gasp for air.

When I come back to his mouth, I make sure to run my hands through his hair too. Then press my nails into the flesh of his back. I am desperately cataloging all the places I want to remember. Places I can explore in view of the public.

My body sinks into his with so little effort. It's a sigh. A release. A homecoming. The kind of reunion that makes choirs sing out *hallelujah*. The fire building earlier has finally sparked, setting my skin ablaze in every place that presses into Ben. His kisses get softer as the urgency between us makes way for tenderness. Our switch is effortless, a smooth glide from intensity to intention. He pulls back to look into my eyes.

There he is.

The Ben in the old YouTube videos I watch late at night. The Ben whose face I've searched for in those pictures online. None of them ever fully capture what it is to see him like this. The way his nose turns up at the end. How his smile lines stay even when he's serious. Memories of his past joys are never far from him. He is so real it overwhelms me. He is so him. And you have to know him to know what a compliment that is.

"So that was definitely you," he jokes.

"Oh, *please*." I plug my ears and turn away. "I can't hear this."

He scoops me up from the back, pressing a kiss to my cheek. "That was you. That was you. That was you," he taunts.

I turn into him and rest my pointer finger on his lips. "That was you and me."

"You and me," he repeats, holding me tight. "I like the sound of that."

19

BEN

Back in the car, we haven't talked about what happened on the bridge. If we did, it would only make things worse, because all I can think about is resting my hand on Dee's leg. The idea of her exposed thigh beneath my palm? It's such a thrill I'm almost feverish. If we tried to put this into words, it would eventually become actions, and we both know what happens after that.

As a kid, I was always looking forward to adulthood, where I'd be that professional-baseball-playing endodontist who ran a physical therapy practice too. The possibilities were so infinite, I couldn't wait to greet all of them. If I try not to think about touching Dee, I end up thinking about everything I was when I last knew her. Because of her, I'm looking back at all my childhood hopes that never came true—the ones that still linger at the edge of my subconscious, buried under my need to keep things light and easy. I have spent the last ten years acting like everything I wanted as a kid doesn't matter to me. Including Dee. And that's not true at all.

"Do you want to get some food to go?" Dee asks, lacking all her usual emphasis. There's a seriousness to her that I know I've drawn out, and it drives me wild to think about other ways I could affect her.

"Let's pick something up, then keep driving until we hit North Platte. We've got a lot to do today," I say.

She thumbs through our agenda absentmindedly. "We do."

We might be on track, but things are not going according to plan. Nowhere on Dee's sheet of notebook paper did we account for how every urge I've suppressed for the last twenty-four hours—or the last ten years, if I'm honest—has been brought to the surface. It's so reckless of me to want her. It goes against everything I hoped to get out of this trip, because this kind of feeling between us has only ever brought destruction. But now that I've kissed her—and slept with her body against mine—there is nothing to do but want more.

She searches her phone for somewhere to eat, and we settle on a sandwich place a few exits off. When I pull into the strip mall where it's located, it's Dee who flies out of the car this time.

"I'll get it," she tells me. "You want a turkey sandwich on whole wheat. Toasted, if possible. Tomato, but only one slice. Extra mayo on both sides of the bread. Banana peppers if they have them."

"I . . . I do," I confirm, stunned.

"Sweet. Stay here. I'll be right back."

My car is immediately empty without her. Full of random things that need her presence to make them complete. Otherwise it's only crumbs and bags. How many miles have I driven without her in the passenger seat? Where was I going? Why was that where I wanted to be?

Through the window of the shop, I watch Dee approach the register. She's wearing a little yellow dress with straps thin as floss. Straps I could break with my teeth. She's got her hair up again, exposing her shoulder blades. As always, her entrance pulls the focus of the whole room. The girl behind the counter leans forward. The guy sweeping lifts his head from the floor to stare. Two patrons stop their conversation to watch her.

Dee sways from foot to foot as she looks at the menu. I can't help but note the way her body moves without me, imagining all the ways I could move with it. I know exactly where I'd hold her. How fast I would go.

Once she's placed her order and paid, she looks down at her phone. **Are you watching me?** she texts.

Yes, I respond.

Good, she writes back.

Her hand grips the back of her neck. There's a sneaky half grin on her face as she does a little swirl, then drops into a curtsy. The guy who is sweeping bites back a laugh.

This is what you wanted me to watch? I text her.

She starts to mark a waltz across the floor of the shop. After a few more spins, she stops to type.

Everyone was staring at me when I walked in

The energy in here is intense

So I wanted to see if they would support me dancing like no one's watching

I want them to think I'm a real Live Laugh Love bitch

The girl at the cash register was into it

She's my Marge

Everyone deserves one

I hoped and hoped

But I never thought it would happen to me

Finally, my own Marge

Hahaha

You know you could have anything you want

Her little text bubbles pop up. Then they disappear. And reappear.

I look up to see Dee staring at her screen. Her posture has changed—she stands straight as a board, one foot right beside the other. Her eyes are squinted in concentration. Then she tucks her phone into her purse and waits with her hands laced together behind her back.

Why did I write that? This is the kind of thing we aren't supposed to talk about. We've never been able to talk about it. Last time, we had sex in Colorado and then drove the entire way back to Illinois without so much as sharing a loaded glance over it.

Once Dee gets our sandwiches, she strolls outside wearing an unreadable expression. The breeze blows gently against her dress, yellow fabric pressing between her legs. She stops in front of my car with her hands on her hips.

I roll down my window. "What are you doing?"

She levels me with a penetrating gaze. "I'm deciding what I want."

There might be a world outside the two of us, but I can't see it. Unless that world happens to be playing our past on a projector screen. Because it's our story being told in this stare. It's her breath hot on my ear. My hands on her waist. Her hips. Everywhere. With one swift pass, she moves from the front of my car to the passenger door, pulling it open and sliding into her seat, tossing the sandwich bag into the space between her feet.

I turn to her. "I hope what I wrote wasn't—"

Her heaving breaths crash against my chest as she puts the full weight of her body against mine. Her tongue slips into my mouth, and I immediately press back with my own. My hands roam across all the curves I watched move in the window as my fingers sink into her skin.

"It's you," she whispers breathlessly. "I want you."

We can't do this here. But I would, if she asked. If we weren't in a parking lot in clear view of the staff at the sub shop, I'd be lifting her dress over her head.

"I want you too." The words taste dangerous coming out of my mouth. These aren't the things I am supposed to say. But I have to. Because if my lips don't find hers again, I think my body will combust.

So we make out. In my car. In the parking lot of a sandwich shop in rural Nebraska. Every kiss from me is a promise for more. A gentle cup of her chest to tell her I'll be back. A quick brush between her thighs to remind her that this is only the beginning.

Abruptly, Dee pulls away from me.

"We need to get going," she says.

I slump back into my seat, breathless.

"You're the one with a sacred sports ritual to attend tonight!"

She has the audacity to laugh. "And I don't wanna miss the trading post either!"

I'd miss the tourist stop we have planned. The baseball game. *Everything.* For her. But I put my car in reverse and set us back onto the agenda, because it's what we said we'd do. And a promise is a promise.

There is a moment on those early morning runs with Darius where I've pushed through the discomfort and I'm in a groove, my speed building as I work my way closer to our designated finish line. That's how it feels with Dee. I see where we're going, and I'm running like hell to get there. But it's also nice right now. Exhilarating. All the difficulty of getting started is in the past. All the hope of something great is soon to come.

When I merge onto the highway, I put my hand on her leg, and I don't let go.

20

DEE

Ben and I kissed again. I touch my lips, and I know that happened. My heart hammering in my chest remembers it even better than my mouth does. But it's all so strange, because not only does Ben seem unworried, he actually seems relaxed. He's leaned into his seat, one hand on the steering wheel, the other on my leg, looking the most content he's been yet.

Meanwhile I'm sitting ramrod straight with my palms squeezed together between my sweaty thighs, only moving to take small bites of my sandwich, then chewing quickly and resuming my frozen posture. He kissed me on the bridge. Or we kissed each other. Whatever. We made out in his car.

All signs point to us heading toward exactly what I planned for, but I should've tossed him in the back seat of this Civic right when we pulled off at our first rest stop somewhere in rural Illinois. I should've had sex with him then, and then said, *Okay, that's good.* That would've been fun. But now I know that Ben will sit on the bathroom floor with me as I rid myself of every whisper of tofu fish sticks. He will hold me in the dark. He will press his lips to mine with attention and care. He can drive the speed limit. I've done the very dangerous thing—memorized my favorite parts of him again, shading in all the spots of my mental

Ben picture that have faded over time. And it's such a beautiful sight. Vibrant and full and far too real.

Our next stop in Nebraska is a town called North Platte. They have an Old West tourist attraction called the Fort Cody Trading Post. Ben used to go as a kid, and he insisted I would enjoy it. He was, of course, correct, because the place looks like it's made from Lincoln Logs. That's something I will always need in my life.

When we pull into the parking lot, there's still a skyscraping statue of Buffalo Bill Cody holding a musket. The whole place is supposed to be like walking into an era long past, but I think of the *Oregon Trail* computer game we used to play during computer class in grade school, which is just as good to me. Probably better.

The parking lot has a few other cars. Ben gets out and immediately takes to looking at each license plate. "Captain Business, we've got Utah," he tells me, pretending to speak into a walkie-talkie.

I pull my notebook from my purse to make furious note of it. There are many things that I want to accomplish on this trip, and while seeing every license plate is not number one on the list, it's definitely in the top ten. "Copy that," I say into my shoulder. "Anything else?"

Ben checks the other row of cars. "Holy shit. There's *Delaware* here."

"Are you kidding me?"

"I promise. Put it down! We've got Delaware! This is huge!"

His earnest enthusiasm makes adding a new license plate feel as monumental as a national holiday. Sweet Ben, genuinely entertaining my little time killers, celebrating with what must be the purest form of joy that exists.

"Do you want to be the one to write it down?" I ask him.

His eyes go even wider. "I get to write in the notebook?"

I hand it over. "Get in there, Mr. Compass. Add Delaware to the log."

Our innocent excitement seems to cut down on the rising tension between us. For a moment, it's good to have somewhere else to put my thoughts. If I didn't, I think I'd dig myself to the core of the earth trying to figure out what Ben really thinks of anything. He told me he wanted me. I need to know for how long, and in exactly what way.

It's the most annoying thing about me. I need to know everything. Then I don't know what to do with the information once I have it.

When Ben is done, he passes the notebook back to me. He's put down Delaware in the most careful version of his handwriting, not a single edge out of line. His handwriting looks award worthy, especially beside my chicken scratch. At the bottom of the page, he's written something else.

You are very funny. And smart. And beautiful.

I like your dress.

He's watching me, waiting for my reaction. When I look up, unable to stop myself from blushing, a pleased grin cracks across the revelation that is his face. He extends his hand for me to hold. I grab on, imagining the lines of my palm aligning with his. All the paths that pulled us apart now meeting again, pressed together, converging exactly where they are meant to converge.

"C'mon," he says playfully, still happy with himself for flattering me. "Let's go."

We walk hand in hand through the museum, learning once again about Buffalo Bill and how he once lived here in North Platte. If time travel is real, this is what it is—doing the same thing with the same person ten years later, feeling everything twice over. Teenage Dee moves in perfect symmetry with the adult, current version of me. It makes all the sense in the world to both of us that Ben and I are here again, fingers interlaced, making our own fun in the middle of nowhere.

There are so many unique things throughout the museum. To us, the most notable is a two-headed stuffed calf that stands surrounded in glass in the middle of a linoleum-tiled room. Fluorescent lights cast rectangular glares onto the encasing. There is something so starkly strange not just about the decision to include this here, but to place it with no real explanation. It's almost melancholic in its oddness.

Ben and I stop to pay our respects. The last time we came, we'd watched other people pass and laugh, but we'd both agreed on a somber tone. It had been one of my favorite memories, our collective empathy for the two-headed calf in the middle of a Buffalo Bill museum. The way we'd said so much by saying nothing. We have always had the ability to make the smallest things interesting. To decide on a mood without words. To appreciate what other people ignore. Together, we can make anything important.

Standing here again, wondering once more about all the odd things in this museum—in this life, really—I realized I've missed Ben so much that being around him makes me feel more than whole. It's why my anger has been so big and my anxiety almost comically exaggerated. He fills up so many spaces that ached in his absence that the relief within me overflows, mixing with all my other emotions. Absence didn't make my heart grow fonder. It made my heart forget. Because if I'd remembered him exactly as he is, I never would have let him walk out on me.

Our last stop is the gift shop. Ben insists on getting himself a Nebraska hat, putting it on as soon as I pay for it. I make good with a keychain. It's something that will fit into that tin under my bed, so I can hide it from myself if I have to, because this isn't a me I know very well. This is me reckless in the one way I don't usually allow myself to be—I'm reckless in joy.

We have a little over four hours to make it to Colorado in time for the Rockies game. It seems impossible, all the places we will have been by the time this day is over.

We exit the store with candy bars to tide us over until we get to enjoy some classic ballpark food.

"Want a bite?" I ask, extending my Snickers to Ben.

He takes it readily, eating right out of my hands. Once he's done chewing, he extends his Twix to me. When I try to take a bite in the same way he did, he pulls the candy bar back.

"Hey! This is no joking matter," I say.

He lifts the Twix to my mouth and presses it there, letting the chocolate melt into my lips until we're both laughing.

The sun has cast a buttery yellow glow over everything, a perfect filter for my joy. This is the kind of weather you wish for when you're caught in the middle of a snowstorm. Effortless perfection.

Ben dutifully wipes the chocolate from my mouth with a napkin he apparently keeps in the pocket of his shorts. When he's done working, he closes his eyes and tilts his face up to let the afternoon warmth cover him.

"Did you know that the sun weighs 4.18 nonillion pounds?" he asks with his eyes squeezed shut.

"Shut up. That's fake. You're making that up."

"I swear." He smiles into the light. "But you're right. It's not exact. We can't ever know the real weight of the sun, because we weigh things based on our gravity, and the sun has its own."

"*Of course* the sun does. That's so like the sun to do that." I reach out and tap his hand. "Thanks for teaching me, Mr. Porter."

"Anytime." He takes a deep breath. Then he opens his eyes to look at me. "I'm really happy you're here."

He can make something so simple it hurts. He can boil something this intricate down to happiness, and he can mean it. It's the exact kind of naked sincerity that rips me open when I least expect it.

"Why did you walk out on me?" I ask, almost whispering.

It's not my well-documented habit of wanting to set fire to the good that makes this question spill out of me. It's that I know if we're really gonna do this, be the type of people who hold hands in public and talk like the 4.18-nonillion-pound sun shines only for us, then I have to know he won't walk out again. I need to hear him say it. Even if it's jarring to bring up in the middle of this beautiful, sun-soaked moment of peace.

"I was young, and I didn't know what leaving you meant," he explains. "I never should have done it."

"You ripped up the Nickelback poster."

I laugh to fight off the urge to cry. It's all so trivial. Irrelevant in the great, grand scheme of things. Unfortunately, knowing that does nothing to make it matter less. In fact, it seems to make it matter more. It's so small it has no right to feel this immense, but here it is, materializing as a lump in my throat.

"I thought you'd find it and be so mad that you'd come look for me to yell. But you didn't," he says.

Maybe our last fight is something like our first kiss, the kind of event we will always remember differently. A situation that happened outside of us somehow—this huge, life-altering moment that we are powerless to understand.

"I'm always looking for you," I tell him.

He puts a hand to my face, cupping my chin with his palm. There are things he tries to say. Words that always get caught under the wall he's built for himself, the pleasant, hardworking guy who can do it all with a smile. He wants to crack, but he still doesn't really know how.

"I wanted to go to prom with you," I continue. It's a sentence that's supposed to open the door to discussing what we won't say. Instead it opens the floodgates. A single tear rolls down my cheek, threatening to multiply. "It feels so fucking ridiculous to say that. I am a full-blown, tax-paying adult crying about my senior prom." I wipe the tear away. "If you tell anyone about this, I'll sue you."

"It's not ridiculous," Ben says, ignoring my attempt to use humor to soften this self-inflicted blow.

"We had this perfect fucking trip," I continue. I have to give in to the madness of this feeling. There is no other choice. "And you still asked Alina Dennis. It made me the worst kind of cliché. The girl who misread something. The one who thought what we had was more than it was. And we didn't even need to be dating to go to prom. I would've gone with you no matter what."

Ben and I got back from our road trip, and three days later he put together a promposal for the girl who sat in front of him in AP English. Alina, with short dark hair and a nose stud she wasn't allowed to wear during school hours. She always stood at her locker and shoved it back in as soon as the last school bell rang. She was someone whose name Ben mentioned in the barest of passing, as casual as I would bring up the weather or my feelings about the texture of ketchup. She was this background character that suddenly became a main player, nearly a villain if I didn't know better, inserted into the middle of a plot I never imagined I'd live through.

"It was so embarrassing," I explain, careful to leave out the whys. Like the dress I'd saved up for, purchased at the second-hand shop by my mom's work. It had been at the store for years, and I'd gone in to covet it so many times that the owners gave me a generous discount, making me able to purchase it. It was long and royal blue, with a beaded bodice and a completely open back. I knew it would look nice with Ben. Even before I figured out I loved him, I knew that. The day we pledged to go to prom together, sitting on the park swings a few weeks after our eighth-grade graduation, I knew that.

On senior prom night it sat in the back of my closet, unused, while I sat in the back of Trevor Williamson's car. Number four of eleven. A few days later, I put the dress in a trash bag and gave it away.

"I'm really sorry," Ben says. "If that means anything."

It does mean something. If only regret could rewrite what happened. Maybe then the past wouldn't scratch up against me as much, sandpaper to the poor teenage soul trapped inside my twenty-eight-year-old body.

I stare at him. "Why didn't you ask me to go with you?"

This is the exact question that ended our friendship. When I asked him last time, I was yelling it at him. He was yelling back. Telling me he couldn't believe I'd ask something like that. Then he walked away from me. And he never came back.

"Dee." He pivots on his heel to breathe into his hands. "I never thought you wanted me to."

Now I'm really crying. Twice in two days. "How could I not want you to?"

Staccato breaths creep out of me in desperate huffs. This perfect Nebraska day, with its dandelion clouds and bleached grass. The smell of wood from the Lincoln Log building. The shadow of the Buffalo Bill cutout shading Ben's car. It's all so fresh. Too pure.

Ben's got tears in his eyes too.

For a flash, I think of Garrett, sitting on my couch only two nights ago. Crying because I told him we needed space. Now I'm begging Ben to explain why he wouldn't keep me close. Why, after everything, I wasn't the one he wanted to hold as we said goodbye to our youth.

"In that hotel room . . ." He waits to make sure I know he means the one we stayed in ten years ago. "I told you that you were the most important person in the world to me. And you said thanks."

I almost laugh. It sounds so absurd explained like this. Void of all the small details, like the way he'd been tracing a circle into my clavicle with his pointer finger. Or how I had my other hand on his head, stroking his curls with the pad of my thumb. We were inches apart as we said this, breath to breath. We were fucking naked. Without all that context, I sound callous.

"I meant it," I insist. "No one ever thought of me that way. I did the best I could with it. I wasn't used to being anyone's favorite."

Ben's the one who does laugh, the cruel kind he directs at the sky, like *Isn't it all so obvious?* "You were always my favorite. Why do you think you're the one I waited for?" he asks.

It's certainly something I've wondered. Why didn't Ben Porter sleep with anyone before me? It's not that he didn't have choices. It's not that he wasn't social enough. Or well-liked enough. Or cute enough to pull literally anyone he wanted. But he went out with girls for a few weeks at a time. Three dates and he was out the door, onto the next. He could've dated guys too. Anyone he wanted. No one ever met his standards. I accepted all of that.

He didn't owe anyone anything. He could be with as many or as few people as he wanted. He could be with no one. It didn't matter to me. He'd always be my Ben. Having him in my life was enough.

"I don't know," I say.

"Because I—because I really loved you then," he tells me.

Then. Past tense.

"I loved you then too," I choke out, careful to use the same distinction he has.

"Do you think that would've been enough? To keep us from breaking? If we'd just said that then?"

I can't keep looking at him like this. Since the car's only a few steps away, I walk toward it, one foot in front of the other. "We probably would've hurt each other in a different way. I certainly wouldn't have made any trips down to Indiana University to visit you." My dry delivery couldn't be more false. But there has to be humor here to cut the edge of the pain.

"You would've liked it there. It was a really nice campus," he tells me.

We get into his car as he says this, somehow returning to our own version of safety—this touch-and-go place where we build fake lives for ourselves atop our real ones.

I don't have the strength to continue picturing this particular revisionist history—a timeline where we don't break each other's hearts at the end of senior year, and we see each other through the years we missed. That's too overwhelming. Would I have run into Javi at that bar? Would we have started our podcast? Would I have made a life for myself?

Absolutely everything I know would be changed by Ben staying.

He backs out of the Fort Cody Trading Post with no real

ceremony to it. Like we're leaving a grocery store after our hundredth run. Because the meaningful and the mundane collide
in the strangest of ways, and where we are no longer matters,
only what we're saying to each other.

With the monotony of the highway to once again lull us into
answers, we press on, collecting our thoughts in quiet.

"I wanted to go with you too. Just like we promised," Ben
tells me.

Ah.

So he *does* remember that part. The part I've been afraid to
mention. We *promised* we would go together. I hear a catch in
his voice, coloring that word. Because that's who Ben is, a man
who keeps his promise. And he knows he didn't.

"That's why you had to keep this one," I say, more for myself
than for him. It's not something he has to answer. I already know
I'm right.

"Everything used to make sense to me. Losing you was the
one thing that didn't. I accepted it, because that's what I was
good at. Accepting things without looking any deeper. And then
I found out my whole life's been a lie."

I've wanted to mention it again, but it's not the easiest thing
to insert into casual conversation. Or even deep conversation.
This is something he has to want to talk about, and I respect that.
"Does anyone else in your family know that you know?"

He shakes his head. "I've thought about bringing it up. I can't
seem to actually do it."

I reach for the hand he's placed on the gearshift, lifting it up
to lace my fingers through his. "It's okay. You can talk to them
when you're ready."

It's a leap to hold his hand. A risk I'm willing to take to let
him know, in spite of it all, I still care. Deeply.

"That's the thing. I *am* ready. But I also don't want any of the mess. There will be so much. I don't know if my dad even knows. I think he does. But Richie . . ." He pauses to think it over. "Richie definitely doesn't know. He can't keep a secret for shit. He's been texting me this whole trip. Begging me to go somewhere with him. I haven't been answering. I don't know what to say anymore."

"Maybe you could make everyone get one of those Ancestry DNA tests, and then freak out when yours doesn't match your dad's," I suggest, only half kidding.

"No. I want to be honest."

It hurts me to know how much he's hurting. I care about him, and I don't want to see him in pain. And he is. And I think I love him.

I test the weight of that in my mind, turning it over like a coin.

I *know* I love him.

Present tense.

Did I Forget to Tell You?

EPISODE 100: HUNDREDTH TIME'S THE CHARM

JAVI: It's our one hundredth episode.

DEE: Yes it is.

JAVI: Do you know what I've done?

DEE: Ordered a cake?

JAVI: Wait. Yes. Did I tell you that?

DEE: Yeah.

JAVI: Damn.

DEE: Do you know what I've done, though?

JAVI: Called Name Redacted and made amends?

DEE: Oh my god! Absolutely not! I'm evolved, but I'm not a *saint*. No, I texted my mom. Obviously this show started with her, and I thought it would be nice if we brought her on again. But she didn't answer.

JAVI: She didn't? I'm really sorry to hear that.

DEE: Unfortunately, no. But . . . I also wrote to my dad.

JAVI: *What?*

DEE: Yeah. I know. It was wild of me. As a refresher, if you're listening to our show for the first time, I've never met my dad. I only know his name because my mom admitted it to me on this very show. Some of you scarily good internet users found him for me. I'm just as good as you guys, but I have no interest in doing that kind of research myself, so I appreciate all of you for sharing your detective gifts. I've had all of his information for a while, sitting in a labeled email folder. Never done anything with it. Until last week.

JAVI: I can't believe you didn't mention this.

DEE: *Did I forget to tell you?*

JAVI: Wow. That was well played.

DEE: It is our one hundredth episode, after all. We have to give it everything we've got.

JAVI: Did he respond?

DEE: He did! He called me! Asked to meet up with me.

JAVI: Oh my god, Dee. Did you do it?

DEE: No.

JAVI: Why not?

DEE: Because it's enough for me to have him know I exist. I don't want to complicate it by having him know me. Or me him. We can be beautiful ideas to each other.

JAVI: Is that really what you want?

DEE: Sure. I mean, honestly, it's harder to let him in than it is to keep him at a comfortable distance. He can't hurt me this way.

JAVI: I mean, you changed this man's whole life.

DEE: Yeah. That's true.

JAVI: If I have a child out there somewhere—which as far as I know is not scientifically possible, but just in case—please don't contact me unless you actually want to know me.

DEE: I think I do. Want to know him, that is. It's scary. You know? Especially since I barely speak to my mom anymore. The idea of another parent letting me down? Another *person*, really. That's a lot.

JAVI: It is.

DEE: Welcome to the chaos of my mind!

JAVI: We're very happy to be here.

DEE: And I'm happy to have you. Stay tuned for the moment I finally shatter these emotional walls like the girl boss I am! Name Redacted better look out!

21

BEN

Did Dee and I really talk through the entire reason for our split without fighting? Not like the last time, at least. This was more clearing the air than an argument. If it's always been this simple, I could scream. When we get into the mountains, I think I will. Just to hear my voice echo the pain back to me. I've spent ten years hiding Dee from my mind and my memories, too afraid to face the well-earned anger she'd have for me, and it's all been solved in less than ten minutes.

She has her lips pressed to my knuckles now, helping me through my current struggle. "Having a different biological father doesn't change the fact that they're your family. You get to decide exactly how much that matters to you. No one else." When I don't say anything, she pokes my ribs. "Do you hear me? Blood does not determine what someone means to you. Okay?"

"I know," I tell her. "I hear you."

"Hear it *and* believe it," she says, more insistently. "Some of my listeners found my dad for me. So I know what I'm saying when I tell you this."

"Wow. Have you reached out to him?"

"Yeah. But I haven't met him in person or anything. And I don't think I ever will."

"Why not?"

"Ben, you know how much not having a dad is a part of my personality!"

It would be easy to laugh. Her delivery is perfect, and she is always funny to me. But I want her to know that I see the seriousness beneath this.

We sit in silence until she adds, "It would be too hard for me to accept that he might be great. He might even love me. After a life without him, I can't find out that I could have had something wonderful, if only I'd looked."

The little waver in her voice breaks me. The world has hurt her so much. So have I. For as good as it feels to be around her, there's still that truth. We have hurt each other so much by staying silent. Which feels like part of the answer to the question I didn't know I was asking—silence hurts.

"You still get to have good things," I remind her. "Even if they come to you later than you deserve."

She smiles at me like I might be that good thing. If silence hurts, I need to keep speaking.

"I'm afraid to tell my family the truth because I've never been the one to make a mess before, and I'm scared they won't react in the way I need them to," I admit. "When something bad happens, we don't talk about it. We barely even acknowledge it. We keep going, waiting for the better days to come. Which I used to think was nice. You of all people know how much Richie fucked up when we were younger. My parents had meetings every year with his teachers to discuss his lack of effort and his troublemaking behavior. After every incident my parents looked at Richie and said, 'You'll do better next time, right?' And let it go. Which is a nice way to be on the surface. Shame doesn't fix things. But neither does apathy. They didn't know what to do with him, so they chose to do nothing at all. Lucky for them, he turned out pretty okay in the end."

Dee brushes her thumb across the top of my knuckles, urging me forward.

"And like with me, I never wanted to cause trouble for them. I used to get so worked up over not getting things exactly right," I continue. "When I'd have a bad game or something, my mom would hold my shoulders and say, 'Aww. Please don't get upset, Benny. It doesn't matter.' But I was sitting there crying. That has to matter, right?"

"Of course it does," Dee assures me.

"Now I wonder if my parents acted the way they did because any real problem would have somehow led to talking about my mom's affair. If my dad knew about it, he obviously made some kind of peace with it that required no one ever mentioning it again. They seemed to decide the only way to keep everything from falling apart was to pretend there was never anything to worry about. Which only ever made me worry more. I could always tell something was wrong. So I spent all my time trying to keep everyone smiling, because when they weren't, they became miserable in a way I didn't know how to fix."

"*Ben.*" Dee says my name so insistently I look away from the open road for a moment to make eye contact with her. Her gaze cuts right through me. So focused. So assured. "You can't fix other people's problems. You really can't. You can offer support, you can even come up with solutions, but in the end, it's not your responsibility. Especially with your parents. And you can believe me on this one, because it's taken me a shit ton of therapy to learn this about my own mother. I finally figured out that I will never be able to make her into the mother I wish she would be. Sometimes the best way to love someone else is by protecting your own peace and keeping your distance. It doesn't mean I don't care about her. As soon as I had enough money to do it, I started supporting her financially. I plan to keep that up. But I don't think I can see her anymore. I've finally learned that being around her will hurt me more than it will ever help me." She rubs my cheek tenderly before saying, "Tell me what happened when Gam got sick."

She's filled me in on her life in her Dee way, tucking information into the corners of a different conversation, leaving it up to me to piece it all together. If she wanted me to ask more about her mom, she wouldn't have steered me away from the topic so quickly. I have to take her lead.

"My mom told us about Gam over text," I say.

Dee gasps.

"Exactly. Richie responded with 'That sucks.' And my mom said, 'Don't worry. We'll get through it.' Except no one had any plans for how. If I hadn't moved Gam in with me, she would have died alone in the mountains."

I hate that memory. The sobering realization that if I didn't do something about Gam's living situation, no one would. We'd get through it by acting like nothing happened, like we always did.

"Now I know the family secret—I *am* the family secret, actually—and if I'm not the one to share it, it won't get shared at all," I say. "I've been lost for months now, and I'm sure all of them can see that. But they haven't asked me what's wrong. They're waiting for me to be better again."

"You know, my whole job is listening to people's secrets." Dee's gentle tone keeps me calm. It's easier to breathe when I hear her voice. "It used to be really shocking to me how many people didn't want to say these things to the people that needed to hear them, because they'd tell me and Javi within an hour of knowing us. I've learned that we all want someone to love us for all our flaws, but we're afraid to ask for that from the people we know best." She leans forward to turn down the music. "You've really never listened to my show, have you?"

"No." I hesitate. "Well, I played a clip from your latest episode as I was walking up to your apartment. Mostly because I wanted to hear your voice. To make sure you sounded the same."

"Did I?"

"Yes and no. You sounded like you, but more mature." It's hard to explain this to her. The details weren't as important as the feeling. Hearing her voice made everything chaotic about my life suddenly seem far away, rendered unimportant.

"That makes sense," she says.

"You sounded happy. And I'm realizing now that I don't know if you were. Or are. I showed up uninvited in the middle of your life."

"You sure did," she says, grinning. "But I'm glad you showed up."

"I'm glad I did too."

More than you could ever know.

"And I'd say that lately, I've kind of been floating through it all," she tells me. "Because in the back of my mind, I'm always waiting for some nameless disaster to strike. I'm not used to things being this steady. I feel like I can never get too comfortable, or the world will punish me for it. So I try very hard to coast. Not happy. But not sad either. Just existing."

"Why would the world punish you?"

"Because I've never been allowed to have good things for too long. They always disappear without warning."

Her words are difficult to hear, but I told myself to keep speaking. *Especially* when it's hard.

"No amount of apologies can ever cover how sorry I am for disappearing on you," I tell her.

"I know," she says quietly. "I really do." She angles herself toward me. "What about you? You said you're lost."

Any other day, any other person, my instinct would be to tell her I'm actually fine. Because who am I to say I'm lost? I own a home. I have a steady job and a great summer gig coaching youth baseball. If I listed it all out on paper, it would look like a detailed map of a steady life. But for Dee, I say, "Nothing excites me anymore."

"What would excite you?" Dee probes. "Endodontics?" Like only she can, she softens my struggle.

"I don't really know. I do like my job. It's just all there is. I go to the gym. I go to work. I come home. That's it. Being around you again reminds me that I used to want so many things at once. And they all seemed possible."

"Dude, you are Ben fucking Porter. They are," she says. "I talk to so many people on my show that do cool things with their life. There's no real common theme for how they got there. Except generational wealth, most of the time. Which you have! But you also have a lot of heart. If you put that toward whatever interests you deep inside your secret, special brain chamber, I bet you'll find something pretty exciting there."

"You make it sound so simple."

She squeezes my arm. "That's because of you! You have this way of making complicated ideas seem really easy to figure out."

"Tell it to the thirteen-years-olds who've learned eukaryotic cell structure from me."

"Well, the mitochondria is the powerhouse of the cell, Benjamin. We *all* know that." She lifts her other hand up to run a finger across my passenger-side window, drawing an invisible smiley face.

"How do we stop you from floating through life?" I ask her. "More time with Garrett Two Hearts?"

She snort-laughs, which is good. It was a risk to say this guy's name, but it felt like a safe one to make with her. The kind of ambitious callback she'd appreciate. I want to soften her struggles as much as she softens mine. I want to do everything for her.

"Oh my god. *Definitely* not," she says. "You know, I never even talked about him on the show, that's how unimportant he was."

It feels like an invitation to ask the obvious. I could avoid it, but I'd be lying if I said I wasn't a little curious. Or worried that Garrett Two Hearts and I fall into the same category. "Have you talked about me?"

She pauses for so long I decide it doesn't matter. What could she even say? I was her best friend, I made a promise that I broke, and we don't talk. It would be boring. Her listeners would not care.

"It's okay if you haven't," I tell her, smoothing over the awkward pause. "I promise I'm not offended. I was only wondering."

"Ben," she says insistently. "I talk about you."

Before this trip, I assumed Dee and I had handled the last ten years exactly the same. We'd put a bolt lock on any mention of each other. We'd watched each other's birthdays pass on the calendar, and we'd made ourselves forget the day had any meaning. The reality is, Dee has never been like me. Which is why we were the pair we were. Salt and pepper. Working well together while never accomplishing the same thing. Maybe she's hated me and everyone knows *except* me. I don't like letting people down as is. I'm not sure I can cope with disappointing countless strangers across the country.

She interprets my contemplation as upset. "I don't use your

real name or anything!" she tells me, injecting cheer into her voice. "No one would ever know it was you! Except for you, of course. Plus, like, Victoria and Javi. But that's inevitable. And everything I say about you is, um . . . *mostly* good."

I gulp.

"I'm so sorry," she says. "I should've asked for your permission."

"No, no. It's not that. You have my retroactive permission, I promise. I just didn't realize you still thought of me that much."

"Of course I do." A loaded silence lingers until she adds, "You really haven't looked me up at all? Like, even a little bit?"

"No. I deleted all my social media before my freshman year at IU. Haven't been back since."

"I mean, Google still works on phones without social media apps. That's how I've found out things about you." She grabs her mouth. "I wish I didn't say that."

"Why?" It's painful to think of her searching for me, shining a flashlight into the darkness. That's Dee, though. She looks where others won't.

"Because I know everything about you there is to know," she tells me. "At least when it comes to the internet. I know where you *work.* Crest Ridge Middle School. Go, Eagles! I've seen your house on Zillow. And BlockShopper. Great job getting a good deal from previous owner Donya Grable! Your Little League team. Way to go on that blowout game last July! Can't believe Timmy Scanlon hit a grand slam twice. What are the odds? I've read every mention of your name in your town's local Patch. Proud of you for founding the astronomy fair. Congrats on making the stars seem cool!" She leans over her legs and buries her face in her hands. "You didn't even type out a single 'Dee Matthews Illinois,' and I am over here with your dental records ready to go."

All the details she's known about me along the way suddenly

make sense. She's Dee of reading grocery receipts. She has kept track of me all this time. She's talked about me on her show without ever saying my name. She's held me close, and I've done nothing but ignore the very idea of her.

"If it helps, I got off-line because of you," I offer.

She peeks up at me through her fingers. "You're telling me that we divorced, and you gave me the World Wide Web in the split? Our precious internet, all for me?"

I put my hand on her back. Her skin is sticky from being pressed against the seat. I wish I was always touching her. I wish I was touching *more* of her. Without much thought, I follow signs for the nearest exit, cruising into a quiet town with wide open roads and no one around to drive on them.

"All for you," I say. We are in our usual sweet spot, admitting the truth through our jokes. "No more Penjaminborter music reviews."

"That was a devastating loss for the YouTube community. The fans were outraged. We all wanted your take on the last two Paramore albums."

"You know I loved them."

"Obviously *I* do. I'm speaking for the community at large."

"Tell them I couldn't handle seeing you online. It hurt too much."

She sits up taller. If she has a joke, she doesn't offer it. Instead she watches me intently. There is no easy way through this. We created our own prison. It would've been so easy to break free, and we didn't. I ignored her. She looked for me everywhere. But she never reached out. And neither did I. We will always have to carry that.

"Does it hurt to see me now?" she asks.

My hand is still on her back. There's so much I want to do.

Hold her. Feel her. Remind her how badly I want to be right where I am. "Not at all," I tell her.

We're on a two lane road now—one coming, one going—and now that we've passed the gas station that was near the highway exit, we're the only car in sight. I drift off to the gravel, my wheels nearing the grass.

"What are we doing?" she asks.

"I don't know," I admit, putting my Civic into park. We stare out the windshield, watching nothing at all. No cars. No people. Not even buildings. "I couldn't keep driving."

"Why?"

"Because I can't stop thinking about how much I want you."

Dee's lips fall open as her stare moves lower. Suddenly, she unbuckles her seat belt and crawls over the console to reach the back of my car. I fight the urge to watch her dress lift up as she moves.

"What are *you* doing?" I ask.

"Waiting for you to join me," she says, soft and serious. She's laid out across my back seat with her legs spread apart. Once again, she's braver than me. She always has been.

I check the windshield and the rearview one last time. No cars either way. Just wide-open flatland and the most beautiful girl in the world in my back seat. I'd be a fool to turn this down. I've spent ten long years being a fool. No more.

I unbuckle myself and crawl in to meet her.

"Two Truths and a Lie," she whispers right as my weight settles atop her.

My hands can barely catch up with my brain, with my pants. With anything. She's so close there is no escaping her. I can't remember a single piece of my life before this moment. The bare heat of her inner thighs could kill me. Her face up close is a revelation. Beads of sweat break and fall from her hairline, glistening as they flow down her shining skin. A drop of moisture catches in the tiniest pucker of a scar above her left eyebrow. I knew once how she got it, but I can't remember. Because right now, the past doesn't exist.

"What letter are we on?" I ask, trying—and failing—to focus.

"I don't know," she teases. "We can play a regular round."

How can she expect me to play a game right now? I see in her eyes she expects it all the same, and I will not let her down. After all, I get to be on top of her, and the longer this lasts, the better it is for me.

Her hand squeezes my backside as she murmurs, "You go first."

"I want you," I say, because it is the only thing on my mind.

"That one has to be true."

"I never want this to end," I continue. She lifts her hips to press harder against my jeans. "I—uh—I don't like lakes."

My inability to come up with anything good makes her cackle. She squeezes her legs around me, and oh god, she has to be careful.

"Are you kidding me? You don't like *lakes*? That's really all you've got?" She lowers her hips while maintaining her wicked grin. "Embarrassing."

She's distracted me well, but she knows I don't like to lose. She's not the only one with good moves. I lower my hand, hovering above the fabric of her dress until I find the hem. She lets out a small gasp of delight when I hike up the bottom. "Is this okay?" I ask.

She smiles at me as she whispers a breathless "Please."

I move her underwear to the side to press my fingers right

onto the warmth that's been waiting for me. "Your turn," I say, teasing her with small, slow circles.

Her breathing turns frantic as she presses against the door. "This . . . isn't . . . fair."

I increase my pace, only slightly. Enough to make her other hand clench around the back of my head. "It's not?"

"I . . . have a . . . podcast," she starts.

I press my lips to her neck, scattering kisses across her clavicle as my hand works faster. When I shift my fingers to the left, her breathing slows a little. Pressed this close, it's noticeable. So I center myself, searching for the point that makes her legs squeeze tighter around my waist. Once I find it again, her eyes roll back. If I do this right, there is no way she will ever complete her turn.

"That's really all *you've* got? Embarrassing," I echo.

Not one to count herself out, she keeps trying. "My favorite . . . color . . . is . . ." She's holding her breath she's trying so hard.

I press my mouth to her ear. "Your favorite color is *what*? Orange? I already know. But you're welcome to keep going, if you'd like."

She knows she can't. She's lost her ability to speak. Instead she sighs out short huffs that build in intensity alongside my work. I love watching her face. The way she tenses and twists, incapable of resisting anymore. I could get addicted to being the one who makes her lose herself like this. Soon enough, she's rocking in tempo with my hand, building the friction alongside me, no longer using words at all. Only sounds. Until finally, she falls apart.

It's then I slide my fingers inside her completely. "You told someone that this is what I was doing yesterday," I tease while she's still wrapped up in her euphoria. "And I know you don't like to lie."

This makes her laugh. My favorite sound. My favorite girl. Always.

Slowly, her body relaxes. She takes my hand and pulls it out of her. "You've won. I assure you. The round. And my approval. All awards go to you." She reaches for my zipper. "Time for your reward."

COLORADO

22

DEE

The border of Nebraska and Colorado is marked with a cross on the ground, surrounded on all four sides by a spiked fence.

"You really have to wonder why they bother with the ceremony of marking this place when the only picture we can take looks like we're standing beside some random cemetery gate," I note, spinning 360 degrees to see which direction will give us the best light.

"It's only for us to know," Ben says.

"That's true. But I'd like us to know in a cooler way."

"I'll call some state officials. See what can be done about this."

"It's the least you can do," I say. And then I kiss him. Because I can. Every opportunity to do this shoots off fireworks in my chest, temporarily stunning me. I get to kiss Ben whenever I want? He has the face of a god and the gifted hands of a red-blooded sinner? This can't be right.

His precious baseball stadium is about three hours from where we are, and our back seat recreational activities have put us even further behind. We can't afford more distractions, no matter how welcome they may be. If we miss the game, Ben will be heartbroken. And I admit that I've been worn down enough that I'm kind of excited to eat stadium hot dogs and to high-five each other when something good happens. Even though I will have no idea what's going on, I will be there with Ben. That will be enough.

We decide to squat down for our prerequisite border picture. It does indeed look like we are beside a cemetery gate, because the fence is wrought iron with golden spikes and little swirling flourishes between each stake.

Ben kisses my cheek. The smile I give is ten times more genuine than I intend.

I shield my eyes from the sun to examine the picture we've taken. It's the kind of photo people post on Instagram and you sigh a little, but you also think, *I might not hate that if it were me.* And I don't hate it. Not even a little bit. It's so good I do sort of want to post it. The listeners would somehow track Ben by the beauty marks on his cheek, and next thing I know I'd have his birth certificate in my inbox with a message like *Is this the man from your picture? Are you sure you want to date a Libra?*

They know full well I am a Sagittarius, and I do.

Suddenly, Ben grabs my arm and says, "Did you hear that?"

We are the only people at this border. Nothing around us but the kind of wide-open space Natalie Maines sings about. We had to drive onto side roads to get here, completely immersed in countryside. Behind us, several hundred feet away, there are a few grazing cows.

"Probably one of them," I guess. Ben shakes his head. Then he puts his hands on the earth and starts *crawling.* "What the hell are you doing?"

It's unclear whether this is a joke or not. If it is, I have absolutely no idea how to partake yet, so I follow on two feet like the biped I am. Lucky for me, this is all undeniably charming to watch. And quite an excellent view.

"There you are," Ben coos. He reaches his hands into the grass patch.

Much to my shock, he pulls out a *cat*. Not a kitten. A full-grown shorthair, long and very thin, coated in white fur with a single splatter of black over the left eye. In Ben's hands, the cat is surprisingly docile for how desperately they meow. It's a sound evidently designed for Ben's ears alone.

"It's okay. I've got you," he says as he pulls the scared thing to his chest.

I approach with caution. It's not that I'm afraid of cats. In fact, I respect them greatly. They know exactly what they want out of life, and I understand I may not be a part of that narrative. This particular feline seems too distressed to worry about me. Unfortunately, that does nothing to soothe my apprehension. Animals are so majestic I automatically assume they think I'm unworthy. Which I am.

The cat's meows get less desperate with every gentle, soothing pet that Ben offers. I watch in cautious amazement, convinced if I try to touch this cat, they will murder me. "What should we do?"

"Will you check if there are any others nearby?"

Unlike Ben—the strapping feline rescuer who can drop onto all fours and start roaming for strays with no notice—the situation is a little more delicate for me. I have on a breathy cotton sundress Victoria forced me to pack, designed for looking casually cool and granting quick access. It is not made for scouring the earth for scared animals.

"When someone drives by and sees my ass, at least it's for a good cause," I announce as I drop to the ground and begin my quest. I inspect a few of the tall grass patches nearby, seeing no signs of life. Ben walks around too, cradling his new friend in his arms like a colicky infant. Our search goes on for a few minutes with no success.

Ben and I lock eyes. His grip on the cat tightens.

"We can't leave him," he tells me.

"Him?"

"Yeah. I checked."

"Wow." I move closer. "Lonely boy kitty wandering around the border of Colorado and Nebraska all by himself. Whatcha doing out here, buddy?"

"I don't think he's been able to find himself any food in a while." Ben holds the cat up to show me his prominent ribs, then returns him to his cradle hold. "His fur is a little matted in a few places too. I didn't see any ticks. They'd be easy to spot with the white fur. He's a pretty chill guy. He must belong to someone."

The cat answers by nuzzling into Ben's chest.

It never occurred to me the Ben effect might work on animals too. He had dogs growing up. They were friendly pups that loved everyone. Even me, though I rarely indulged in a pet, too afraid that they might second-guess their decision to be sweet. This cat met Ben like five minutes ago and seems to have already formed some kind of soul tie with him. Join the club, kitty. I'm the founding president. We meet on Friday mornings to google Ben's name and cry.

"We have to get to the game," I announce.

We missed it last time because I'd begged Ben to let Gam make us lunch, so this sentence sounds extra absurd coming from me, noted game-missing enthusiast.

Ben squeezes the cat tighter. There is something he wants

me to suggest. He can't do it himself, because it's so completely off the wall that it's not a possibility. Which is why I'm the one to say, "Let's take him with us."

Ben's eyes light up. "Really?"

"Dude, I don't know," I admit. "We can't leave him."

"We can't," Ben confirms.

"Let's bring him with us, and we can find a vet nearby and check for a microchip or whatever, and then he can be reunited with the family that surely loves and misses him."

It's not lost on me how dejected Ben looks at the idea of this cat having a family.

"Okay," he says softly. "Yeah."

We don't really have time for this. But this poor cat is cute and scared and obviously in need of help. Neither of us is capable of ignoring him. So we carry our new friend toward the car. Our first guest.

Outside the passenger door, Ben realizes he has to surrender the cat to me in order to drive.

"I'm scared to hold him," I admit. This is likely the first time I've ever willingly said these words aloud.

Ben treats the moment with the reverence it deserves, taking a very serious step forward. "Don't be afraid. This cat will love you—"

He leaves the sentence hanging. I can't help but imagine that the intended ending is *as much as I do.* That would mean Ben loves me present tense.

There is no way that can be true. No streak of luck could be that great, that Ben and I would find each other again, at a time when both of us are on the same page about our feelings.

To smooth over the heavy pause, I close my eyes and reach out my hands, waiting to be attacked by this scrappy, majestic being we've stumbled on in the middle of nowhere. Suddenly, there is a bundle of soft white fur and sharp bones in my arms. His body is so light he may as well be a paperweight. There is no tension in his slinky frame. He sinks into my chest, letting me hold him.

Ben is right. This tiny wonder must be protected at all costs.

The cat doesn't even mind as I scoot into the passenger seat and buckle myself in. In fact, he folds himself up into a little white bread loaf between my legs. Gingerly, I stroke his soft fur, amazed each time to be met with no resistance.

"We can't name him, right?" Ben asks as we get back onto the highway. "That would be weird."

"For sure."

"But what about Abe?" he overlaps.

This makes me laugh so hard our poor kitty does move a little. Ben reaches a protective hand across the gearshift to calm him down. Or me. Or both of us.

"I want to start by establishing that I don't think it's a good idea to name someone else's cat," I say. "But *please* talk me through that name choice. I have to know."

"It's what came to my head when I first found him."

"Wow. Okay. You've had this picked out for a *while*. When were you going to tell me?"

"Probably never," he admits.

"That can't be true. You caved with literally no pressure from me. In fact, you suggested the name game."

Tentatively, I lean forward to get a good look at maybe-Abe in my lap. He has a slim face for a cat, soft whiskers that cascade proudly out of his sharp cheeks. His eyes are a bright, yellowish green, and his ears are two pointy triangles. I look at him, and

I think, *Cat*. Which is why I'm not the one who has secretly named him.

"Hi, Abe," I test. "Like Lincoln?"

Ben shakes his head. "No."

"Like the Bible guy?"

"No. Just Abe the cat. No relation to anyone else."

"I don't understand, but I don't need to." I stroke Abe's back, this time with confidence. "We're gonna get you home, Abe. It's gonna be great. You picked the right people to help you. We do this all the time."

Ben smiles as he reaches over to scratch Abe's head. He appears to be physically incapable of keeping his hands away from this cat. "We actually took this trip to cat hunt." He stops. "Sorry. That came out wrong. We hunt for lost cats we can help."

"Yes. So don't go thinking you're special or anything, dude," I tell the little prince between my knees. "You're a dime a dozen to us."

Ben moves his hand to my bare shoulder. "Now that's too far."

"I'm sorry, Abe." I scratch under his chin, which he welcomes happily.

Look at me, a cat person!

"This is what we do," I continue. "We make things up. You'll get used to it soon enough."

"You will," Ben assures him.

And so we drive, Abe the stray cat in my lap, on our way to the nearest vet clinic that's open on weekends. Exactly like we planned!

23

BEN

The vet is nothing like a hospital, not in any meaningful way. Still, the first thing I think about is Gam. It must be the sterile environment that takes me there. Or the hostile, tangy smell of whatever products they use to keep everything sanitized.

I can't believe how much I miss her. I'd say she'd never believe I'd be here, but she could always see for me all the things I couldn't. Somehow she would have predicted this situation down to the color of the walls in this clinic, a calm grayish blue, similar to her eyes. This must be exactly what she envisioned when she asked me to go after what I really want.

"We are hoping to get this little guy back to his family," I explain to the woman working behind the desk. She's dressed in paw-print scrubs.

"And you found him where?"

Her gusty sigh triggers my guilt. They aren't open long on Sundays. We've gotten here minutes before closing.

"At the state border," Dee explains. The woman nods and steps into the back. Dee eyes me. "This will be fast, right?"

"I think so," I lie. Even if it's not, it's the right thing to do. It would be the same if we found a wallet. I'd stop everything to make sure it got back to where it needed to be. This is exactly like that.

The woman leads us into an examination room and tells us the veterinarian will be in shortly. She closes the door, and Dee starts casing the place like she's searching for clues at a crime scene.

"Looking for anything in particular?" I ask.

"I never know what I'm looking for until I find it."

"Deep."

"That's right. You are back in the River Dee, where your feet will never touch the bottom of my depths." When she's satisfied with her assessment of the room, discovering nothing interesting aside from a jar of Q-tips she finds "aesthetically pleasing" but ultimately not worth keeping, she comes over to give Abe another head scratch.

His disposition hasn't changed since we got here. He's still subdued in my arms. Maybe a little put off by the fluorescent lights, but not worried in the way most animals are when you take them to the vet. Which makes me think he's never *seen* a vet before. Our dogs used to panic at the sight of the entrance. The older one, Daisy, the sweetest chocolate Lab you ever met, would whine and pant the whole way in. The younger one, Duke, a very spirited Chihuahua-terrier mix, would cower in the corner, rubbing his nose raw on the edge of his carrier.

"We've almost got you home, little guy." Dee plants a gentle kiss on the top of Abe's head.

"Hey now," I say.

"What? Are you jealous of a cat?"

"Of course not. I just don't know if we should go kissing other people's pets."

"But we can name them?" she teases.

"I never said we had to keep calling him that."

"You said it with your eyes." She gets up on her tiptoes and kisses me this time. "Is that better?"

Before I can answer, the door swings open. In walks a smiling woman with long blond hair pulled into a ponytail and a much better concealed, but still noticeable, air of annoyance. "I hear you've found a friend." She shakes my hand, then greets Abe with a friendly pat on his back. "I'm Dr. Henry." She extends her hand to Dee.

Then we all stand in silence.

Dr. Henry breaks it by saying, "Would you mind putting the cat on the table for me?"

My laugh comes out nervous and unsteady. It didn't occur to me that I would be the obstacle here, a loose nail even in the vet's office.

The first thing Dr. Henry does is confirm Abe is male. Then she gets a good look at his teeth. "He's about three years old, by my guess." She scans his body for any visible fleas or ticks, or any injuries, finding nothing wrong aside from his clear malnourishment. Then she gets out her microchip tester and begins her scan. Every few inches, she presses a button on a device that looks like a very large television remote. The tester beeps as results flash across a green screen at the top.

Click. *Beep.*

No ID found.

Click. *Beep.*

No ID found.

Click. *Beep.*

No ID found.

"It seems like your friend doesn't have a chip," Dr. Henry announces.

Dee and I exchange a loaded glance. This is not the result we expected. I can't tell if that's a good thing or not.

"Doesn't mean he doesn't have a home, though," Dr. Henry continues. "If you leave him here, we can keep him overnight, then do the work of passing him onto the nearest shelter. If you decide to hold on to him, you'll need to take some good pictures of him and post them everywhere you can. Local Facebook pages. Craigslist. Any of the missing-pet websites. Just to make sure he doesn't belong to anyone else. You should give it about a week, and then I'd say it's safe to call him your cat. At that point you can bring him back to me and we can get him set up with all the shots he might need. Neuter him. The good stuff."

It's a lot of information to take in. We've been holding Abe's fate in our hands since we found him. It's only now I feel all that power. What I want to do makes no sense. It's the wrong choice.

"We'll keep him," Dee declares at once. She squeezes my hand, then scoops Abe up in her arms, kissing him on the top of his head several times in a row. For a girl afraid of cats, she's found her comfort zone quickly. Then again, Abe is unique. Or I'm biased. Maybe both.

"That's what I was hoping you'd tell me," Dr. Henry replies.

"But we don't live around here, so we can't bring him to you next week," Dee explains. "I hope that's okay."

Dr. Henry doesn't seem too bothered as she says, "Not a problem at all."

Dee asks if we can purchase some supplies for Abe while we're here, and Dr. Henry directs us back to the woman at the front. She sells us cat food, water, a bowl, a small pet bed, a soft-sided carrier, a brush, a toy, litter, and a litter box. "Otherwise known as *the works*," she tells us, still mildly annoyed at all she's accommodating.

I try to turn the conversation to how her day has been as Dee hands over her card to pay for everything. The front desk attendant visibly softens as she talks me through this morning's successful emergency bird surgery.

Shockingly, Dee says nothing. Not even about how happy she is to pay. We haven't made eye contact since she said we'd keep Abe. My face is probably as blank as my mind, void of any substantial thought beyond the tired, hungry cat in her arms.

Facts will ground me in this moment. Dee and I are on a road trip that will end soon. We don't live in the same city. We don't even live in the same state. I know nothing about cats. I had no idea I liked them this much until twenty minutes ago, when I found Abe in a patch of grass at the Colorado border. There is still a chance he belongs to someone else.

I think again of Gam. Her wind chime laugh knocks through all the facts I've laid out for myself. She'd tell me it's all so obvious. She'd tell me this is me going after what I really want.

Apparently, I really want a cat.

Once everything is gathered up and paid for, Dee and I say our goodbyes to the clinic staff. I carry our new belongings to the car, and Dee keeps her arms wrapped tightly around Abe. Into his fur, she whispers words I can't hear.

We don't speak about what she's agreed to do, only about how to best accommodate our new road trip companion. Abe's domain will be the back seat, we determine. A place Dee and I will no longer be able to use like we did earlier. We start setting out all the stuff she's bought, deciding what goes where.

"We're not putting the litter box out, right?" Dee asks me.

"I'd love to not have that in my car, if we can avoid it."

"Yeah. We can keep it in the trunk and fill it in later."

"Right."

Maybe I should be the one to say we can't do this. Or that we shouldn't. But that would be a lie. Because we both know Dee did this for me. She said what I couldn't, in the way only she can. She jumped all the way in for me, like she always does.

As a result, we now have a cat.

It makes no sense. In fact, it makes so little sense that it circles back to making perfect sense. This is what happens when Dee and I are together. The strangest, best things.

Did I Forget to Tell You?

JAVI: After many years of saying I wouldn't, I must admit that two days ago, I passed by a pet adoption pop-up, and I got a dog.

DEE: Don't you have something else to say about it?

JAVI: What?

DEE: You know what!

JAVI: Oh. You want me to say you always knew I would.

DEE: Yes I do.

JAVI: That's true. Anytime we see a dog on the street, I stop and pet them. Dee always asks me when I'm going to get my own. And I say that I'm not. And she says, "Oh yes you are." And I tell her I don't want to go outside when it's cold to take a dog for a walk. But now I'm a dog parent, and I will walk through the seventh circle of hell for my little Cheddar.

DEE: Tell everyone why you chose that name.

JAVI: Because she looks like a cheese puff. She's a very cute mixed-breed rescue pup with fur the same color as Dee's hair.

DEE: My dog sibling, Cheddar. She's scrappy like me too.

JAVI: Now that I know the highs and lows of parenthood, the joy and grief, the pain and glory, I'm wondering what's holding *you* back, Dee? You were the one who kept insisting I wanted this for my life, and you were right! What about *your* life?

DEE: Oh, I couldn't handle a dog. No thank you! Respect to all those who can, but it's not me.

JAVI: There are other kinds of animals, you know.

DEE: Of course I know. I just never had any growing up. We couldn't afford it. And I can't now either. So I appreciate all of them from a comfortable distance. Even Cheddar. She doesn't need a pet from me to know I love her.

JAVI: What if someday in the future you can afford it? Would you do it?

DEE: I don't know. It would really have to be the right circumstances. And those circumstances seem pretty impossible to me.

24

DEE

By the time we get near Denver, Abe has eaten two full wet food containers. As a result, the car smells like tuna. He's also peed in the back seat. Which does make me regret saying we don't need to put the litter box out. I look at Abe's cute face, with the black smudge over his eye and the dainty whiskers jutting out around his prim little nose, and it's impossible to be mad at him over it. Luckily, Ben keeps cleaning products on his person at all times. If anyone could be prepared for a surprise pet, it's him.

The Rocky Mountains are now in full view. Their jagged outlines slice into the sky, making everything look immense and wondrous. I take pictures through the windshield even though they don't capture a fraction of the beauty.

The GPS says we're fifteen minutes from Coors Field.

"Are you sure you want to go?" Ben asks.

I pretend to check my forehead. "I must have a fever. Surely you're not the one asking me this."

"I know, I know. It's just—" Ben makes a gesture to Abe.

Oh, Abe. I've taken all the necessary pictures and posted on the sites Dr. Henry recommended. So far, there has been zero traction. Which continues to be a surprising relief. Not that I can take on a pet right now. It's probably that I don't want Ben to have him without me. And aside from the peeing in the back seat—which does make sense all things considered—our buddy seems genuinely friendly and well-behaved. He has to belong to someone. Other than Ben. Or me.

"We can't leave him in the car," I say.

Ben shakes his head fervently. "Absolutely not."

"Should we check into a hotel and put him there?"

"What if he starts meowing, and they take him from us?"

"That would be very bad."

"Yeah."

"So what do we do?"

The miles between us and the ballpark are ticking down too quickly. This is the *one* thing Ben insisted we do. The one thing we missed last time. His favorite sport. His favorite activity. We have to go. I know we do. But we also can't.

Unless . . .

"We take Abe with us," I say, the idea forming as haphazardly as every one I've had before it. My brain is a confusing maze of impulsive decisions, long-held grudges, and inappropriate questions.

"There's no way we can pull that off." Ben's voice lacks any real conviction.

"I think we could do it if we really wanted to."

I improvise an admittedly terrible plan, which is to stuff Abe into my shirt. To my surprise, Ben does not reject this idea. In fact, he welcomes it, a sly grin spreading across his illegally handsome face.

As a teen, it was always *way* too easy to convince him to do wild things with me. Which is why I refrained from it as often as I could. I liked knowing how soft he was in this world, and I didn't want anyone to break him. *Especially* me. Part of what's been so comforting about seeing him now is that I know the world has hurt him, and he's still the same way with me. Gentle and willing.

We park in the back of the stadium lot. I hurry to our trunk and open my luggage, getting out my tightest tank top and a pair of jean shorts. I pull the shorts up my legs and then put the shirt on over my dress. *You served me well, yellow dress. Thank you for your award-winning work in the back seat of Ben's car.* With a devastating lack of grace, I shimmy the dress out from underneath my new outfit, tripping on the fabric as it reaches my feet.

Ben, of good hand-eye coordination and fast-twitch muscles, catches me.

"Do you have a jersey I could wear?" I ask him, my head inches from the pavement.

He leans down and kisses me so hard he almost knocks the breath out of me, then sets me upright. "Of course I do."

With impressive ease, he opens his duffel bag and lifts up neatly folded piles until he lands on something royal blue. He spins me around to put me into it, guiding my arms through the holes.

The fabric is perfectly loose, ideal for disguising the way my undershirt will stretch when I drop Abe down through my chest. I will basically become a kangaroo, with Abe as my little joey.

Once I'm suited up in my baseball fan uniform, Ben goes back into his bag and pulls out yet another jersey for him to wear. As if he had planned all along for this.

"Home and away," he says as he shows me his. It's white with pinstripes.

At first, I take the phrase to be some sort of really deep

interpretation of what we are doing on this trip. It turns out to be the names for the different jersey styles. He is wearing a home jersey. I am wearing an away one.

"Guess it's time to put Abe in my shirt," I say. I get him from the back seat, and he remains completely unaffected when I drop him inside my tank top. For an animal we found through his insistent meowing, he has been nothing but chill since. He looks up at me with his keen cat eyes, and I see a portrait of contentment.

It's Ben who grows nervous. He starts gripping my hand so hard I'm losing feeling.

"If anyone notices, we'll say I'm pregnant," I tell him. In a way, it's true. I am indeed carrying a living thing in my stomach. Unfortunately, this idea seems to knock Ben into the stratosphere. His grip on my hand goes slack, then comes back twice as strong.

We are steps away from the check-in line when he tugs me off to the side. "Is this cruel?" he whispers urgently. "The kind of thing that PETA would hear about and attack us for?"

I pull my shirt wide enough that Ben can see straight past my chest to see Abe curled into a ball at my gut. He's right that Abe shouldn't stay here for hours, but he is absolutely as pleased as a cat can be for the moment.

Ben gets flustered in a new way. I am not wearing a bra, which had not occurred to me until after I flashed him my tits and my feline baby all at once. Ben cracks up, so I do too, until we are laughing so loud that the people waiting in line glare at us.

"We're being suspicious," I say.

"We *are* suspicious," he reminds me.

"No comment on my boobs?"

"I have many comments."

This is not the place to be flooded with want, yet here I am, standing beside a baseball stadium with a cat in my shirt, wishing for Ben to tell me exactly how I've affected him. But this is a mission I've accepted, and it's a mission I will complete, so I say, "Now is not the time," and bring us to our place in line.

Muttering prayers I've invented solely for this occasion, calling upon deities I know and some I make up, such as the god of baseball security, we make it into the ballpark without incident. It's truly *so* easy it's almost upsetting, like we should go back through again to really feel like we've worked for this.

The interior walkways are concrete, with large green beams above. There are vendors all along the sides: food, drink, and apparel. Nothing for cats, though. Something I never would have noticed before. Things really change when you've got a living thing pressed against your rib cage.

Now that the hard part is over, the reality has settled in: I will be watching hours of baseball—a sport I care about very minimally—with a cat in my shirt. Which may be at least fifty percent less exciting than it originally seemed.

Turns out, Ben's got his own surprises. When we're right outside our section, he whispers in my ear, "I stuffed Abe's carrier into the back of my pants. I was worried about him being in your shirt for too long. And I figured if we got in, no one would really bug us after." He reaches under his jersey, contorting his hand around his back to pull out the crumpled soft-sided carrier. With a few tugs, it's easily restored into its proper shape.

My sweet Ben. Taking my terrible plan and making it somewhat reasonable, as only he can. He hands me the carrier and I bring it into the nearest bathroom. Once inside a stall, I free Abe, who remains as nonplussed as ever. He accepts a quick head scratch before being zipped up. I take off my jersey and drape it over the carrier, then walk out of the stall.

Ben shakes his head when he sees me. "You have to put that back on." He points to the blue fabric.

"I don't know. I think it goes against our plan to root for both teams. Plus it hides Abe."

We walk hand in hand to our seats. Once we get settled, Ben places Abe's carrier behind his legs. "He's hidden down here. No need for him to be covered by your jersey."

"*My* jersey?"

Ben puts an arm around me. "Oh yes. It's all yours. This is my chance to make a baseball fan out of you."

"I always liked watching you play," I tell him.

It's possible I've never said anything like this before, because he appears deeply moved by my admittance.

"What? Don't act like this is a surprise," I continue. "You looked great in your little pants. Home and away." I have decided this phrase does in fact have some great meaning. What it is, I don't know. I'll keep using it until I decide.

Ben laughs in the exact way he should. He gets it. As always.

"These seats are so good," he tells me, like I'd know the difference. "Third base line."

"Totally," I say, smiling. "Exactly where I wanted to be."

25

BEN

It's 0–0 at the top of the eighth.

This has not been an exciting game for a newcomer to watch. It's a pitchers' duel, which means there's been no offensive push from either team. If you don't know the value of a perfectly executed changeup, it's pretty much a bunch of guys playing high-stakes catch. As soon as I reminded Dee that foul balls don't count for anything other than the first two strikes, and fly balls are easily caught, she hasn't even had an opportunity to grip my arm in anticipation.

Thank god for beer.

The beer has made her happy.

On a rare occasion, she would come to watch my high school games. Since I was never in the crowd with her, I had no idea what she was thinking up in the stands. When I'd peek my head out of the dugout to look for her, she always had her attention on the field. Afterward, she'd comment on something no one else would ever notice. I was rubbing my eye a lot during the third inning, or my coach had a habit of putting his left hand in his back pocket when he was stressed. She never mentioned the game itself or how I played. Too prideful to ask, I let it be. It meant a lot to me that she was there at all.

I used to think enjoying something meant I had to be the best at it. And anytime someone didn't tell me I was the best, I thought it meant I'd failed, and I wasn't allowed to enjoy that thing anymore. But Dee never cared about how I played.

"Oh my god, I found one," she tells me, grabbing my arm.

So far, the only thing to truly spark her attention tonight has been hearing my limited knowledge on the players' personal lives. She's been on Instagram most of the time, looking at some of their pages, then clicking over to their wives' pages.

She points to a wife she thinks she's spotted in the crowd.

Because baseball players are very habitual, a lot of them marry their high school or college sweethearts. If a relationship works, they lock it in for life. It becomes a part of the routine like anything else: their lucky socks, their game-day breakfast. That wasn't something I ever wanted. For all the ways I liked a life that made sense on paper, that was one place I planned to be different. It was all those game-day talks at first base that did it, chatting with a whole host of guys from different schools. It was so easy to be friendly, but it all felt meaningless to me. I didn't want to be someone you could talk to for five minutes and have all figured out.

Now I look at the girl I loved in high school sitting beside me, and I wonder what the hell I was thinking back then. There are no rules for when someone amazing is allowed to come into your life. Sometimes it really does happen when you're a kid.

"Makes sense that you were able to find those Patch articles about me," I say to Dee as she zooms in on a photo of a beautiful woman.

"*Please.* That was beginner stuff." She zooms back out. "Okay, yes." She holds up her phone to compare the image to the woman she's been watching. "That's definitely her. Right?"

"Whoa. It really is."

Dee polishes off her fifth beer with one long, triumphant gulp. "Me sitting in a crowd of like twenty thousand people and spotting a player's wife three sections over? *That's* the real stuff." Her words slur together.

"Thank god I gave you the internet in the friendship divorce." I may be a little drunk myself. Nothing that finishing *my* fifth beer won't fix.

"Truly. What else would we be doing here?" She anticipates my wince and picks up my ball cap to run her hand through my curls. Her touch is so nice. She is so nice. "Don't worry, this is home and away an enjoyable experience for me." Off my amusement, she says, "I'm still workshopping how I want to use that phrase."

"Well, home and away, I do know that the baseball wives usually have to buy their own tickets. Which is why we've ended up with better seats than her." I realize too late that I am yelling into Dee's ear. The people in front of us turn around to give me a dirty look.

Dee, oblivious, grins. *"Our power."*

The crack of the bat pulls our attention to the field.

There's an unmistakable thunder to a home run. It always sounds to me like both dread and relief, because the noise is the same no matter the team. Dee and I bolt out of our seats as our eyes gaze upward, tracking the small white ball across the night sky. It sails effortlessly over center field. The Rockies' outfielder is sprinting, desperate to catch what he knows in his heart isn't his to have.

The ball glides over the wall. Dee screams as I lift her off the ground.

"Yes!" she yells into my ear. "I love baseball!"

I don't even care what she's said, or that we've finally scored the first run of the game. All I can think about is how much I love *her*. I was gone the moment I showed up at her door. Out of the ballpark the second she let me inside her home. There was never a chance for me.

Dee breaks from my embrace to squat down and check on Abe.

I love you, I think again, such an ordinary phrase turned revelatory.

It's something I've said to past girlfriends. Something I've meant each time. Not in the way I mean it with Dee. The words don't capture the immensity of this feeling. My heart beats in double time when she laughs. My throat goes dry at every chance I get to be near her. The way she smells. The sound of her voice. I can never begin to wrangle her in or make sense of a single thing she does. She will never stop interesting me.

I expect her to reach a finger through the front of the carrier. Instead she unzips it completely and pulls Abe out. My head is so light that I can't grab hold of the new voice in the back of my head—the low, urgent one trying to distract me from the chorus of *I love you*s singing at full volume. The new voice is telling me this is a bad idea. But Abe doesn't seem upset. He's not even confused by the noise and the crowd and the lights. Other than when we found him in the field, he has remained the most casual cat that's ever existed.

He is a cat at a baseball game, the voice reminds me. *And cats aren't allowed to be at baseball games.*

Normal Ben would be concerned. Right now, it's very funny. Because the girl that I love holds Abe like he is Simba, letting him see all of Coors Field. What's there to worry about?

The guy sitting next to us doesn't share this sentiment. He tries to reach for Abe.

"Please don't touch him," Dee warns.

This upsets the man. He puts a hand on Abe again, trying to shoo him off. This time, Abe startles at the forceful, unexpected touch. In an instant, Abe is out of Dee's arms and onto the ground, sprinting.

My first thought is *Wow, cats are so fast.*

My second thought is *Wow, Dee is fast too. I love her.*

She's reacted as quickly as Abe, jumping over seats and running down the steps to chase after him. The protective netting that surrounds the inner field ends almost exactly where we are seated. Both Abe and Dee capitalize on this. Abe makes an impressive jump over the barrier. Seconds later, faster than the security guards can process, Dee does too.

My third thought is *Wow, I am really fast.* Because I am running right behind them. Where is Darius? He would love to see this. Everything we've ever worked for is happening right here.

Abe reaches center field and comes to a complete stop. It's so instantaneous that Dee and I have no time to slow our own momentum, and we end up sprinting past him. When we arc back around, Abe is rollicking around on the turf like the happiest cat in the world. He rolls side to side, fully stretched out, in complete bliss. The crowd laughs and cheers at a thunderous volume.

The Rockies decided to pull their pitcher after the home run, so there is no current baseball-related action happening on the field right now. It's just Dee, Abe, me, and the entire Rockies defensive team spread out in playing position.

I once hoped to be like these guys, living my life under stadium lights for six months out of every year, playing this sport for a crowd of thousands. If a cat ran had run onto the field near the end of a tight pitchers' duel, followed by two drunk fans, I'd probably laugh just as much as the current players do.

I don't know if I'd laugh at the two security guards charging toward me at full speed, though. Probably not.

"Uh-oh," Dee whispers through her teeth. She scoops Abe up right as the guards apprehend us both.

26

DEE

After a brief but memorable back-and-forth, two security guards escort Ben, Abe, and me off the field and through a mysterious side door. The rowdy crowd soundtracks our every move until we are plunged into the eerie quiet of this ballpark's inner workings. The guards lead us through long corridors, headed toward an unannounced location.

They've allowed me to keep hold of Abe because he remains docile in my arms. On the field, one of the guards tried to grab him, and he hissed for the first time in our short but storied life together. I am not sure I have ever felt more proud of anyone, animal or human.

As the four of us walk, our shoes squeak so aggressively against the concrete floors that it actually embarrasses me. All of this is very serious while managing to be spectacularly awkward. I already struggle with this combination when I am sober. Being a little drunk does not help.

We reach a bland, unmarked office. Confident we aren't going to run off, one guard lets go of me, saying he's "going to go get the paperwork." These are the first real words spoken since they tried to grab hold of Abe.

The other guard, a gangly younger guy with glasses and a

potent nervous energy, releases Ben, then asks us to sit in the two chairs that are set out in front of the desk. He walks around to the other side and pulls an ancient-looking digital camera out of the top drawer. It might as well be Ben's old Nikon from ten years ago.

"I need to take pictures of you both," the guard tells us.

There's a slight waver in his voice that does nothing to help with the whole embarrassment aspect. I bite the insides of my cheeks to keep from laughing.

Rushing the field is dangerous. And wrong. If I were even two percent more sober, there's no way it would have happened. I no longer consciously cause chaos of this magnitude.

Unfortunately, everything changed the moment we found Abe at the state border. The multiple beers without any real meal to support them certainly did not help things. At least I am not vomiting tofu fish sticks. Judging by the way things are going, that's the only victory I am going to get tonight.

There is also a part of me that knows this is all my fault, and my guilt sometimes manifests as amusement. When people are laughing, they're less likely to be angry. Although sometimes, laughing makes things worse. If effort counts for anything, even cosmically, I really am trying my best to remain as neutral as Ben, who has become that unreadable, poker-faced version of himself that gives me a headache.

He gets up first, offering his image before we've even given our names. I'd think the first order of business would be finding out who we are. But I'm not the ballpark security guard tasked with processing our crimes, am I? My therapist would tell me I am not required to do other people's jobs for them. My astrology friends would say it's the Capricorn rising in me that thinks I should.

The flash goes off. Ben stares into the camera, hard-eyed.

"Okay, you next," the guard tells me. When Ben and I pass each other, I squeeze his arm, and he doesn't react.

Nervously, wildly, and downright enthusiastically, I *smile* for the photo.

Abe remains lazy and content in my arms.

Then I return to sitting. In silence. Ear-gnawing quiet. Similar to the suffocating feeling of being left alone with a friend's friend, straining so hard for conversation that you just give up. The nervous guard opens his mouth periodically, like he wants to offer up some insight, but he seems to second-guess himself.

When the other security guard returns with his aforementioned paperwork, every single one of us seems to let out a breath we all knew we were holding. Even if the news is bad, at least it's happening. The guard is followed closely by an important-looking man in a suit.

Now the real show begins. The suited man seems born for this kind of pageantry. Maybe even a little excited by the prospect of issuing our punishment. He's older, with a steely glare and a penchant for mouth breathing, and he has admirably opted to wear a baseball-themed tie tonight. The bats look phallic.

Good for him.

He begins explaining the seriousness of what we've done. As he speaks, I stare at my hands, having flashbacks to middle school, when I spent a good amount of time in the principal's office. I'd do really wild, rebellious things, like get up and go to the bathroom without asking for permission, and I'd end up down there being scolded for believing in my own bodily autonomy. The final straw was a cold January afternoon in seventh grade, freshly returned from winter break, when a very nice cafeteria worker named

Evelyn decided to break form and offer me hot lunch instead of the standard peanut butter and jelly they were required to give to the poor kids who couldn't afford a meal. Evelyn lost her job. For feeding me.

That was the day I decided I wouldn't cause trouble anymore. Not on purpose.

Mr. Bat Tie gives what must be the rehearsed speech he uses for all ballpark vagrants. He explains that most people who rush the field are issued a lifetime ban from Coors Field. The gravity of that statement bottoms me out. Ben and his beloved baseball.

"Your situation is unique, though." Mr. Bat Tie's voice ticks up to convey what I read as optimism. "You were chasing after a stray cat."

"He's not a stray," Ben says firmly, in his first words since we were apprehended. He must be even tipsier than me, because the stronger choice would have been to let everyone think we are impassioned animal lovers, not two weirdos who willingly snuck a possibly feral but rather adorable cat into a baseball game.

Mr. Bat Tie stares at Abe in my arms. If anyone bothered to look at where we were sitting, they'd know we brought a carrier, which would be a dead giveaway of our culpability. Then again, no one even knows our names.

"So this is *your* cat?" the man asks, incredulous.

"Yes," Ben says.

"Really?"

"Yes."

"Well, then I'm afraid I'm going to have to proceed with the ban," the man explains. "Since you brought your cat into the game . . ." He lets the sentence linger, waiting one last time for an objection from us. When neither of us challenges him, he reaches for the paperwork and scoots it toward us. "Go ahead and look this over."

The document states we agree to be banned from this ball-park. If we are caught returning, we will be arrested for trespassing. Our names (ha!) and pictures will be circulated among the ballpark staff. My laughter threatens to surface again, almost out of panic as much as guilt.

I haven't even finished trying to read, fighting against the alcohol that makes my brain swim, before Ben is taking a pen to the document to carefully write the neatest version of his signature onto the designated line.

I gape at him. He continues avoiding my eye. I'd expect to find Ben utilizing his friendly demeanor to the fullest—the affable, beloved everyman. Maybe even a version of Mr. Porter the middle school science teacher? Something other than the sullen, withdrawn Ben only I know. This isn't the time to reveal his emo heart to the world. He thinks baseball is sacred. He believes his team represents who he is as a person. And we're now tucked into some dark, nondescript office in the bowels of a ballpark, signing a piece of paper that says we are troublemaking baseball criminals who can never again return, and he has no desire to lead with love?

In a brief moment of levity, Mr. Bat Tie informs us that the TV coverage of our escapade has already started to go viral. "We don't normally televise people rushing the field, but the situation was unique, since we thought you were chasing after a stray. People really like your cat," he says. "They can't believe you scooped the little guy up like that."

A genuine "Oh god" slips out of me. There may not be a ton of crossover between listeners of my podcast and baseball people, but there could be some. And sometimes these kinds of videos make their way past their target audience into a more general online community. With no real conviction, I emptily hope I am unrecognizable in my silly little sports jersey. Maybe the cameras only saw me. Maybe Ben kept his eyes on his feet. Maybe, maybe, maybe.

I sign my version of the document.

This is when they request our IDs. I say, "I thought you'd never ask," and absolutely no one reacts.

Both of us happen to have them. Ben's is always in his back pocket, and mine, normally in a purse, has been stuffed into my jean shorts. The nervous guard leaves to make copies of them.

Mr. Bat Tie reveals the cherry on top of this disaster sundae— we are being issued a $2,000 fine for rushing the field. "It's on the lower end," he says, like that's some kind of accomplishment.

My stomach still somersaults at the number, instantly thinking of the Dee who couldn't even afford a train card and would walk untenable distances in the Chicago winters because she didn't want to hop the turnstile and get fined. Lucky for me, I can pay this fine now. But I know deep in my bones what it feels like to have your entire world changed by a single bill, and that feeling never leaves you.

This is all so bad. This is me and the nice cafeteria worker all over again, except the cafeteria worker is Ben, the man I secretly love in present tense. I've brought my signature brand of destruction back into his untarnished life, and there's no way to fix the mess I've created.

When it's all said and done, the two security guards silently escort us out of the ballpark. At my request, they've retrieved our cat carrier from our seats, and standing beside Coors Field—a ballpark I guess I will never again enter in my life—they watch as we stuff Abe back into it. Then they close the mysterious back door on us forever.

Ben looks so handsome under the glow of the moon, even with his unreadable expression. He takes off into downtown Denver, and I follow him, matching his pace as well as his wordless intensity. We cross the nearest intersection, taking us away from the ballpark and into the city. Who knows where we're going, but we're getting there fast. It's almost a sprint.

Then, suddenly, as if we have passed some kind of invisible threshold, Ben stops to look at me. And he laughs.

No, it's more than that. He erupts with joy, like he's been holding in the biggest joke of his life and it's all spilled out exactly as planned. Normally the sight of him this amused would make me laugh too. I'm so confused right now that all I can do is breathe heavily and stare.

He reads my confusion and places Abe's carrier on the ground to hug me. He squeezes my body with such tenderness. Such *relief.* The gesture brings tears to my eyes, all my fears dissolved by the total assuredness of his arms around me. Even the fervent beat of his heart feels like home.

"I thought you were mad at me," I whisper, devastated to find myself crying for real.

Ben pulls back to look at my face. "Dee, I would never be mad at you."

"Well, let's not *lie.* I don't have the Cheez-Its."

"You know what I mean."

"Honestly, I don't. You were so quiet in there. I thought you were furious."

"Are you kidding? This was the funniest thing that's ever happened to me. And the best baseball game I've ever been to." He kisses my cheek. "Because of you."

It's a relief to receive tenderness when I've expected anger, but it's also unfamiliar. This level of care has not been extended to me in a very long time. Maybe ever.

"I got you banned from this ballpark," I remind him, searching for a pressure point. I look off to the side, at the imposing shadow of Coors Field. "I never should've taken Abe out of the bag."

"You wanted him to see the game." Ben relays my own actions like I made the obvious, relatable decision. "How could I ever be mad that you want our cat to know baseball?"

Our cat.

We don't know who Abe really belongs to, but Ben saying he is ours makes me cry harder. Thankfully, this isn't a plaintive, chin-shaking cry. It's just a steady stream of tears pouring out of my eyeballs, dripping onto the concrete beneath my feet.

I've rented apartments with shitty roommates, cobbling together a home consisting of Craigslist thrifts and furniture found on the sidewalk. Even still, when it came time to move out, it was always clear who owned what. There was never any confusion. Never even a graceful *Oh no, I think those spoons are yours* or *Did you buy this shelf?* Even if it's only for the night, this is the first time I've ever owned something with someone else.

Ours.

What a beautiful, frightening idea.

"What should we do?" I ask. "We can't drive. But they're probably gonna tow your car or something if you stay in the lot overnight."

"Then we better sober up." Ben turns around and pats his back. "Hop on." When I don't move, he repeats the gesture. "Let's go, Matthews. Your ride is right here."

Ben carries me piggyback through downtown Denver as we

window-shop for some dinner to help offset the expensive ball-park beer we will never again have.

All the while, the words *I love you* are desperate to pour out of me. It feels so obvious. Like there's nothing else I could possibly tell him after all we've been through on this trip. But I resist. Because maybe I only love this circumstance. The spontaneity of all our plans getting disrupted. The thrill of adventure. And the relief.

Is that what love is? Relief?

Either way, it's not what I should say. Even if it's present tense, who knows what the future brings. We're both far from home, miles away from our regular lives, building a temporary shelter out of each other.

I will enjoy the ride instead.

27

BEN

Once we get some food into our system, and lots of water, I am sober enough to move my car. I don't feel comfortable going far, so we find a hotel right beside the ballpark with valet service, and I'm able to hand off my keys within minutes. In addition to being down the street from Coors Field, the hotel is also pretty high end.

When we get into our room, Dee and I are in hysterics. We're staying at a five-star hotel because we got drunk at a baseball game and rushed the field with our cat.

"Remember when we got banned for life?" Dee asks me for the fifteenth time tonight. The question has not lost its effectiveness. It probably never will.

We both laugh so loud that someone knocks on our shared wall to get us to quiet down.

Dee presses a finger to my lips. "Yeah, Ben, be *quiet*. The wealthy elite are trying to *sleep*."

"We're here too," I remind her. "Are we the wealthy elite?"

"We are tonight."

Giggling, she unzips the soft-sided carrier and lets Abe roam free. He wanders curiously through our room, passing both of our beds to sniff the corners. Then he plops down near the air

conditioner and sprawls out wide, revealing the soft white fluff
of his belly. I would pay to hear his thoughts. Does he know the
chaos he's caused? Does he care? If his actions are any indica-
tion, he doesn't.

"I mean, look at him," Dee says. "Happy as can be. *That* is a
privileged cat."

"Any responses to our posts about him?" I ask her.

She pulls her phone out of her pocket and takes a quick scan
of all the missing-pet websites and pages. "Nothing yet." She
grins as she puts her phone away. Then she gets Abe's litter box
and food all laid out for him.

You'd never know she hasn't had a pet. Or that a few hours
ago, she was scared of him.

It's obvious she loves him as much as I do.

"Oh, hey," I say casually. "Remember when we got banned
for life from Coors Field?"

Dee pretends to think as she fights off another bout of laughter. "*Hmm.* I actually don't. When was that?"

I come up behind her and scoop her into my arms. "It was
tonight, strangely enough."

"Are you sure? I only remember being with you and our
cat." She turns so we're chest to chest. "I'm tired," she whispers,
sleepy-eyed.

I clasp my hands together and pull her in tighter. "Me too."

We are almost sleeping standing up, supported only by the
firm hold we have on each other. It's been such a long day, full
of adventure. It's exhausting to imagine moving from this spot.
The ritual of preparing for bed seems like the hardest task in the
world to complete. It's so much easier to be here forever, wrapped
in the arms of the woman I love.

It's funny that Gam told me I was doing what was safest,

because it's not actually true. All this time I was making myself uncomfortable on purpose, for no reason other than I thought that I wasn't allowed to let things be easy. I saw what easy did to my family. It made us hollow. We never talked about what really mattered. When I knew Dee as a teenager, I tricked myself into thinking that our relationship was too easy to be real. I did what I learned from my family—the very thing I've come to hate. I cut her off without a word. Moved on without looking back.

Being with Dee again, I remember how much I crave it— safety. Dee is a harness of a human, holding me to the world, showing me everything without letting me run. Letting her go wouldn't be the safe choice. It would be the uncomfortable choice.

Safe is holding her.

28

DEE

Last night Ben and I fell asleep in our street clothes, much to his mortification. He took an extra-long shower to make up for this choice. *His* choice. He was the one who didn't want to let me go, and I certainly wasn't going to object.

Today we wind up through the Rockies until we reach narrow streets with hand-lettered signs that have lived through more decades than me. It's so surreal to be in Gam's small mountain town again, knowing this picturesque place has continued to exist without me, exactly as lovely as I remember. Maybe even more so with the June sun dominating a cloudless Colorado sky, turning everything golden. The drive makes my chest ache with wonder. I pick up Abe so he can see what I see.

We pull into Gam's long driveway. My *Birdhouse*. There are so many ways I wanted to be protected as a kid, and I wasn't. For those two days we were here, Gam gave me that. Tears spring to my eyes at the memory. It's only now that the real idea of her loss has hit me. She won't be in the house when we get inside.

The exterior is still painted lavender, chipped from years of neglect. She filled the yard with wind chimes and different statues—gnomes, flamingos, and even miniature bears, tucked between dead flowers and overgrown vines. Her husband died long before Ben was born. She told us that after he passed, she decided to decorate how she wanted, which is why this looks so much like an extension of her. A physical representation of the whimsical, colorful way she filled up a room, unique and unforgettable. Even without her here tending to all of it, the house still glimmers with the brightest pieces of her.

The trees that frame the driveway seem to bend at the weight of our task. A strong breeze dusts us with leaves as we get out of the car. We promised to come back, and we have. Where last time we came to enjoy time with Gam, now we're here to take what's most precious and leave the rest for a new family to use.

"How are you holding up?" I ask Ben. He's standing with his mouth slack.

"Just missing her." The simplified truth delivered as only he can give it.

Eventually, delicately, we make our way inside. The first thing I notice is how small the place is. If I broke it down to square footage, there is probably the same amount of room here as the house where I grew up. Single story. Two bedrooms. One bathroom. A tight kitchen and a strangely shaped living room. But my house held curses, and this house holds only good memories.

"I haven't been here in years," Ben tells me. "When Gam got sick, I paid to fly her out to me."

I can only imagine how he feels. The interior looks as though someone pressed pause on her life. There's even a coffee mug out on the kitchen counter, waiting to be filled. It gives me peace to know that Ben took care of Gam. In the end, she was with the person who would do whatever was needed to make sure she was comfortable. But it hurts me to think of how much of himself he surrendered to that task.

"I don't even know where to start," Ben says finally. He's not withdrawn Ben. Or friendly Ben. He's stripped of all of it.

"Hey." I come close to hold him. "That's okay. It doesn't all have to be done at once."

When he presses his head onto my shoulder, his chest shakes against me. He's crying. My need to help him grows desperate, and I wrap my arms around him as tight as I can, anchoring him to my steady breaths. I run my fingers through his hair in soothing strokes.

We're in the middle of Gam's kitchen. Where there aren't cabinets, there are photos. Dozens of them, all in different frames. Most are of Ben and Richie, but there are some of Ben's parents too. I am so used to hearing secrets that when Ben told me about his dad, my mind turned it into a story. Something that could be told on the podcast over the course of an hour, interrupted only by ads and other anecdotes. The reality is, it's his life, told here in snapshots on Gam's wall. The history behind these pictures all rewritten with one revelation.

Ben pulls his head off my shoulder. "We need to go to the backyard."

"Of course. A promise is a promise."

He smiles as he leads me out the back sliding door. There's a jaw-dropping view of the mountains right beyond the fence. That's why this place always felt so large. I think of the night we sat out here, warm around the glow of a fire. I'd caught Ben's eyes over the flicker of a flame and thought to myself that life couldn't get any better. It's definitely gotten worse at times, but it's also improved in ways I never would have anticipated.

Ben goes to the back corner beside Gam's small shed. There are dead azaleas along the wall. I see them shriveled up and feel a need to cover myself, suddenly exposed. It's the same flower that's tattooed on my forearm. There's so much more of this house in me than I even consciously realized.

Ben opens the shed and finds the shovel we used to bury the time capsule. Gam cooked up the idea right as we arrived, and she made us follow through with it the day we left. She had such a gentle power about her. When she spoke, she did not suggest. She commanded. Softly, but confidently. She told Ben and me that we would never regret capturing the trip. That when we came back in ten years' time, we'd love seeing what we'd left for ourselves.

"What did you write in your letter to me?" I tease as Ben digs. That was Gam's most important request—we write each other letters.

"I honestly couldn't tell you. What did you write in mine?" He breaks the earth with a good amount of effort. The dry soil coughs up less than it should for how hard he digs his heel into the shovel.

"I don't remember either. I was hoping you would. I also don't know what else we put in the capsule. I'm kind of excited to see it."

Ben grins. "Me too."

When the shovel finally hits the spot, we both gasp. Eagerly, we drop down on all fours to use our hands instead, tossing away dirt until we reveal a large butter cookie tin. Even this is something I've paid homage to without realizing. The tin beneath my bed, stuffed with all my precious memories. I got that idea from here. This one is rusted from its time in the ground.

"I don't know how well everything in here held up, considering the shape this is in," Ben says as he pries off the old cookie tin's lid.

"Good thing Gam made us put everything inside it into Ziploc bags."

"She knew *that* would outlast us all." Once the lid is free, Ben hands the tin to me. "You do the honors."

"With pleasure."

Our two sealed envelopes sit perfectly preserved in a bag at the very top. My name is written in clean block letters—Ben's perfect penmanship—and his is scribbled out in my gorgeous doctoral handwriting.

"We should read them last," I say, my heart racing. I don't remember what I wrote, but I remember the feeling. Like I wanted to capture everything he meant to me and turn it into a perfume that would cover him as he read, impossible to wash off.

We dig into the rest of the tin. There is the mix CD I'd made, titled *Here Goes Nothing,* with all the tracks written in numbered order. We laugh looking at it in the clear plastic container, a relic rendered irrelevant in the current digital age. Ben made one too, called *Spring Break Driving Mix for Dee.* He left the track listing a mystery, though I'm not above admitting I remember each song.

"Penjaminborter would die to get his hands on these one-of-a-kind collector's items," I say.

Ben grabs it. "Penjaminborter is holding them right now."

"Review coming soon?"

"You wish."

There are other relics of the time inside the tin. A stack of the animal-shaped stretch bracelets that I unironically loved and wore from eighth grade through senior year. Ben's oldest Cubs hat. Two tickets to the baseball game that we never attended: Rockies versus Diamondbacks. An unopened bag of Sour Patch Kids, for reasons neither of us can remember. And finally, a picture of Ben, Gam, and me standing in front of her house. It was taken on an old Polaroid she'd held on to for so long that by the time we came to see her, it had circled back to being cool again.

There's an authentic faded effect that makes all three of us look like we're from a different era. Only my fire-engine red hair really gives it away. Ben is Ben, in a plain green tee and his favorite pair of jeans, ball cap fixed over his curls, smile beaming. Gam has on sturdy overalls atop a flowing white blouse. Her hair is wrapped up in Dutch braids. She stands barefoot in the middle of Ben and me, splitting the difference between our heights. Her head is tilted toward Ben, but her hand is wrapped around to pinch my cheek, drawing out a much bigger smile than I usually gave at age eighteen. The image so perfectly captures how the trip felt. Sun drenched, a little hazy, bursting with unexpected emotion. Ben looks at it for a long time. At one point he pulls it so close to his face I think he might be smelling it.

"Are your eyes going bad?" I ask him.

"No. Just wanted to see you up close."

My cheeks warm. His sincerity always cuts right through me in a way no one else's can. He has a direct line to my nerves.

"Well, I guess it's time." I pass him the letter I wrote. His is already carefully positioned across my lap, waiting for me. He never put much into his yearbook messages. Junior year, his entry was so short I've since memorized it.

Captain Business,

Another one is in the books. Here's to many more to come.

—Benjamin

He never signed my senior yearbook.

I have no idea what to expect from the contents of this envelope. We wrote them after we'd slept together. We'd stayed at Gam's for the first night and a hotel the second, just because Ben always wanted to, but his parents never let him when they came along.

When we returned to Gam's for a farewell breakfast, we assembled the capsule. Ben sat in Gam's kitchen privately cowering. He had his arm hooked around his paper like it was a test and he didn't want anyone to cheat off him, which was surprising, because he always let me cheat off his real tests.

When he finished, he kept a hand over the places where the ink might be visible, not allowing me to see a single word. He slipped it into his envelope and then wrote my name tall and tidy across the middle.

I break the seal and begin reading.

Dee,

Before we left, my mom asked me why I wanted to go with you instead of driving alone. I think she was checking (for the hundredth time) that we weren't dating and I wasn't going to be creating her first grandchild on this trip or anything. Which is kind of funny now.

I shouldn't be writing any of this.

Okay, Gam won't let me get a new piece of paper. I'll leave what I wrote. Only cowards cross out entire paragraphs. And you know what Richie would say about me. "Ben's not a chump! Ben's not a chump!" (Future Dee, do you remember that? Summer before sophomore year, at Gavin Dilmore's Fourth of July party? When he made me do the Jell-O shots between cannonballs into the pool?)

Back to my point. I told my mom I wanted to take this trip with you because you make life interesting. Maybe that sounds too simple. There have been times where we've been annoyed with each other, or mad about something small we both know doesn't actually matter. But I've never once been bored when I'm with you. It's not possible if you're in the room. I've taken this road trip so many times with my parents. It's a boring trip. You've made it seem like something brand new. You're the only person in the world who can do this, I swear.

When we come back here in ten years, we'll be twenty-eight-year-old billionaires. I'll have turned Gam's house into the mansion of her dreams. Maybe you and I will take a flying car here? (Please don't laugh. I'm not good at making up things about the future without your help. I just know I won't be driving a Civic.) All I know for sure is that our next road trip here will be just as good as this one. Because you will be taking it with me.

I really hope I didn't change things between us this morning when I told you that you were the most important person in the world to me. I know now that it sounds intense. I wish I could take it back, because I don't ever want to do anything that makes me lose you. You're the most important person in the world to me.

Oh no. I promise that was an accident. I can't believe I did that. You're staring at me right now as I write this, because I just swore out loud. I guess I can't take it back. I really mean it. There's no other way to describe you, except *for the obvious stuff, like funny, and smart, and beautiful. You're all of that too. But more than that, you are important. The most important. I can't imagine a time in my life where I don't think this. So when you read this in ten years, it will be equally as true then as it is now.*

Okay. I think I'm done embarrassing myself. Hopefully in ten years, you laugh at this. Because your laugh is my favorite sound.

Sincerely,
Benjamin Nathaniel Porter

29

BEN

What did I put onto that paper that's made Dee's brows scrunch down into her nose and her mouth hang open in a long O shape? Her eyes dart back and forth so quickly it doesn't seem possible she's reading at all.

For as obvious as she thinks she is, I've never quite been able to figure her out. I don't know if I'd want to, though. To know her is to be constantly surprised by how she sees the world.

When she finishes, she gazes at me with the kind of intensity that could break a lock. "Did you read mine?"

"I was waiting for you to finish," I tell her.

"That's what she said." When I crack a smile, she melts into a quick, pleased grin. "Well, get on with it, then! We don't have all day!"

"Yes we do," I say as my thumbs work the edge of the envelope.

The paper is warm from the sun, and the handwriting is even smaller than Dee's now—so tiny that to read it, I have to move into the shade, needing to be free of all possible distraction.

Benjamin,

How official of me to start this with your full name. Then again, this is a pretty official task your grandma has given us. She's very cool. I'd say I want to be like her, but she's doing such a good job of being herself that I think it would be an insult to try and copy. I'll settle on being myself too. That seems like the most fitting tribute.

We're supposed to be thinking about our futures here. She wants us to make some ten-year predictions for each other, I think? If I'm honest, I'm not really good at this. It's hard enough for me to imagine the next month, much less the next decade. But for you, Benjamin, I will try. Isn't that the theme of my life?

We already know you're going off to Indiana University in the fall with a whopping academic scholarship. You don't have a major yet. So either you're gonna pick up endodontics again and make sure I never suffer with a root canal like you once did, or you'll become a baseball man. OR!!! In my heart of hearts, you will become a famous online music reviewer. You'll take Penjaminborter mainstream, and the internet faithful will fall at the feet of your musical opinions. That is my prediction for you.

But really, whatever it is you do, you'll be good at it. Because you're good at everything. (Except bowling.)

I have to imagine that when we come back to look at these letters, we're not going to remember what we wrote in here. Right? Like if I tried to remember something we did ten years ago, I couldn't. We were eight. Was that the year you were obsessed with dinosaurs? Actually that lasted a couple of years. Maybe you should become a paleontologist . . .

Okay, so since I'm not going to remember doing this, I'm going to write something really embarrassing I've never told you before. That seems like the spirit of this kind of activity.

Here goes nothing.

Sometimes when we drive to school together, I close my eyes and picture you and me. I imagine us doing really simple things like folding laundry or painting a wall or something. And it's always taking us too long. But we're laughing so hard our stomachs hurt. And you stop to smile at me in a way that makes me feel more alive than I've ever felt before. You look at me like you see me. And then I throw something at you, acting like I hate it. But I don't. Of course I don't.

So yeah. Whenever you think I'm sleeping, that's what I'm doing. I'm thinking of us.

I also want to say, probably ten years too late because I am nothing if not a stubborn girl, that I'm sorry for not saying more to you this morning. You don't know what you mean to me, Ben. I don't think you ever have. It would've killed the moment if I told you.

Hopefully when you read this, you are an extremely cool twenty-eight-year-old, and you are laughing at me, because we are still the best of friends and we've long since gotten over that whole sex and Twizzlers moment. Maybe we've had sex again and it was better. I think I've got better in me.

Also, I hope we're talking about prom night, and how we had so much fun at that dance together. And how we were so hot at graduation. Literally, because it's gonna be outside, and also figuratively, because we are probably very sexy teenagers right now and we don't even know how good we've got it. So much great stuff is gonna happen between this moment and the future. I can't possibly imagine it, because like I already told you, I'm not good at seeing the future. But I know it'll be me and you through it all. I don't have to be a mind reader to see that.

You're not the most important person in the world to me. You are the world.

XX,
Dee

30

DEE

When Ben finishes reading, he looks at me like I put the nuclear codes into that letter. It's funny how we're both holding on to each other's secrets right now. My whole life's path started right here, scribbling my heart words onto a sheet of loose leaf, then promptly forgetting all of it.

Back in Nebraska, Ben and I admitted we loved each other when we wrote these. It's a whole other thing to read it straight from teenage Ben's mind. His nerves vibrated off the page in between the lines of tenderness. It's bittersweet in the worst way. This aching feeling within me should be dulled by now. Instead it's amplified by the repeated proof that it all could have been so much easier than it was.

"Should we swap?" I ask him. If nothing else, let me see what kind of chaos teenage Dee was wreaking.

Ben moves from the shade back into the sun, and we exchange papers with a ritualistic emphasis. As soon as I look at my own work, I am struck by the urgency of my writing. This is the penmanship of my fastest thoughts, when I'm scribbling my real secrets onto the pages of my diary. I know I loved him then. It's overwhelming to see how much, because the feeling still lives a single layer beneath my skin. It gets exposed every time I so much as exfoliate too hard. To read it so plainly lays me bare.

Ben was the world to me then. That was true. My show has since taught me that no good comes from giving someone else every single piece of you. No one should be your entire world. What good comes from holding on to everything, though? I've kept it all inside because once, when I was eighteen, I felt too much for the man who stands before me now. As a result, I've given nothing to anyone else. Sex and conversation without any hint of true connection. That's been good. And, at times, fulfilling. But it's never lasted.

"Dee?" There's risk in the waver of Ben's voice. The dip of his chin. He's about to leap. "I can't keep it in anymore. I—"

"I love you," I blurt, cutting him off. "Present tense. Probably future tense. I love you, Ben. I have to guess at this point I'll always love you, because I keep thinking about the years you weren't here, and it's like reading a book that's missing important pages. The story is still good, all the characters come through, but there are details you're not meant to live without. *You* are the details."

He shakes his head, biting back his choir-of-angels grin. "You're not supposed to say it before me."

"Yes I am. Because you said it first last time," I remind him. "Thanks for calling me interesting, by the way."

"Thanks for calling me the world," he mutters softly.

"We were eighteen," I say.

"We're not anymore."

We really aren't. For as much as I feel that Dee with me, she's no longer running the show. It's *my* thing now. What's happening with Ben and me stands all on its own.

Warmed by the sun, and the intensity of this feeling between us, we make our way back inside, where Abe has curled up on top of Gam's table. He's wrapped into a perfect cinnamon roll shape, so sweet and cute I could honestly scream.

"Hey, Dee?" Ben prompts.

"Yeah?"

"I love you."

I beat him to the chase solely because I knew when he said it to me it would turn my insides into liquid, and I'd melt through the floorboards. And I was right.

"I love you too," I can't help but say back. "Home and away."

He smiles. "Home and away."

Since he showed up at my door, we've spent almost every single second together. For as beautiful as it is to feel like we've healed, I need some time by myself to process the immensity of all of this. Solidify myself again, so I don't turn into a perpetually liquid human, pouring out emotion at the sight of anything meaningful. Next thing I know, I'll be leaving earnest comments on random Facebook pages, and no one will be able to stop me.

"Do you want some time here alone?" I ask Ben. He's come here to do so much more than share his feelings with me. This has to be overwhelming for him too.

"I tell you I love you, and you're trying to leave me?"

"Yes," I say back dryly. "My work here is clearly done."

He comes up and kisses the top of my forehead. We hold each other, and the liquid feeling within me turns into adrenaline. My legs actually shake from the shock of it all. The Ben who holds me is a Ben who loves me. This Ben stops me from floating through life. He keeps my feet on the ground.

"I can go to that little diner we went to last time," I say. "And I'll look for an Airbnb or something for us to stay in tonight.

While I do love Gam, this place is not fit for current living." We both look up at the water-stained ceiling. There are enough marks up there to make a map. Not to mention the dust that's gathered on the ceiling fan blades. "I bet I can find us somewhere cute around here."

Ben makes no effort to loosen his hold on me. "If you insist," he says reluctantly.

"This is all an elaborate ruse to get you to let me drive your car. The whole trip, I've been scheming. How can I get behind the wheel of Ben's Civic?"

This is what convinces him to let go. He grabs his keys and tosses them to me without a single comment on how I've invited myself to drive. His trust in me is so complete, and frankly, so unearned, that he really must love me.

"Text me when you want me to come get you," I say.

The reality of being at Gam's seems to have settled in for him too. He knows he needs this moment to himself, and he knows I've recognized that for him before he has.

I love how well I know him.

I love him.

"Can I take Abe?" I ask at the door.

Ben picks up our lazy, happy cat and drops him into his carrier. "I'm gonna miss you," he says to me and to Abe.

"Easy now. We're not abandoning you."

Ben grimaces. Completely by accident, my joke has hurt a bit. There are still a few sharp edges from our past we have to be careful not to catch.

He kisses me farewell, and I set myself on the road without him, hands fixed far too tightly around ten and two. Abe sits in his carrier, riding shotgun beside me. Anxious thoughts spring up as I navigate my way through this postcard town. What if I wreck? Or hit a curb? Or blow a tire on a nail?

Amid my self-created dread, there's a peace in knowing that even if the worst happens, Ben will help me handle it. Ben will not be mad at me. With him, I am always safe.

Barely one mile away, I think I already miss him.

I follow the GPS directions to our favorite place on Sixth Street. It's in the national historic district, giving me all the best views of this former mining town. There's so much history here, I opt to sit outside and soak up the views. My Chicago high-rise shows me Lake Michigan and traffic. This place shows me tree-covered mountaintops. Both are beautiful to me in different ways. Both seem impossible. There's still so much of the world I haven't seen, and the idea of getting to see it *with* Ben excites me more than anything has in a very long time.

After roughly ten minutes of quiet reflection, I am already at my limit. "Okay," I whisper down to Abe. "That's enough me time." I slip in my headphones and call Javi.

"Finally," he booms.

"I'm sorry. I needed time to think."

"All we do is think, Dee! I hope you've taken some time to feel too, if you know what I mean."

"I've taken lots of time. For lots of things."

"That's my girl."

"I miss you," I say. "What's going on? How are you?"

"I miss you too. Nothing's going on. Sitting on my couch with Cheddar, bored. Spending too much money on dinner. Trying to stay off Twitter and failing."

"This is the longest I think I've ever gone without checking any of my stuff," I realize.

"Yeah! Because you have something to do!" He pauses to let out a single staccato laugh. "Vicky told me you called her."

"Of course she did."

"Did you invite Ben to her reunion?"

It's satisfying to hear Javi call him Ben and not Name Redacted. "I keep forgetting."

"You better do it."

"I will."

"You know she doesn't like to work this hard. This is her one thing. Other than her wedding."

I stay silent, knowing I've earned this warning.

"Also, I saw you on Twitter," he adds.

My insides somersault. "What do you mean?"

"At a baseball game. With a cat?"

The somersaulting turns into a full-on gymnastics performance in my stomach. "Does everyone know it's me?"

"Actually, no. No one's put it together yet. Your face isn't clearly shown. But I saw your tattoos, and the red hair, and the whole Colorado of it all. And Ben. So I knew I was right. I thought you didn't like cats."

"It's not that I don't like them. I'm afraid of them." Abe is quite literally purring at my feet right now in between bouts of excitedly meowing at passing birds. "But I've pretty much gotten over it."

"You sound suspicious."

"Oh my god! I'm telling the truth!"

"Not all of it, though. That's okay. When I see you, I will know." He lets out his signature cackle. "If you're worried people can tell it's you, I can send you the clip. You can't see Ben in it very well either. Only the cat."

"Definitely send me the clip."

"By the way, I've got a show idea," he tosses out.

"You do? You've been more productive than me. I haven't come up with anything."

"I think we should do a ten-year reunion episode," he tells me. "We can talk to all of your classmates. Or at least the ones you think would want to do the show. And that you'd want to come on. People would eat that up. And we could maybe have Ben—"

"No." I cut him off, not intending to sound even half as harsh as I do. "I don't want to have Ben on the show." There's no reason for me to object, especially since one of my most enduring thoughts has been how Podcast Worthy this whole trip has been. It just seems ugly to me to try to turn this very real, very private part of my life into something I can sell.

Javi is quiet, likely deciding how he wants to play it. "Okay. We could do other people. Vicky can come back on. Whoever else. Maybe, as a gift to me, we get Derek Blake. I'm just saying . . ."

"The whole reason I don't want to go to this reunion is because I kept all the high school friends I wanted to keep. Which is your sister. And you. Even though you weren't in our class. But you know what I mean. Now I've got Ben again. There's no one else I need to see."

"It doesn't have to be about making friends with them. Maybe just hearing from them at all? Since you kept your circle so small?"

It *is* a good idea. It has that sparkle of something that could be really challenging, in a good way, which was the whole point of the show, once upon a time. To challenge ourselves to examine the parts of our lives we kept locked up.

A list of names has already begun forming in the back of my mind—all the people I never really spoke to or understood in high school. Hell, maybe I could even bring on Alina Dennis, Ben's prom date. It could be kind of cathartic in a way. Maybe I've held on to even more than I realized. More than Ben.

"I don't know . . ." My words lack any weight.

"You're the one who said you hadn't thought of anything. So my idea takes the lead here. And I promise if we are still doing the show by the time *my* ten-year reunion rolls around, we will do the same thing to me."

"Only if your mom comes on to talk about the tornado incident," I counter.

"Are you haggling with me right now? Does that mean you're on board?"

"It means I am considering it. Nothing more."

"I'll take it."

There is a pause that could turn us to a new topic, but that overshare button that only Javi knows how to press prompts me to admit that throughout the trip, I've had thoughts about Ben coming on the podcast.

Javi lets out a low hiss of betrayal. "And you got all defensive with me for suggesting it. We can do a Ben episode *and* a ten-year reunion episode."

"I said I'd never talk about him," I try.

"Yeah, and somehow he's become the one person you reference almost every single episode."

It's harsh, but it's honest. By not talking about Ben, I have instead made him the most present part of the entire show. Maybe doing an episode would help. We're supposed to be taking this break and then beginning a new era. What better way to start than by reversing the redaction? The idea needs to simmer a little longer, so Javi and I call a truce for the time being and catch up on other things.

When we wrap up our call, I text Ben to ask how long he thinks he needs. He doesn't immediately answer.

We didn't use our cell phones in high school the same way we do now. I never got a chance to learn his texting style. On our trip, I've seen him on his phone maybe only two or three times total. We texted in the sandwich shop, but that was a different kind of thing. We were both watching each other as we did it. In everyday life, he might be a slow texter. Or worse, an anti-phone guy. Those things would be tough for me to overcome. Though I am willing to try.

Javi forwards me the baseball clip. After at least a dozen rewatches—including one slow-motion scrub through of all forty-six seconds—I decide that contrary to what Javi told me, I am very identifiable, and it is only a matter of time before someone figures it out.

It would be good to get ahead of this. If Ben is open to it, maybe we *could* do an episode together. A short one. The old-school way. Him, me, and my iPhone's microphone.

31

BEN

This place is so full of Gam it's like she's breathing down my neck. I don't know if I believe in ghosts, but I know that energy is real. So much of hers has remained here that the second I walked through the door, I expected to see her. Because for the first time in months, I could *feel* her.

For a long while I sit in the quiet, soaking it all in. This is a place where she was happy and healthy. I remember her sitting on the couch with her legs propped up on the coffee table, blurting out *Jeopardy!* answers and never getting them right. Or standing in the kitchen with one elbow leaning on the counter, yelling at her recipe book for lying to her about how much flour to use. Ever since she died, my sadder memories of her have been determined to take up permanent residence in my mind. It's nice to remember the sweet stuff again. The little things that made her who she was.

Being here again, I can see how grief has built a barricade around my heart. I've been afraid to show too much joy, because then people might think I've never known loss. But I've never wanted to seem too sad either, because I don't want people to think I'm not grateful for all the good things I have. I've been putting limitations on myself since the day I shut Dee out of my life, and slowly, mile by mile, I've been shedding them.

My peaceful reflection is interrupted by the crackle of Gam's gravel driveway. A souped-up Dodge Ram has pulled in much farther than someone would if they were trying to turn around. Only one person I know drives a truck like this, with blue lights under the grille and a dancing lady atop the dashboard.

Richie.

Sometimes my students will come up to my desk in a panic, holding their backpacks open for me to see inside: *My homework's gone! I swear I put it in here this morning!*

That's how it feels to see my brother hop to the ground and take off his aviators. He'd sent me so many texts asking if I was planning on meeting him. All texts that I brushed off with fast replies and lack of attention, because I thought he meant driving into Illinois to meet him at his favorite bar or at the park district to shoot hoops. I'm sure some of the texts were about that. He meant meeting him *here*?

I press my back against the wall to collect my thoughts.

"Damn. The exterior looks rough," I hear him say. When I peek out the blinds again, it's not only him standing in Gam's driveway. It's my mom too.

"Oh, c'mon," Mom says in her most soothing voice, the one she's always used for Richie, forever treating him with kid gloves. "No one's been here to take care of anything."

If this were up to only me, I'd slip out the back screen door, hop through the neighboring yards, and walk myself to the diner where Dee is waiting. Which is exactly why I don't. Because Dee is here with me, even when she's not physically in the room. She'd want me to straighten my spine and open the door to this opportunity.

So I do.

Richie—never surprised even when it's an actual surprise—hugs me. "Dude! You decided to come!" He looks back at Mom. "See? I told you he'd come around. Damn! I'm really happy to see you. This is awesome!"

My mom walks up and cups my chin in her palm. "Hi, Benny." She kisses my cheek.

My brain works like a calculator, trying different thought combinations, hoping to come up with a result that makes sense. My mom and Richie are here, and they thought I would be too? I knew ignoring my brother would eventually become a problem, but I never expected it to be like this.

"Where's Dad?" I start, not sure how much confusion I want to give away.

"He's down at the diner," Mom says. "He wanted to pick up some food before we started. How long have you been here?"

"Not long," I say. "I got in a few hours ago."

"Perfect timing. We're definitely gonna need you," Richie says. "I can't pack all of this up by myself."

Somehow we're all here for the same thing, which is the most confusing reveal of all.

32

DEE

I don't know a lot of things, but I know faces. And the rugged older man that's strutting through this parking lot in steel-toed boots is absolutely Ben's dad, Garth Porter. He still has an unmistakable handlebar mustache, now gray instead of brown. He continues to wear buttoned shirts that he tucks into his jeans in a way I can only describe as inspiring. Which might seem an impossible accomplishment in stiff, boot-cut Levi's, but Garth makes it happen.

In my mind, this town has always belonged to Gam and Ben. Only now does it occur to me that this is where Garth grew up. It does make his entire aesthetic suddenly way more logical. He is legitimately a cowboy. Or a rancher? Mountain man? Whatever they call his kind around here. In the Chicago suburbs, he was just one hell of a unique dude.

If Ben knew his dad would be here, he said nothing. Considering all I have learned about Garth in the last few days, it does seem like something that would have come up.

My heart starts racing, puzzling together what I'm seeing with what I know. There's no obvious connection aside from the need to pack up Gam's house. If I were here on my own, I'd probably march up to Mr. Porter and ask him what's going on.

But I'm here with Ben, and my protective instincts are kicking in, and it seems of the utmost importance to me that I don't give myself away. So I dip my head low as Garth walks past me, staring at my phone screen with its startling lack of Ben Porter texts, selecting the first available Airbnb I see—a tiny home perched on a river.

I book it, because sure. Why not?

Garth picks up a to-go order, leaving as quickly and mysteriously as he came. All the while, Ben doesn't text. Or call. Or send up a flare from Gam's corner of the mountains. It's all more than a little strange, and possibly connected, but I don't know how.

I finish up my meal, get an extra slice of apple pie for Ben, then decide to drive past Gam's and check things out. There is a giant truck in the driveway, and the entire Porter family stands in tableau in the living room, visible through the drawn curtains of Gam's front facing window. Those were closed when we arrived.

Instantly, I picture Mrs. Porter—Denise, with her perfectly layered brown hair, always salon fresh—getting in and saying something sweet and practical like, *Oh, Benny, I hope you weren't sitting in here in the dark,* then pulling the curtains wide to let the sun shine through.

Ben's family hosted me for more family dinners than I can possibly count. The Porters always seemed so aspirational I sometimes thought I was imagining them. Ben's parents never fought. His dad hardly spoke, in fact, and his mom kept the conversation afloat with her breezy questions and easygoing curiosity. Ben's brother has always been the type of person I would politely label as a complete goober, but he was surprisingly harmless considering his penchant for muscle tees. He's even wearing one now, and it doesn't set off my alarm bells like it normally would.

As a teen, I romanticized Ben's family an unhealthy amount. They were everything I never had on my own, and for a few nights a week, I considered myself lucky to be in their orbit, always hoping their familial harmony would eventually rub off on me. Now I know Ben's family wasn't as perfect as they seemed to me then. They seemed so pleasant because they never acknowledged their own problems.

I cruise down Gam's street a clean two miles per hour, staring. Ben has his hand on the back of his neck. He looks more overwhelmed than when I left him. He might be telling his family the truth, and while I've got a noted flair for inserting myself into people's personal drama, this isn't the moment for Dee Matthews, notorious question asker and occasional human tornado, to enter the scene.

I go to the Airbnb I got us instead. It is indeed perched on the river. And it is indeed very tiny. Though Ben and I do just fine in close quarters.

If Ben is going to come at all.

Not that I am worried.

Not at all.

Did I Forget to Tell You?

EPISODE 125: PSYCHIC ENCOUNTERS

JAVI: So I went to a psychic yesterday.

DEE: Oh my god. Why didn't you invite me?

JAVI: I was having a main character moment! I wanted to be by myself so I could ask her questions about my breakup, then get in my car after and cry.

DEE: That's fair. Everyone deserves that moment. What did the psychic tell you?

JAVI: Oh, it was so good. You've got to go see this woman. She did a tarot reading, and she told me that my time with Green Eyes isn't over.

DEE: You're right. I *do* need to go see this woman. Because I need to yell at her. We've worked too hard to have her unravel your path to healing with one flip of the Three of Cups.

JAVI: I knew you were going to say that. Which is why I've held on to the second part of what she told me.

DEE: Which is what?

JAVI: She said that my time with Green Eyes isn't over because even if we don't resolve our conflict in this life, we are going to get another shot at it in the next life. Basically the problem will keep rolling over until we figure it out. Even if we're born as siblings next time around. It won't be exactly the same, obviously, because if we're brothers it's not gonna be that he's afraid to commit to me. It's gonna be that he doesn't show up when it matters, or something. And I'm sure whatever problem he has with me, which I can't begin to imagine because I am a flawless individual with innumerable merits—but should it exist to him—either we have to figure it out now, or we're gonna be stuck with it when we are eventually reborn into this cruel, cruel world.

DEE: I don't know. I don't like the idea that all conflicts can be explained as some sort of cosmic grudge that travels across space and time. Sometimes people are just bad, and we don't need to assign universal meaning to it.

JAVI: I agree with you. And the psychic even said it doesn't apply to every relationship in your life. If a man on the street harasses you, he's an asshole. Plain and simple. It applies more to the relationships that you know are a big deal. When it feels like something unexplainable has gone wrong, like there's some wedge there that neither of you really put in place. You know?

DEE: Okay, okay. *That* I understand.

JAVI: I know you do.

DEE: So you're saying that if I don't fix something with a certain someone who need not be named, that I'll have to struggle through all of that in another life? Put me on the first spaceship to Pluto, please. I can't do this again!

JAVI: The other option is to resolve it this time. With the name that's very obviously been redacted from this story.

DEE: Hey now! You're the main character of this, remember? This is about you and Green Eyes.

JAVI: Yeah, yeah, yeah. It is. But we all know that for you, it's always about Name Redacted.

33

BEN

I know that Dad isn't my biological father," I blurt out, right in the middle of Mom explaining what Gam wanted us to do with her antique china.

Earlier, Mom insisted we go into the living room because it has the best light. She deemed the furniture too dusty for sitting. Now all four of us are standing scattered throughout the space, smothered in sunbeams and too confused to move. My dad still holds his takeout bags.

"Benny," she whispers. She is definitely my mother, because she searches for words the same way I do, all the hard things caught at the base of her throat, stopping her from saying anything more.

"I'm serious," I say to Richie. He might believe that this is some strange joke. He's the living embodiment of *hey, things aren't so bad*, and a dark part of me wants him to know that this isn't something he can protect me from with his misplaced optimism. That doesn't make it any easier to watch the way my words wipe the grin off his face.

Before I spoke, Richie wanted to take the picture frames from the kitchen and hang them in his condo. Dad planned for us to eat the takeout on the back patio to enjoy the mountain view. Mom cared about letting the light in and staying away from the dust on the furniture. Now I've stripped the color from her cheeks and the shine from her eyes.

Tears burn the rims of mine. "Why did Gam tell me?" I ask, knowing Mom can't answer. I look around the room at Dad and Richie, pleading with them to feel something. "Why am I the one who helped her after she got sick? Who saw her die? You all want to be here to pack her away, when none of you came to my house to see her through her last days."

Telling the truth has dislodged everything I'd buried underneath the secret. I'm so confused. And so, so angry. It didn't have to be this way. I shouldn't be a full-grown adult tasked with handling this gracefully for the comfort of the person who kept this from me. And I shouldn't have to explain to my family that they should have shown up more for Gam. I told them to come visit her. Many times. I asked as nicely as I could. I don't have any niceness left in me.

"Did you know?" I ask Dad.

The way he holds my gaze tells me he did. All my life, he's known this.

He drops his food to come up and hug me. He's so strong, with hands calloused from a constant need to build. They wrap around me as he says, in his low, husky way, "It never mattered to me. I hope you know that. You were always my son. And you always will be."

Suddenly, the hug has multiplied. Richie is on the other side of me, squeezing with all his strength. "I didn't know. But you know I love you."

Even now, they're ready to bandage over this life-changing wound of mine, accepting it as if it's as simple as me declaring I want to be a teacher or I've decided to lease a new Honda. "Stop it," I say, pushing out of their hold. "Stop acting like this isn't a big deal. It might not have mattered to you, but it matters to *me*."

Dad is startled. Richie is shocked. Wordlessly, they back up.

Mom has slumped down on the dusty couch to cry into her hands, so worn down she's forced to show something dark.

"This is my whole entire life right here," I say. "I remember the Christmas cards from him. How you'd throw them away. That man is my father, and you never gave me a chance or a choice to know him. You decided for me that he meant nothing. Now I have to deal with the fact that every single adult I trusted as a child was lying to me. Did you hope I'd never figure it out? What if there was something medically wrong with me that could be traced to him? Would you have told me then? Everyone made a decision about my life without me, so you'll forgive me if I don't feel like hugging it out and moving on."

No one has ever heard me speak like this. This is everything I've never allowed myself to be. All the fights I walked away from suddenly make sense. I've conditioned myself to do exactly what they did to me. Push the problem aside and move on without a word. It doesn't feel natural, and I already want to smooth it all over by telling my mom and dad I still love them. But I hear Dee's voice in my head telling me to hold my chin up.

"There's no such thing as easy. Sometimes life is shitty for no reason. In this case, you're the ones who made it shitty, and you have to face that." I look back and forth from my mom to my dad. "You need to own up to it, or we're never going to be able to move forward together." My eyes are already swollen from crying, and my voice has turned hoarse. "We have to be able to talk about this. I have a lot I still want to say. I'm not ready now. I need to know that when I am, you'll be willing to hear me."

Finally, my mom speaks. "You're right. We should have told you. I should have been the one to do it."

As she says it, I realize nothing could ever be enough right now. Even if she fell at her feet apologizing to me, it still wouldn't fix the pain she caused. It doesn't make me feel any better or worse to get proof this has hurt her too.

"It was never about wanting to keep it from you," my dad interjects. "It was really about me. I didn't want to lose my family, so I agreed to stay with your mother after I found out. But I didn't want other people to know my wife had stepped out on me and I'd taken her back." He's crying now. He didn't even cry at Gam's funeral. "I was a coward, Ben. I'm sorry."

We all have pain we can't fix. We have to overcome it, and it's going to take a lot of time. And patience.

It's going to take conversations. Many more than this one.

My parents have made a start. For the first time, my mom and dad have agreed to acknowledge the flaws of the past. Even Richie registers the gravity of this. He's now slack-jawed, eyes darting back and forth between our parents and me, soaking it all in.

From this moment forth, we are a completely different family than we've ever been before.

And not a single one of us knows what that means.

34

DEE

It's overwhelmingly quiet up here in the mountains. The only sounds outside come straight from Mother Nature—the gentle flow of the river and the persistent bristle of trees.

Ben has not responded to a single text. Not that I've sent that many. I've forwarded the address of this Airbnb. And told him I saw his dad. And asked if he was okay. That's it. Obviously his entire family has shown up, and that is a notable occurrence. He's probably very busy with that.

If only these logical thoughts made my mind stop racing with worried thoughts. Ben's family drama has nothing to do with me and I know that, and still I think that this glimpse of his normal life, the one that's existed without me all this time, has reminded him of how much life we've lived apart.

Abe purrs peacefully beside me. *Our* cat. If nothing else, Ben will want to come back to see him.

I've been trying to rest on this tiny couch in this tiny home. My tiny wish for a tiny new reality has kept me from getting a single minute of sleep. After a literal decade of promising myself I wouldn't do anything like this, I've created a fake Facebook page and requested a friendship from Richie and from Ben's mom in hopes that either of them have posted about their trip. I may or may not have also dusted off my fake Instagram to find Richie there and do the same.

Why would he have a private account? What is he hiding behind that lock? A photo of him holding a fish?

Unfortunately, neither of them accept any of my various requests within five minutes like they should. Don't they want to add an account with a flower as the profile picture, and no followers or friends? There's nothing suspicious here!

A loud engine rumbles outside. Abe gets down on his haunches, fixing his eyes on the front door. Heart in my throat, I stand up and tiptoe toward the window beside it, pulling back the gingham curtain only a sliver, just in time to see Ben hop out of the same Ram that was parked in Gam's driveway. He holds two bags—one containing takeout boxes, the other holding some sort of alcohol— and I don't know if I've ever seen a more emotional sight considering how aggressively my stomach rumbles. He knocks gently, no idea I'm watching him, then leans his forehead against the door. The pressure is so featherlight, but so bone weary, that it shatters me a bit.

I open the door.

"Hey," he whispers. "I'm so sorry. I brought pasta. Do you think you could let me in?"

The fact that he believes this is even up for debate loosens any residual upset I've been harboring. It's clear from his shadowed eyes his day has been much longer than mine. And he's still shown up.

"Of course," I say. "You don't even have to sit outside for an hour while I think."

He offers me a small, tired smile. "I think I might have fallen asleep if I did." I step aside for him to enter the tiny home, and his first words about it are, appropriately, "This really is small."

"Not a lot available around here on such short notice."

"Good thing we're used to tight spaces." He takes a cautious step toward me, questions lighting up his eyes. *Do we still get to touch?* he seems to be asking me.

I close the distance and press my lips to his, tasting the relief as he sighs into my mouth. "I missed you," I tell him. This is a fascinating version of me, heart on my sleeve, and I don't even mind it. "I got you some pie."

"Perfect." He opens up cabinets until he finds plates.

It's so downright domestic of us, this mealtime preparation over low light in a tiny kitchen decorated with various deer and elk figurines. I think of those little mental vignettes I used to make up for us on the car ride to school, a memory reignited by rereading my old letter to him. There has always been something irresistibly meaningful to me about doing mundane things with Ben. Sharing a quiet life together. Talking about our day while spooning takeout onto matching plates.

"So you know that my family is here," he starts as he hands me a heaping serving of pasta. The smell is so beautiful and again, so homelike, I swallow back the urge to cry.

"Did *you* know your family was here?"

He rubs his mouth as he fights off something like a laugh. "Not at all. Although according to my mom, I've been on an email chain about it since April. I guess I knew without processing it. Turns out, my idea was actually theirs."

"Oh no."

"Yes." He then pops the cork on the bottle he's purchased and pours out two glasses of red wine. He takes a quick sip. "This is nice."

I pretend to have any sort of discernment for wine myself,

swirling mine around. When I drink it, the taste is as bitter and unappealing as I expect it to be. *"Hmm,"* I say. "It's . . . good."

Ben cracks up. "You hate it."

"I'm not a wine person."

He quirks his head. "Really? I just assumed."

"So much we don't actually know about each other, huh?"

"Yeah."

He's so much more open right now, worn down. It's like looking at the realest piece of him. Peering right into his sweet, gentle heart. To put it in Ben-speak, he looks sad. Nothing more to it.

"I told them all that I know," he says. He tries to take a bite of his food, but he has to put the fork down.

I stand up and come around to his side of the table, wrapping my arms around his neck. "How did it go?"

His shoulders tremble gently beneath my hold. "I don't even know why I'm still upset."

"You can be upset for as long as you want," I tell him as he begins to cry.

His body shakes in my arms as quiet sobs work their way through him. I've always worried about being able to repay him for all he gave me, when the truth is we aren't indebted to each other. There is no way to measure this kind of care. Whenever he needs me to wrap him up in my arms, I will. And he's already shown he will do the same for me.

"Do you feel like you got everything you needed out of the moment?" I eventually ask, accidentally slipping into Podcast Dee voice.

Not now, I tell myself. *Not here.*

Ben's crying has died down, but he is still too in his head to catch the shift. "Not really. I still feel overwhelmed." He wipes the last of his tears onto the sleeve of his shirt. "Nothing ever goes the way I think it will. Like when we talked about our high school fight."

The words *high school* set off my internal alarm clock. I have to tell him about the ten-year reunion. Vicky will never forgive me if I don't. I can't interrupt this discussion by bringing the reunion into it yet. So I bookmark the task, suddenly nervous about mentioning a future for us beyond this trip.

No. I'm not nervous. I'm hopeful. That dreamy, imagined place of mine—where I see Ben and me doing small tasks—fills with the image of us walking into the dark high school gymnasium arm in arm, met by quiet gasps from our shocked classmates.

"I was so afraid to bring it up to you," Ben continues. "And talking about it ended up being the best thing that's ever happened to us. But with my family, it doesn't feel like the hard part is over. It feels like the hard part has just started. Now we have to actually change and connect with each other. And I don't know yet if we will change for the better."

"What do you think comes next?"

He sighs. "Can I be honest?"

"Cheese crackers to the throat if you aren't."

"I don't want to talk about this anymore tonight," he admits. "I just wanna be here with you."

"We can do that." I kiss the top of his head. "We definitely can."

I move back to my seat, and we finish eating our meal, with Abe happily collecting as many bread scraps as we will offer him. He makes figure eights between our legs until he lands at my feet for a nap. The ten-year reunion sits poised at the tip of my tongue, chased off by Ben's sudden need to make our conversation as lively as ever. He is overcompensating for his sadness, and he clearly needs me to embrace that. I do, gasping when he tells me he saw a Minnesota license plate on his way here. My response excites him so much he takes the initiative to get my notebook and write it in himself.

"I'm afraid we're not going to finish this," he says.

"Maybe on the way back," I respond.

"You think we'll see thirty-eight states driving home?"

"Anything is possible."

"You know, we've got a lot of time now," he comments. "And nothing planned anymore."

"We could plan right now," I suggest. "If you want to be the one to write it out, by all means."

He sets my notebook down. "Maybe later." The way he looks at me is so dangerous. Like there is something very obvious we could do instead. With our bodies. He scans me up and down to make sure the message is clear, taking his time to appraise my every inch.

"I think I'm gonna go shower," I say suddenly. My chair screeches against the hardwood, the floor itself protesting my abrupt, aggressive motion. We have spent way too long cursed with inconvenient circumstances. This is no different. No matter how valiantly he tries to cover it up, Ben is sad. Overwhelmed by his day. If I stay in his presence for a moment longer, I won't be able to honor any of this knowledge.

He puts a hand on my arm. The pressure seems intentional. "Are you sure?"

"I do indeed feel very connected to a desire for cleanliness, yes," I confirm as I slip out of his hold. Free me from this prison of desire. Please. It must be the sips of wine. Going straight to my head.

Ben walks right behind me. Not that there is a ton of space in this house. It's not the modern, HGTV-approved idea of a tiny home, complete with shiplapped walls and a farmhouse sink. It is an old, incredibly small cabin decorated to pay intense tribute to the majesty of woodland creatures. He follows me into the closet-sized bathroom, which is squirrel themed, and not in an ironic way.

"Did you . . . need to shower first?" I ask, confused.

He closes the door on us, pressing us chest to chest in the small space.

"No," he whispers into my ear. The wavy feeling in my head rushes straight down through me. With breathless ease, he lifts me up and sets me onto the counter, making good use of the little room we have in here. "I would actually like to do something else."

There's no stopping me now. I wrap my legs around his hips, holding him to his wishes.

He kisses my neck, working his way across my clavicle until he's reached the strap of my tank top. He pulls it down with his teeth, and I could genuinely become oblivion itself. His mouth works one side as his hand does the other, and next thing I know, I am topless in the squirrel bathroom, and it's the greatest thing to ever happen to me. Who cares about decor when our bodies are this close?

"You're tired," I say to Ben, for no real reason other than self-destruction. No single part of me wants him to stop, yet here I am trying.

Ben laughs into my skin. "I promise you I'm doing great. And I believe I owe you some compliments." He kisses his way across my bare chest. "Excellent boobs. Ten out of ten." He cups one in his hand. "Perfect shape."

"Goddamn," I laugh. "You are something else."

He presses a finger to my lips. "Silence, please. I'm working here."

And so he continues, praising me as his fingers burn across all the skin he can touch. It's eager and silly but still so gentle, so Ben, tender in a way that continues to unnerve me. How can he have this much care within him? After all the ways I've tested his patience?

"I'm sorry I tried to rush us in the car," I gasp out, seeing now what Ben can do when he has more time.

He drags his mouth back up to mine. "Don't be. I've enjoyed everything we've gotten to do. And I will enjoy everything we do tonight." He backs away from me without breaking eye contact. Smoothly, his hand reaches behind him, pushing the shower curtain aside and turning on the faucet. "You said you needed to get clean?" With one swift motion, he pulls his plain cotton tee over his head. "Mind if I join you?"

As he stands before me shirtless, unbuttoning his pants, I think briefly of his list. He's slept with four people. Counting me. Which really means three, because I didn't get to show him much beyond the basics. With a quick glance skyward, I pay silent tribute to my three fellow comrades, who seem to have given Ben a refreshing, earned confidence in his abilities, from which I will now benefit greatly. Comrades, your work is seen and known.

I leap off the counter and remove the rest of his clothes. "I think I'd like it better if you go first."

Look at him. This handsome man, with the trace of hair between his pecs that I once wondered who else had memorized. Forget all the people who've come before. For either of us.

He grants my wish and steps under the running water. It's colder than he expects, and he gasps, then adjusts the knob to settle into it. When he showed up at my apartment only a few days ago, I watched as he twisted rainwater out of his hair. Never in my wildest imagination could I have foreseen where that would take me, watching him naked, waiting for my every command.

I can't help myself. I climb into the shower with him. My shirt is still pulled down, halfway around my midsection. My denim shorts instantly grow heavy from the weight of the water.

"Couldn't wait your turn?" he asks.

"I think I've done plenty of waiting when it comes to you."

He cups my back, pressing me into the orange shower tiles. "Your favorite color," he reminds me. Then he guides both of my arms up. He wraps his hands around the shirt bunched at my waist and pulls it off me as slowly as he can. Each inch becomes revelatory under his careful pressure.

"Thank you for showing up," I say. My voice is soft against the pulse of the water.

"I'm sorry it took me so long." He presses in close, leaving barely enough room for him to undo the button of my shorts.

As he lowers himself to take them off me, he keeps his lips on my body, dragging down against my skin until his mouth is below my navel and my shorts are at my feet. I step out, one foot at a time, but he doesn't stand up. Instead he moves lower, kissing and touching in all the right ways. Then he comes back up with that dangerous, mischievous grin of his.

"We can't stay in here," he tells me. "Do you feel clean?"

We haven't touched a single bar of soap. He knows the answer to this question. It wouldn't matter if we had. He stops the water and steps out, toweling himself off, then handing the towel to me.

"To think I had you crouching behind a bed in Iowa, afraid to let me see this," I say as I dry myself. No amount of water can cool the heat within me.

Ben laughs at the memory. Our whole history is in this laugh.

It amazes me how we never stop evolving. We carry it all with us, and in the times the weight of our past gets too heavy, we share the burden together. We will always have our laughter. Sometimes it's a shield. Right now, it's a balm.

Ben takes hold of my forearm, the same way he did that night in Iowa, when he'd caught my wrist, forcing me to have the good bed. This time, he leads me to our shared bed. It's covered in a patchwork quilt that might be older than us.

"The lady promised me she washed everything before we got here," I tell him.

"Dee. I'm not worried. About anything. Not when I'm with you." He spins me around to lay me down softly.

"I have a condom in my bag," I tell him. "Right there, beside the dresser."

He quirks his head. "You came prepared."

"What can I say? I was hopeful."

He's back on my body before I have a moment to second-guess what I've said. "I packed some too," he murmurs as he settles atop me. "In case we had another reckoning."

"Oh. There's much to reckon with right now."

We smile at each other. We both knew this is exactly where we'd end up, and still, every moment is a welcome surprise.

Lying here with him, I feel cared for and safe. His wish to make me feel loved comes through with every word, every touch. The only thing I can do is make sure he feels the same from me. There's nothing to worry about. Nothing to fear. We've seen each other through our worst, and tonight, skin to skin, we get to be at our best.

When he is finally inside me, it's been so long, yet somehow, no time at all. There are no Twizzlers or sweaty teenage nerves. We both know a lot, and we move with that knowledge. Time doesn't matter in this tiny cabin in the mountains. We can take as long as we'd like.

We change positions, using hands and mouths to help things along, laughing between the moments of passion. We work ourselves to the edge, then we change tempo. We break to talk about nothing important. Then we get swept up in each other again.

"I knew if we ever got the chance to do this again, it would be amazing," I tell him as he finally falls apart, moments after I have.

"You have no idea how long I've wanted this," he says, gazing up at me.

I brush the curls off his forehead. "Oh, I'm pretty sure I do."

He laughs into my ear as I rest my head beside his. "You are my favorite," he tells me. "Home and away."

35

BEN

The next morning, I roll over to discover Dee has gathered up all the pillows for herself. The bedding is also on her side, and she's smiling in her sleep. She knows exactly what she's taken during the course of the night.

I make my way into the kitchen, where the unfinished wine bottle sits on the counter. There is still so much more I have to learn about her. It's hard to believe this trip started with me in Walgreens staring down the snack aisle, wondering if she'd hate me for picking the wrong snacks. Last night we spent several hours together in bed, nothing at all like that first time, while not being that far from what I remember. Dee was still Dee, fitting right into all the places she's meant to go. Making me laugh while driving me wild.

The fridge is bare aside from butter and a few condiments, but the cabinets are stocked with a pancake mix and oil. It's enough to get a decent breakfast started.

Five minutes later, drawn in by the smell, Dee emerges with a quilted blanket wrapped around her. Pushing past me in the tight quarters, she starts rummaging through the cabinets. It takes me only a second to realize she's casing this place like she did the vet's office.

"They had a pancake mix in the cabinet," I tell her.

"And syrup?"

"And syrup," I confirm, winning a smile from her. "I would never make you pancakes without."

"Very good."

Content with that information, she sits at the table to watch my breakfast-making skills. The pressure of her gaze still intimidates me. No matter how long we've known each other, or what we've done together, I still want to be someone she admires this way. Openmouthed, without reservation. It's fun to entertain her, flipping the pancake using only one hand, being greeted with her hearty applause. She has always been my best audience.

When I nearly miss one, flipping it too high and catching the edge of it with the pan, I tell her, "This reminds me of the last game of mine you ever watched. It was a double play, and I almost fucked it up and dropped the ball because I was looking for you in the stands."

She gasps, punching the patchwork bedding until she's free. "*Shit.* I have to ask you something."

"About high school baseball?" I question, trying to figure out what train of thought led her to this level of urgency. "Anything you want to know."

"No." She starts fidgeting in her seat. "Would you ever . . . wanna . . . go to the ten-year reunion or anything? It's at the end of the month."

"Of course I'll go. Victoria would kill me if I didn't."

"Yeah . . . she would . . . How do you know that, though?"

"Because she already asked me to go," I explain. "She's the one who gave me your address. You told me when I showed up that you didn't want to know how I found you. I didn't mean to keep it a secret. I was only honoring your wishes." All her focus goes inward. "Are you okay?"

"It's not you," she assures me. "I'm just surprised. Victoria didn't tell me any of that. And she had *many* opportunities. She begged me to convince you to go."

"She didn't need to do that, because I already said yes to her. She was the one who messaged me, actually," I say. "Sometime last year. Right before Gam died. She found my work email and sent me a really nice note asking me to come to the reunion. I was so wrapped up in my personal life, I didn't answer. When I came up with the idea to take our trip, I finally responded to her. She told me she'd only give me your address if I promised to come to the reunion. There's been so much going on in my life, I forgot all about this. I'm sorry."

"No, no. No need for you to be sorry. You didn't do anything wrong. Well, some people might think it's inappropriate for you to show up at my door. Those people probably don't know us. Maybe you could have started with a phone call. I think you and I both know I probably would've hung up on you, though." She pauses to marvel. "I can't believe Victoria kept this from me."

"Think about what you just said. You would've shut her out the same way you would have done to me." I put up my hands. "Not that I'm saying I didn't earn it, but you know. She did what she had to do to get you to go to the reunion. I don't think it was ever about me. It was about you."

"You're right," Dee admits. "Damn you for being right." She starts composing a text to Victoria, reading it out to me as she works on it. "'Hello, Mrs. Class President,'" she speaks. "'One Benjamin Porter has informed me you already invited him to the reunion. Months ago, in fact.'" She stops to look at me. "What should I say next?"

It's no small honor to help Dee compose her thoughts. "What do you want to do? Tell her you're mad or confirm your attendance?"

She squints at me as her thumbs hover over the keyboard. "Damn it, Ben. That's a really good question."

She settles on confirming her attendance.

Victoria responds instantly. Dee shows me the screen, where Victoria's written, **Thank you for agreeing to come. You know I did what I had to. Love you!** finishing it off with a kiss emoji.

I'm admittedly a little impressed with myself. "Didn't I just say that was why?"

Dee rolls her eyes, then gets out her notebook. *"Moving along,"* she says pointedly. She turns the page and scribbles the date onto a fresh sheet. "Since you didn't want to plan last night, we still don't have anything on the agenda. What's the plan, Mr. Compass?"

"I'd argue I had plans for last night," I tease. Dee can't help but smile. "I don't think we need to go back to Gam's today. My family and I left it on okay terms last night, but I'm not ready to see them again yet."

"Understood. What do you want to do with the day, then?"

"Spend it with you," I say. "Head into town. Look at the mountains from a comfortable distance. You know."

She puts a hand over her heart. "Thank god. I thought you were going to suggest hiking. And I was going to have to let you down easy."

"I might not know everything, but I know you like pancakes. And you don't like hiking. Or wine."

"Good work. That's really the whole list." After a quick beat, she says, "I'm lying. It's a long list." She leans across the table to plant one quick kiss on my cheek. Then she pulls back. "Hey, so, I actually have something else to ask you."

I hand her a plate of pancakes and the bottle of syrup. "Lots of questions for me this morning. Can I say yes to it all? I already know it's a yes. If it's you, it's a yes."

She blushes in the exact way I'd hoped. It's so hard to get her bashful. I love that I'm the one who can do it. I love *her*.

"I'm still going to ask, because we know consent is important, Benjamin!" She fights to keep her face straight as I challenge her with my biggest, eyelash-batting grin. "Oh, cut it out. I'm asking my question now!" She lets the silence settle until the stage is set for her. "Would you ever want to, like, do my podcast with me?"

"Sure," I tell her, as easily as I promised I would. "What would we talk about?"

The podcast has been something I've quietly put into a Dee-only category. It's the same place I imagine she keeps baseball and science for me. These are things we can respect without having to invest at the same level. She already told me she's talked about me on there. Hearing it for myself would feel like reading her diary. I trust her enough to know she'd never say something I wouldn't want anyone to know.

"Us," she says quickly, stabbing at her food with a fork. "And what if we, like, talked about what happened in high school? Would you hate that?"

"I don't think I'd hate it. I don't know if what I'd have to say would be very interesting to anyone, though."

"Oh, Benjamin. You sweet October child. You truly have no idea. It would be *very* interesting. You're kind of a mystery to the listeners. It's become a whole thing. They really want to know who you are. They've begged me to talk about it. I've never done it. But now I think . . ." She shakes her head. "Never mind. I've kept this boundary up for a good reason. I shouldn't break it now."

"I hope you're not saying that because of me." I settle into my seat with my pancakes. "I really will try. Especially if you think that people would want to hear it. Maybe I can teach them about the three kinds of rocks too." She eyes me emptily. "Igneous, sedimentary, and metamorphic."

"Easy now, Mr. Porter," she says as she bites back a grin. "What if we did the podcast right now?"

"Is this something you've been planning for a while and you haven't known how to ask me? Like the reunion thing?" The shock on her face tells me I am right. "See how well I know you?"

"Too well," she says with a fake shudder. "Basically Javi and I are supposed to take this month off to recharge. And we want to come back with a bang. But I also want to find my way back to what drew me to starting the show in the first place. And that was talking to someone I love about something I don't know. This will be easy, though, because you and I have already discussed what happened between us. The listeners don't know that, though. We would talk about the fight, and how we've reconnected."

"Sounds simple enough," I say as I bite into a pancake. "Don't forget, though, I'm just a guy who teaches seventh-grade science in Indiana. My favorite color is blue. I had a dinosaur phase. None of this is interesting."

"Dinosaur phases are inherently interesting. Societally, we don't spend enough time really reflecting on their existence."

"I love you," I say, laughing.

"Home and away," she responds.

36

DEE

It's not very hard to turn a tiny bathroom into a makeshift recording space. I cover the window with a blanket to dull any
outdoor noises, and the space is pretty much ready. We are so
immersed in the wilderness out here that a few bird chirps will
no doubt make it into the recording. At least twenty people are
going to be furious with the sound quality no matter what I do,
so I call it good and yell for Ben to come join me.

"Maybe we shouldn't do this in here," I say once he meets
me in the setup. We have to share a pair of my corded headphones, which means we need to keep very close to each other.
There isn't a lot of room to comfortably do that. "I don't want to
make you stand for an hour, but I can't in good conscience
bring you to another bathroom floor on this trip."

"You can bring me wherever you'd like." He grabs my hand
and lowers us to the ground, then reaches up and pulls my
phone down from the counter. It's perfectly centered between
our folded legs. "I still think no one will care what I have to say."

"I don't know how many ways I can tell you they will care."
We each put in an earpiece. "You should listen to a full episode.
Or go onto Reddit and poke around at the Name Redacted sub-
thread."

"Really?"

"Actually, no. Absolutely not. Never do that."

Making sure he sees, I press record on my phone. Sometimes it takes a few minutes for me to warm up a guest. Without even trying, we've already found a great entry point into this conversation.

"What I've said about you on the show was the truth then, but it's not now," I start. "You don't have to listen to it."

"I would, though. If you wanted."

"It's okay. Maybe you can start listening from this episode forward. The beginning of a new era."

"I like the sound of that." His smile pierces through me, so bright and lively. "Hi, listeners. Dee looks very beautiful today. You can't see her, so it's important to me that I tell you about it. She's wearing a nice green shirt. It's kind of loose. It shows one shoulder. Very good shoulder. She has her hair up in a ponytail. I'm making her blush. Did you know Dee could blush? Probably not. I bet you think she's a force of nature. Which she is. But she's soft too. How is that for a secret?"

I rub the sweat off my forehead. "I hate to tell all of you this, but I *am* blushing. Because Name Redacted is very good at this." Saying his code name lands wrong. "No. I'm not going to call you that," I explain, both to Ben and to the future audience who will hear this episode once it's cut together. "Sorry for the lack of a grand reveal, but his name is Ben. Or Benjamin. Or Mr. Compass. That's who he really is. To call him anything else would be wrong, and I don't want this to be a lie."

"Dee gets really angry about lies. She starts throwing finger foods," Ben tells my phone. He really is so good at this. He knows there is an audience, and he sits with his spine straight and his smile wide, giving everything he's got.

"It's all been necessary," I assure everyone.

"She's right," he confirms. "She usually is."

"Ben and I are currently in the middle of a squirrel-themed bathroom in a Colorado mountain town. And I want us to try and explain how we got here."

"Well, we drove my car," Ben says, playing the beat perfectly. "A Honda Civic. Which I recently learned is a great disappointment to the eighteen-year-old me. But I want to tell him, and any eighteen-year-old out there, that a Civic is a very reliable car with a really solid warranty."

"Not only secrets here today, but life tips too. What can't you do, Benjamin Porter?"

"Do you want me to answer, or you?"

"He can't bowl," I say.

The two of us share a secret kind of smile. The listeners won't ever see the looks on our faces, but they're getting the heart of who we are to each other. And it's exhilarating. We finally have an audience beyond ourselves.

"I'm working on it," Ben tells them. "Hopefully Dee will continue to teach me."

"Hold on a second. Before we jump to future plans here, we need to take it back to the past."

The mood falls, which is to be expected. This will never be easy to address. We will have to deal with the gap for as long as we're alive. Maybe even in the next life, if Javi's psychic is to be believed.

"Up until this week, Ben and I hadn't seen each other in person in ten whole years," I continue. "From the sounds of it, Ben hadn't even seen a picture of me."

"Not a recent one," he clarifies.

"Did you keep an old one?"

"Of course. I have a bunch of them."

My ability to guess what a listener wants to hear rapidly disappears. Personally, I could have Ben describe, in excruciating detail, every single picture in this stack of photos he apparently has. Where does he keep them? How often has he revisited them? Which one is his favorite? Why?

I don't know if that's interesting to anyone but me. Ben is already worried he will be too boring, so I go with saying, "Me too. I keep a tin under my bed with all kinds of pictures and mementos."

Ben gazes sadly at me, feeling the weight of what those pictures mean to both of us.

"I got the idea from Gam," I add quickly and quietly, shifting in my seat so the audio is too muffled to use. This is only for Ben to know. I settle myself with a sharp exhale and set the official conversation back on track. "So you decided to come find me, with the help of one of my best friends, who listeners know quite well. Yes, that's right, our very first friend of the podcast, Victoria Hernandez-Jay, was the one who told Ben how to get in contact with me. We all went to high school together. She gave Ben my address—*secretly*, I might add—and he showed up at my door to fulfill a promise we made ten years ago."

"Take a road trip from Illinois to Colorado," Ben says. "And visit my grandma's house again."

I reach across the phone to put my hand on his forearm, mouthing, *Do you want to talk about that on here? I forgot to check with you.*

Yeah. It's fine, he mouths back. Then, aloud, he says, "She died this past January." He pauses, making a decision. Then he sits even taller and continues. "I was lucky enough to spend the last year of her life with her. Right before she passed, she told me I'd been playing it safe for way too long, and she asked me to go after what I really want. When my school year ended, I finally followed her wish. I found Dee again."

I should chime in, but I'm so overwhelmed I can only listen.

"On our first trip here, she made us bury a time capsule in her backyard," he continues. "So we came back this time to dig it up. In it, Dee and I had written each other letters predicting the future. But mostly talking about how we felt about each other. We were in love." He says all of this in his softest, dreamiest voice, tinged with a bit of sadness.

My eyes do that miserable, unwelcome thing where they fill up with tears. Strangers don't need to know this much. To the world, Ben is a walking hug. That's a choice he's made intentionally. Because I've asked him to do this show with me, he's put his arms at his sides to show something else. Something secret.

"We were," I whisper, knowing I need to muster up the energy to confirm this for my audience, because *love* isn't a word I've ever uttered on my show. Not in an earnest way. Even when I've been in committed relationships. To not include it now would be a glaring oversight.

This has always been about love.

"There's no way to explain what went wrong between us except that we were teenagers, and we were scared." I'm feeling my way toward an explanation that will satisfy both the listeners and me. "Ben tried to tell me how he felt back then, and I kind of shut him down. I said thanks."

In any other episode, this would be labeled a textbook Dee moment. Javi would go, *Oh my god. Of course you said thanks. Like you've grabbed your mobile order from Starbucks, and you're jetting to your next location!*

And I'd laugh aloud, but inside, for a quick, panicked moment,

I'd reflect on how right he is, then take it to my therapist to unpack. She'd mention that I've never been able to hold myself to a single person for too long, and we'd dig into the why. I'm sitting in front of a major part of the why right now. Ben leaving me changed the course of my entire life.

"I made mistakes too," Ben offers, not allowing me to shoulder the blame. "I asked another girl to prom a few days after we got back. Even though Dee and I had promised back in middle school that we'd go together. I pretended like I forgot. But I didn't. I was scared too."

Podcast Dee would come up with a nickname for Alina Dennis in this moment. Maybe Nose Piercing or even Random Student. Podcast Dee would make her sound like a morally ambiguous character—not a villain, but not someone worth rooting for in this scenario. The reality is, Alina Dennis was a cute girl who had a lot of classes with Ben throughout the years, and she was probably really excited to go with him. He almost certainly gave her a fantastic night, and I hope when she thinks back on her senior prom, she smiles.

I say, "Ben and I tried to talk about what happened, and we ended up yelling at each other. Then Ben walked out on me. He doesn't know this, but I'd actually bought a prom dress to wear. It was blue, and I loved it so much, I saved up for it for an entire year. I thought it would look so nice with Ben. It's his favorite color. But it sat in the back of my closet on prom night. I didn't go to the dance. A couple days later, I put the dress in a trash bag and gave it away. I still think about it sometimes, wondering if it's sitting in a landfill decaying. Or if someone ever wore it. How's that for a secret?" I ask right as new tears break through, rolling down my cheeks and dropping onto my phone as it records every word.

Ben's eyes have gone glassy.

For a while, neither of us says anything. Even the trees outside don't whistle in the wind. Not a single bird chirps. The bathroom is so warm I'm sweating through my clothes.

"I . . . I think I'm more overwhelmed than I realized," Ben finally offers.

"Do you want to take a break?"

"No. It's okay," he says.

I should stop recording. Ben will always say he's okay. And he will do it so well that you think he really means it. He doesn't mean it, though, and that's clear from the way he's started rocking side to side.

"I slept with Trevor Williamson that night," I tell him instead. There's an unhealed part of me that wants him to feel it. To *really* know what happened.

"Oh." He looks up at the ceiling. A red splotch has started blooming across his neck.

"It wasn't very good. Actually, pretty bad." I realize I've accidentally said Trevor's real name without his permission. "Let's bleep that out," I say, speaking to the editor who will cut this episode together.

Abruptly, Ben shoots upright. His headphone gets yanked out of his ear, flinging down onto me. "I think I should get some air."

All the while my phone keeps recording, picking up nothing but dead air and maybe, if it's strong enough, the faintest echo of Ben's footsteps as he pads through the house. Soon, the sound of him gets lost to the flow of the river.

What is wrong with me? Suddenly, I feel so terrible—so *selfish*—for asking him to do this. He's grieving. His life is chaos. And I pushed this too far. I told him a secret that should've stayed private, revealing it for an audience instead of only him. Then I had the audacity to make it worse. I know better. But I didn't *do* better.

I tear down our small setup, yanking the blanket from the window and stopping the recording. When I go outside, I find Ben sitting by the river with his arms wrapped around his legs and his head propped onto his knees. He's staring out at the water in that classic, pensive Ben way.

"Ben, I'm sorry," I say immediately. "I know you want some air. I just had to come say that. I knew I shouldn't have asked you to do the show. But I still did. That was really shitty of me." He doesn't move. "I understand if you're mad."

Right as I turn my back to him, he says, "I don't know how we will ever get over it."

This stops me in my tracks. "What do you mean?"

"No matter what we do, we missed so much. Birthdays. Weddings. Funerals. There are going to be so many things that come up, reminding us. And every time, I will feel as terrible as I do now. And that sucks." He tosses a rock into the river. It skips perfectly across the water until it reaches the halfway point, where it sinks down with no ceremony. "I hate how I let you down. I didn't know about the dress. Or Trevor. That really kills me, Dee."

"I shouldn't have said it."

"Yes you should have. It's the truth," he counters. "I thought I'd made my peace with our past, but it's really hard to know I've caused you this much pain. I was sitting here thinking about what it takes for me to look at my mom and dad right now. They've lied to me my whole life. But all I really want is for them to know that I still love them. I don't want to be mad anymore. It takes up too much energy. I hate feeling this way. Like I'm angry at the world. I want it all to go away. That's kind of fucked up, isn't it? That's exactly what I don't want them to do to me, and I'm doing it to myself, trying to erase all of this so it's easier. I shouldn't let them get away with it, but I'm going to, because that's who I am. And with you and me, I'm the one who let *you* down, and you're the one who is looking at me like you still love me. Like you'll let me get away with it. I don't feel like I'm worth that."

"You are," I insist. "And you're not getting away with anything. We are still figuring this all out. Just because it's hard doesn't mean we should stop trying."

"What if I do it again?" he asks. "What if I get scared and leave?"

"Please don't." The possibility dredges up latent terror hiding in the pit of my stomach. "Never leave without talking to me about it."

"I don't want you to feel stuck with me," he tells me.

"I don't feel stuck. Do you?"

"What if I lie to you?" he continues, ignoring my question. "And I don't even mean to? What if it's something you can't forgive, but you still do, because you think you should?"

He's feeling the kind of hurt I know well. It's a soul-deep pain that's finally surfaced, and no Cheez-It reference or mention of Birdhouse can help. He has to let it out. The best thing I can do is get out of his way, because the longer I stay here, the more Ben mistakes his family problems for our relationship problems.

"I'm going to go back inside, okay?" I tell him.

He says nothing.

The rocks beneath my feet are determined to keep me unsteady. Every step I take becomes some kind of miscalculation. It's a perfect metaphor for how this feels. Like suddenly stumbling over terrain that should be easy to walk across.

Back indoors, as I sit on the couch and attempt to watch TV, all the charms of this tiny home have worn off. What was once quaint now feels suffocating. Everything is too close, somehow exaggerated by the fact that Ben is all of fifty feet away but might as well be on another planet. This must be how it felt when he sat in my hallway, waiting for me to open my door. Except for me, with every minute that passes, doubt blooms. I panicked during the podcast recording. He is panicking right now. If it's this easy for us to still get scared of each other, do we really stand a chance?

When Ben finally returns, he walks past me like I'm not even here. Even Abe makes note of it, craning his neck to watch Ben go into the bedroom.

"What are you doing?" I call out. He doesn't answer, which only annoys me further. This place isn't big enough for him to pretend he hasn't heard me. I stalk back into the bedroom, where I find him stuffing his discarded clothing back into his travel bag. "Are you *leaving*?"

"Only for the night," he mutters. "To clear my head."

"You cannot do this again. I told you never to leave without talking to me."

He stops. "Dee, I *promise* I'm not. I just need some time."

"What a good idea," I say. "I think I do too."

I match his actions, packing up the shirt he worked off me yesterday. My jean shorts, still damp from the shower. We move like this—him defeated, me newly furious—gathering our belongings until nothing's left but Abe. We both stand in the living room, looking at him curled up on the couch, sleeping.

Our cat.

The sight of him de-escalates this faster than any of my hard-earned therapy tactics have. Instantly the two of us freeze.

"What's happening right now?" I ask.

"I don't know," Ben says.

For some reason, the both of us laugh. Softly. Not because it's funny. But because it's not funny at all. Then Ben reaches for my hand. It's so simple it devastates me. His palm pressed into mine will always be a revelation.

"I really want to get this right," I tell him as more of my stubborn tears push their way to the surface. "Probably more than I've ever wanted anything."

"I keep getting in my own way," he responds. "Like I always do. I don't know how to stop myself. Gam used to call me a loose nail."

I grab his other hand until we stand face-to-face, palm to palm, like we're marrying ourselves to this moment. "Ben, I am not in any way a professional, but I do know *you*. You worry entirely too much about who other people think you are, and not enough about who *you* think you are. Gam lived a beautiful life, and I know you took care of her in the exact way she needed, right up until the end. But her last words are not some kind of prophecy you are required to fulfill. And little things she noticed about you aren't your destiny. You don't have to stop being a loose nail, whatever that means."

"She meant that I cause trouble without meaning to," he explains. "And that's exactly what I'm doing right now."

"*Ben*," I say again, whispering his name like it's the most sacred prayer I know. "You're not the only one who is freaked out right now."

He stares at me.

"I'm terrified," I admit, my voice shaking as if it's trying to prove my point. "You know better than anyone that when I'm afraid, I like to scare off what scares me. I get angry. I make myself intimidating. And I'm trying like hell not to do that right now, because it would be so easy for us to let this go exactly the same way as last time. We're already trying to, even though neither of us wants that."

Ben looks down at our hands.

"If you listen to one last piece of insight other people share with you, let it be this—all you *have* to do is take care of yourself with the same level of care you give others," I tell him. "All of your jobs are about helping other people. What about yourself? How do you help you?"

He blinks once. Tears roll down his cheeks.

"I want you to take time alone to figure that out," I tell him, surprised by my own words. I'm even more surprised to realize I sincerely mean what I'm saying. "I don't want you to panic. And I don't want to panic either. If we're talking about fear, you know how scared I am of losing good things, and you're the best thing that's happened to me in a very long time. I'm asking you to take time apart from me because I love you. And I know that right now, our love is so fragile, it's distracting you from this situation with your family."

This level of maturity is very unlike me. Everyone who knows me would be proud of this moment. But for the first time, I don't need to tell them about it. So much of my life is about me seeking validation for my choices too. Holding the mirror to Ben has shown me my own truth. I turn my life into stories for other people's entertainment. I catalog my actions by how interesting I think they'll be to an audience.

We *both* need time to gaze within.

My phone starts buzzing in my back pocket. It's an unknown number with a Colorado area code. When I pick up, a woman gasps with relief. "I think you have my cat," she says.

Suddenly, I forget how to speak. To move.

"You posted in a Facebook group," she continues, paying no mind to my stunned silence. "It looks exactly like my Piddles. We lost him three days ago, and my kids have been sobbing ever since, because we never got him chipped."

Ben can hear her voice too. He sinks into the couch.

The woman gives me her address, and I quickly scribble it into our trip notebook, all of today's plans replaced by returning Abe— no, *Piddles*—to his family near the Colorado-Nebraska border.

"I'll take him back," Ben says once I hang up.

"By yourself?"

He doesn't answer, because he doesn't have to. He's taking me up on my word. I've asked him to take alone time to figure out what he needs, and he's going to do it.

I pick up Abe's carrier and drop him into it, planting one last kiss on his sweet little head. There can't be a lot of ceremony to this goodbye. It already hurts too much. Our cat was the one thing we shared—binding us to this trip, to each other—and he isn't even ours.

Ben gathers up his belongings, most of which he's already packed.

"Don't worry," I say as I hand him the soft-sided carrier. "I'll clean everything up here. And I can take a Lyft to the airport. Or a cab. I don't know what they do here in the mountains, but I'll figure it out."

"I'll send you some mon—"

I cut him off quickly. "Don't you dare say that."

"I'm sorry," he says. "Force of habit."

"You don't have to be sorry. I know what you meant." I kiss him, tasting the salt of my tears as our lips press together. "Goodbye, Ben."

Two words I've never said before.

"Goodbye, Dee."

Our time together ends the same way it did ten years ago, with Ben abruptly walking out on me.

Only this time, I've asked him to leave.

Did I Forget to Tell You?

EPISODE 176: NAME REDACTED

DEE MATTHEWS: It's been a long time since you've heard an episode that's anything like this one. It's only me and my phone's recording device, telling you the raw, unfiltered truth.

In the time since Javi and I started this show, we've accomplished almost everything they tell you isn't possible when you start a podcast. It's not that it's impossible. It's really, really hard, though. It requires you to give over a lot more than you realize you'll be giving. It's also been wonderful. You all know how much it's changed my entire world. But behind all of that, Javi and I are still two people in our twenties trying to figure out what the hell life is supposed to be. Javi is going to have something for you soon. Today, it's only me, Dee Matthews. Giving you the most personal piece of myself I have ever offered.

I've been thinking a lot about how I have commodified my pain for you. Tied it up into a bow and sold it as my brand. For years, I've been offering up way more of myself than I should, holding back next to nothing. I've used this space to process things I should have kept private. I've spoken about my complicated relationship with my mother and the many ways she's let me down. You all know the exact moment I chose to distance myself from her because I realized she was never going to be the person I needed her to be. I've walked you through my struggles with money. I've even told you all about my biological father, a man I've never met, whose presence in my life—or lack thereof—is surely something I should have worked through on my own.

But I worked through it here. Because I knew it would get people to listen.

For privacy reasons, most of the other people that enter my and Javi's lives have gotten little nicknames on the show. We've got Starbucks Girl, the Squealer, Doctor Serious, Green Eyes, One and Done, Mysterious Woman, and more. They are real people I've turned into entertainment devices. Even though I've gotten their permission to talk about them on the show, I've still made our relationships into bite-sized pieces meant for all of you to digest, giving away every detail aside from their real names. Although some of them have revealed that too. They have every right to do that. We all get to tell our own version of the story of our life.

Most famously, though, there is Name Redacted.

He—yes, *he*—has been the one person I've kept a true secret from all of you. I've never told you how I met him, or what he really means to me. I've alluded to plenty, but I've never revealed anything detailed. I've left lots of bread crumbs, though, more for him than you. Small pieces of us only he would recognize, in hopes that one day he'd come back. And I have to say, even the keenest of you missed them. Then again, there was no way for you to know what I wouldn't allow you to see.

What you also don't know is that he is—was, no, *is*—my best friend. And for ten whole years, I didn't speak to him. Not a single word. Only hidden messages tucked inside the stories I've told on this podcast and whispered words into the darkness of my bedroom after a few too many cocktails. Then he appeared at my doorstep unannounced, exactly the way I always hoped he would. We took a trip together. A trip I'd normally walk you through in explicit detail. There were so many moments I wanted to. More than I care to admit, I found myself thinking, *This is*

Podcast Worthy. But I stopped myself. Because I'd long ago decided that you'd never get to know Name Redacted. But you already know me, so you've always known him. He is so much a part of who I am that it's impossible to name a corner of my world he hasn't touched. My music taste, my humor. My insistence on categorizing things. All of that comes from him. And so much more.

I realize that this also counts as me oversharing. I am working through something deeply personal on air. The difference this time is that I don't feel like I owe it to you to say this. I owe it to myself. Because there were many reasons I never made it clear who Name Redacted is, but the number one reason has always been fear. I have always been afraid of the immensity of my own feelings for him.

So he showed up at my door, and we took a trip together. And everything I remembered about him was true. He is so kind it almost makes me want to punch things. He has the best smile of anyone on earth. Sorry to anyone who may have been voted Best Smile in high school. Your classmates lied to you. But the most amazing part about him is that he always sees the good in me. Even when I can't see it in myself. He doesn't let me get stuck in my darker parts. And when I am with him, I don't want to be stuck there. I want to see the light and feel the joy.

Because I love him. More than I've ever loved anyone else.

The thing is, my friends, I messed up. Really bad. I tried to bring my work into that special, secret place of ours. I asked him to record an episode of this show with me. He agreed to do that, even though I could tell he wasn't comfortable with the idea. For me, he tried. Really hard. And he was so good at it. You can't believe how good. Everything was going well until I tried to take us through what happened to make us stop speaking ten years ago. I told him a secret he'd never heard. It hurt him. I knew I was once again turning my private pain into something I could sell, but that didn't stop me. He saw right through me. He asked me to stop. Not with words, but his body language. I know better than to ignore that, but I did. Because deep down, I've always thought that love meant destruction. That's all I've ever known. So when things went south, I let the bomb explode. If I couldn't have him, at least I could have a good episode to give you. Which is so broken. Twisted and wrong. Then I caught myself. For maybe the first time in my life, I was able to stop myself from creating an even bigger mess.

In the end, the both of us still needed some space. He didn't walk out this time. I asked him to leave. After ten years without him, one week together doesn't feel like nearly enough. But for now, it has to be.

He gave me permission to share our original conversation with you. I won't be doing that. Because even if it's the truth, it's not what I want to say right now.

What I want to say is this—Name Redacted, you are not a character to me. You are a person I love. A person with hopes and dreams and interests. And hurts that matter to me. Hurts that need to heal on their own. Take as long as you need.

I used to think that letting go of something without a fight was the fastest path to resentment. That taking the higher ground was not grace, but avoidance. I know now that not everything can be healed through baptism by fire. I am sorry I tried to do that to you at first. I am glad we were able to reach a place where we could both step away without bitterness. It's the most mature thing I've ever done, and I am glad that it was with you. Another milestone of ours to add to the list.

Thank you for the best week of my life. Again.

If the space we take from each other somehow turns into forever, know you are always with me in all the ways that count. In the Birdhouse. On the road. Whenever the light turns green and someone floors it to get through.

That's you and me.

And thank you for coming back into my life. For stopping me from floating. What I've learned about myself has been nothing short of revelatory. We'll get it right in the next life. I have to believe that. Home and away.

ILLINOIS

(FOUR WEEKS LATER)

37

DEE

The last of my belongings wait beside my front door, neatly packaged into a plastic storage container labeled ESSEN-TIAL DEE. These are the things I can't part with until my very last day in this apartment. Unfortunately, I have to dig almost all of it out to find my best pair of high-waisted pants. If I am going to be around my high school classmates again, I need to be my favorite version of myself—well-dressed, quick-witted, and a little bit emo. No ripped tights, though. Just a formfitting black outfit and more eyeliner than I'd normally wear.

Once I'm fully clothed and ready to go, I shove everything back into the box and sit atop it, taking a long look at this place. There are some things you know are meant to last, and some things that serve only as a bridge, taking you from one chapter of your life to the next. That's this apartment, with its drafty ceilings, exposed pipes, and shitty, judgy neighbors. Very soon, I will be moving into a brownstone condo up north. A place I own that's *all* mine.

Tonight, I head downstairs and climb into my ride, on my way to the suburbs for an evening with my graduating class. I scroll through social media for the entire drive. Richie, god bless him, eventually accepted my follow request from my fake Instagram.

Even though I know I shouldn't, I go back to his recent post about selling Gam's house.

Your boys got it done! he wrote beneath a picture of him and Ben with their arms around each other's shoulders. *Put this place on the market two weeks ago and already closed yesterday. #stayreadysummer*

The picture is a re-creation of a photo they took as kids. He's posted the original alongside the new version, so I swipe back and forth between the two, bookmarking the differences for no real reason other than it amazes me to have known both of these Bens. It's good to see him smiling with his brother again. It looks to me like the smile is real. I hope he's happy. I hope he's healing.

Selfishly, I also hope he's listened to my podcast. The Name Redacted episode went up last week. He's about the only person on the planet who hasn't reached out to me about it. Even my mom called, which might be the first time in her life she's had a question for me that didn't secretly have to do with her.

More than anything, I hope he comes tonight. We've only spoken once since the day he left Colorado. He sent a text asking me to tell him when I landed back in Chicago. So I did. And he heart-reacted to it. No words. Nothing more to say.

My first instinct was to text him again. Ask for one last picture of Abe or an update on Gam's house. But silencing my first instinct is still a gift I possess, and the more I thought about it, the more strongly I felt that I couldn't say what I needed to over text message. So I put it into my work. And now I'm wondering if I should have waited for a third instinct to emerge, because he has not reached out like I hoped he would. I know I can't make him heal on my time. I just want him here with me.

Contrary to what I first thought, this high school reunion is *not* at our school, which is both a relief and a disappointment. I won't get to have my dramatic walk through the gymnasium doors, but I'm glad I won't be overwhelmed by the nostalgia of that building. I step out of my ride, black heels on the concrete, and strut toward the front entrance of our local banquet hall instead.

Victoria is positioned in the center of the lobby. She sits behind a cloth-covered table with a stack of name tags and drink coupons for everyone who enters. "You're *early*," she says.

"Anything for you."

She leans over the table to hug me, then sits back to take in my outfit. "Very good. Very you."

Javi scares the shit out of me by popping up next to her. "Sorry. I dropped some of the drink tickets." He places a pile of them on the table, then walks around to pull me into a hug, which is a large departure from our usual greeting—a head nod as he enters my apartment with his own key. "Derek Blake is already here," he whispers into my ear.

This isn't a hug. This is an information session. "Are we getting queer vibes?" I whisper back.

"Definitely." Then he tilts his head at a backward angle, and I look behind him to see Derek only a few feet away, nursing a cocktail beside the open banquet hall doors. "I already asked him to do the podcast. He said yes."

Victoria clears her throat. "Deandra," she sings out. "You need your name tag." Javi lets me go, hurrying back to his spot.

"I hope you didn't write that on there," I say.

"I will if you don't stop gossiping with my assistant."

"*Volunteer* assistant," Javi clarifies.

Victoria hands me a sticker that says DEE MATTHEWS. "If you're extra nice, I'll give you more drink tickets."

"How do I be extra nice?" I ask as I slap the sticker onto the left side of my silky V-neck tank.

"It's easy. You willingly socialize with the seven other people who have already arrived."

"*Seven?*" I back away from the table. "Oh no. I am way too early. I can't go in and talk to *seven* people. You might as well ask me to lead a seminar on how the mitochondria is the power-house of the cell."

Without really meaning to, I've brought up Ben again. It's been happening with alarming frequency. Javi's already warned me that I keep figuring out ways to mention that the sun weighs 4.18 nonillion pounds. Yesterday afternoon, he caught me *watching baseball*.

"It's not that bad," she tells me. "Alina Dennis is already here. Wasn't she one of the people you wanted to invite onto the show?"

"Oh god. That's worse. I can't talk to her until I'm wasted and we bump into each other in the bathroom and have a come-to-Jesus moment."

Victoria flaunts *eight* drink tickets.

The money-conscious person that will always live inside of me cannot resist the sight. "Fine," I say as I snap them out of her hands.

"Have fun in there!" she calls out, more of a demand than a wish.

38

DEE

Now that I'm three drinks in, the conversations flow a lot easier than they did when it was me, Derek, Alina, and five other alumni in a room built to hold five hundred. We're about two hundred people closer to capacity now. The music is good. And the night is surprisingly fun.

There are several round tables set up around the dance floor. Victoria has lovingly collected personal photos from our classmates and displayed them all throughout. She's even got some up that I loaned her from the tin beneath my bed. I've put my belongings down at the table that features a picture of Ben and me on one of our countless school field trips to the Field Museum. We're holding up peace signs in front of Sue the dinosaur (the dinosaur!). If he's not here in person, at least he is here in memory.

And he's definitely here in conversation.

Victoria was correct, there are more podcast listeners in our class than I ever would have guessed. Every single one of them that is brave enough to talk to me about it correctly guesses that Name Redacted is Ben. I don't bother lying, but I make a point not to confirm their suspicions either. It's basically a lot of me saying, "That would be amazing, wouldn't it?" and them being too confused to push it further. Unlike what I expected, no one has realized we're the people in the cat video on Twitter.

Contrary to Victoria's wishes, I have also been pointedly avoiding Alina, who is wearing a flowy floral dress and a sweet little nose stud, dancing with her *husband*, posing not a single ounce of a threat to me. It's more that she represents my greatest vulnerability, and she has no idea. I'm worried I will sound too intense no matter how I approach her, so I've taken to staring at her an almost uncomfortable amount, sipping on my free drink ticket cocktails.

At one point, Javi comes up behind me to whisper in my ear, "What if you're actually in love with *her*?"

"That would be a lot better than me just being a weirdo who is afraid of her," I tell him.

"She looks very nice. Eco-conscious. She definitely rinses out her yogurt containers and recycles them."

"I do that," I say defensively.

"Well, maybe that's how you get the ball rolling. *Hey, girl, how much do you love playing a minimal role in aiding our global plastic crisis? Do you wanna come on my show?*"

"You make it sound so easy. Maybe you should ask her."

He wags a finger in my face, then walks off to further mingle with Derek.

Alone again, I take time to look at all the pictures Victoria's set out throughout the room. It's hard to understand why the idea of this event terrified me. As I glance between these teenage candids and the crowd of twenty-eight-year-olds scattered throughout, it's very clear they're all like me—a little lost, a little overwhelmed. Doing their best with what life has given them.

I expected them to still see me as the girl with a chip on her shoulder. Or the one whose clothes were a little ragged at the seams. Authentic rips and tears I played off as intentional fashion choices. When I look at these pictures, remembering who they all were ten years ago, I feel nothing but wonder for the people they've become. We've all got our secrets. We're all carrying our hurts in backpacks we never get to stuff into a locker and forget about. But we're all here, paying tribute to how we've grown up. And that's really beautiful.

Teenage Dee would have found this insufferable, but she doesn't define me. I can pay tribute to her tonight and she has no say in the matter. She can roll her eyes all she wants. She's not me anymore.

"Dee?" I startle out of my nostalgic daydream to find Alina Dennis standing before me. Her hair is shorter now, cropped right below her ears, with bangs perfectly organized across her forehead. She wears a sweet, tentative smile as she tucks a stray piece behind her ear.

"Hey!" I say, too enthusiastically, like we're old friends who've run into each other at the mall. Maybe we could have been. Maybe one day we will be. There's a lot of hope in this *Hey*, and I'm okay with how excited I sound.

"I thought you'd be here with Ben!" Her voice strains from yelling over the music. The DJ has started "Mr. Brightside," the millennial's siren song.

"Yeah!" I yell back. "Me too."

"I hope you weren't mad we went to prom together." She touches her hair again. "I was so shocked when he asked me. I always thought he was so cute. And that he loved you."

She leans in enough for me to smell the liquor on her breath. It warms me to her more than she knows. Bless her liquid courage. It's stronger than mine.

"He talked about you so much that night that I told him he

needed to go to the parking lot and call you," she tells me. "That made him stop."

It's a risky thing to say, but she shares it with the right touch of deprecation, granting us both the freedom to laugh. I can picture this Ben so perfectly, his brown eyes saucer wide in mortification and his hand grabbing his mouth as if he could somehow swallow back his words and reverse the course of their night.

"After that, he went out of his way to make sure we had fun," Alina continues. "He asked me what my favorite songs were, then convinced the DJ to play every single one. Whenever I'd go to the bathroom, I'd come out to find him waiting for me with snacks. We went to the after-party together, and he never made a single move on me. At the end of the night, he walked me to my door, kissed me on the cheek, and thanked me for a perfect night. But I could tell . . ." She slurs a bit here as she points from her to me. "He wished it was you."

I'm suddenly overcome with the kind of overwhelming sentimentality I get when I'm drunk, and I'm barely tipsy right now. "Can I hug you?"

"Of course!" She squeezes me tight enough to rearrange some of my vital organs.

When I pull back, we end up doing the thing where we're holding each other's forearms, and it makes me so happy that it's almost comical. "So I do this podcast, and I'd really like it if you'd come on the show. Is that something you'd be into?" I ask.

"I listen!" She tells me enthusiastically. "I'd love to come on!"

We exchange phone numbers as I tell her I'll text her with more information soon. Then she invites me onto the dance floor for the remainder of "Mr. Brightside," and we jump and sing like we were always friends. Like this is a re-creation of our past brought to life.

When the song finishes, she hugs me again. "Maybe you should go to the parking lot and call him," she suggests.

It feels like a flashing neon sign, blaring and obvious, begging me to do the scary thing and talk to him directly. So I do it.

I go to the parking lot and call him.

39

BEN

Rochelle kicks her heel into the back of the driver's seat. "Dad! Stop it!"

Darius has on Jackie Wilson, and he's belting at the top of his lungs just to embarrass her. When Jade starts singing backup, Rochelle folds up into the corner of Darius's SUV. She takes out her phone to scroll in vengeful silence.

"Sorry, baby. We've gotta keep the mood up," Jade yells out as Darius hits all the post-chorus ad libs. "Ben has a big night ahead of him."

For the last few weeks, I've been bingeing Dee's podcast. The internet is an amazing, overwhelming place, and I found a guide to all the times Dee mentions me. I plan to one day listen to the whole show, but there are 176 episodes total. Most are more than an hour long. Hearing how she's felt about me for the last ten years seemed like the right place to begin. This afternoon, I finally got to the most recent episode.

Darius couldn't handle one more phone call about it.

"I love you, man," he said. "But I don't even talk to my mama on the phone half as much as I talk to you these days."

"Do you think . . ." I started. Then stopped. Then started again. "Do you think you could drive me to my reunion?"

Darius laughed. When the line went quiet afterward, he realized I was serious.

Then the whole Carlson family showed up at my house to give me the very ride I once promised Darius I would never need. Proof some promises have to be broken. I told him if I drove alone, I might second-guess myself and turn around. Now we're all on the road together, only a few miles away from the reunion, and I know I was right to ask for their help, because my legs are shaking the same way they did when I sat outside Dee's apartment door. I was so anxious when they picked me up I even forgot to grab my phone. If I was alone, I'd have to pull over right now and do sprints in an empty parking lot or something. I'd never arrive on time, and for this, I can't afford to waste one more minute.

"We could play a car game," I suggest to Rochelle as a way to distract us both. "I Spy?"

She shoots me a deadly glare. Being a teenager is hard. These days, no one remembers that more than me. When I catch a glance at her phone, I see she's on Dee's Instagram page. Even if Rochelle doesn't want to talk, she *is* invested, which means a lot to me. Quietly, she shows me a selfie Dee posted to her story an hour ago. Dee's wearing a low-cut black top, and she's placed her head beside an old picture. *Lotta memories here tonight,* she's written.

Rochelle clicks out of it.

"Hold on," I say. Rochelle opens the story up again, even letting me hold her phone to look closer. Dee is posing next to an old photo of her and me at the Field Museum. She looks so beautiful. So her.

She asked me to take care of myself. And I've been trying. On my suggestion, my family and I started group therapy last week, which is maybe even harder than I imagined it would be, but we're all making it happen. My mom and I have even started discussing if and when we can tell Dr. Ward the truth. It's a very delicate situation, and we know that. He has a family of his own, and we want to navigate that as respectfully as possible. As daunting as it all is, I've found that the more I push myself to face difficult things, the less scared I become of failing.

I'm doing it for me. Not for anyone else.

After we sold Gam's house in record time, it inspired me to look into listing mine. I have all this space and nothing in it but memories of the last year, watching my grandmother fade away. I want something new.

Darius gets off the highway and navigates through my hometown. We pass all the places I used to know like my own reflection. So much has changed, yet the feeling always stays the same. This is the place that made me who I am.

When we pull into the banquet hall parking lot, my heart races at the sight of all these cars. Cars mean people. And the people here are friends I pushed away for no reason other than I believed I should. Because I used to think a fresh start meant getting rid of everything old. Now I know that good things are worth bringing with me wherever I go.

Darius stops in front of the entrance. "We're just gonna drop you off."

This pulls Rochelle out of her sulking state. "What? No we're not! We need to go inside with him!" She turns in my direction, eyes piercing through me. "Right, Mr. Porter? Why else would we be here?" She's used my last name to make a point. To her, I will always be a teacher. Even though she'll never again be in my class, she still expects to learn a lesson from me.

I put my hands up. "I have to go with whatever your dad tells you."

Jade laughs. She turns around to look at Rochelle and me in the back seat. "Oh, we're going inside."

"Never mind," I say to Rochelle, who is already unbuckling her seat belt and smiling.

Darius finds an open spot near the back. The four of us walk through the dim parking lot side by side. There's someone walking down the next row of cars, but it's dark, and they're too far away for me to make out who it is.

"What are you gonna do?" Rochelle does a quick skip of excitement. "Are you gonna, like, propose?"

My face gets hot. "I need to find her first. Then I'll know what to do."

"I hope so," she says suspiciously.

There is no one at the check-in table when we arrive. Victoria might kill me for bringing extra, unpaid guests. Now is not the time to worry about that. We keep going until we're right outside the banquet halls, where the thrum of music pulses against the closed doors.

I turn to face Darius's family. "Thank you," I say. "I know I've been a mess for a while. This means a lot to me."

Rochelle sighs. "We don't have time for this!" She swings open one of the doors and urges us into the low light of the party, where everything is washed in a soft purplish blue.

The faces blur by me, memories swirling as I lock eyes with my former classmates. They all greet me with enthusiastic waves, then immediately ask, "Oh my god. Are you looking for Dee? She was just here."

She was just here.

Where is she now?

No matter where we search, we can't seem to find her. Every second that passes is one second too long.

The four of us stop to hold a conference beside the dance floor.

"What now?" I direct the question straight to Rochelle. "I don't have my phone."

"You have to go up there!" She points to the DJ booth. He's dead center in front of the dance floor, elevated on a platform a few feet off the ground. "We know she's here. Use his mic and ask for her!"

Long before I was Mr. Porter the science teacher, I used to hope my one-on-one friendliness would be enough to keep my friends and teachers from wanting me to speak to large groups. This is exactly why I turned down class president. When I look at a crowd, I can't see the individuals anymore. They become this blob of expectations that feel impossible to meet. What do they want from me? How can I make all of them comfortable at once?

"I don't know," I say.

"Yes you do," Rochelle urges. "We didn't come all this way for nothing!"

Darius and Jade stay silent. They won't interject. This has to be my decision.

"Hi," I say to the DJ, who is midway through playing a Vampire Weekend track off an album Penjaminborter once gave five stars. "Could I use your microphone for a second? I'm trying to find someone."

The DJ assesses my sobriety with a suspicious eye squint. "I don't know, man. That kind of thing is never a good idea."

"Please," I beg. "I am completely sober. I just got here,

actually. With the very nice family standing right over there, waiting for me to do this." I point to the Carlsons. Only Jade waves back.

The DJ winces. "Yeah. That doesn't sound good."

When charm doesn't work, money does. I dig into my pockets and find my wallet. "I'll give you fifty dollars to let me use your microphone."

He hesitates.

"A hundred." I jump up, wincing. I promised myself I would be as financially smart as possible until my house sells, because I have no idea where I'm moving.

"Pay it first and then I'll let you talk," the DJ says.

I give this man one hundred American dollars. He turns down the music and hands me the mic.

"Hello," I call out. A wave of ear-piercing reverb silences the crowd, making everyone wince. Then someone yells out, "Ben Porter! What's up, man!" And the tension melts away. The crowd reassembles, gathering around the platform booth like I'm about to perform a legendary set for them.

The DJ, who has kept his hand hovered beside his microphone, pulls it back, impressed.

Someone else yells, *"Ben's not a chump!"* Richie's famous Fourth of July quote, and everyone cracks up.

What else do these people remember?

A third voice—this one a woman's—shouts, "Ben! She's here!" The woman wears a long flowing dress covered in flowers. She works her way toward me. My former classmates shift to allow her space to pass through.

It's Alina Dennis. My prom date.

"She was looking for you," she tells me when she reaches the front.

I lean toward her, pressing the mic to my chest. "Is she still inside?"

"I don't know," she tells me. "But I can text her." She's already on her phone, typing. "She'd definitely want to hear from you. I think we all would. *Name Redacted*."

When I stand in front of my students to teach a lesson, it doesn't stress me out, because I always have a clear agenda. It doesn't matter if they're sleepy or they're not focused. It's my job to make them learn. Now that I'm aware of what this particular crowd wants from me, I'm confident I can deliver. They are looking for me to be the man from Dee's podcast. And that's who I am.

"Hey, everyone," I start again. I stand up straight, gazing out into the sea of faces. They are all pieces of me. Memories of who I used to be. And that doesn't scare me anymore.

"Porter!" The first voice shouts. It's my old teammate, Bobby Ramos. Our power-belting third baseman. He has a glass raised to me. "Miss you, man!"

"I miss you too," I say, meaning it. All I've done is shut these people out of my life, and all they're giving me is kindness.

"In high school, I coasted on the comfort of my surroundings," I tell them. "I used to ignore problems to keep the peace. I thought it would make everybody happier if they never knew when I was upset. We all got along great because none of you actually knew all of me. Except for one person. The most important person in the world."

Countless versions of this speech have been running through my head over the last three weeks. The words flow fast and free, no room for second-guessing.

"She's brave in the face of every challenge that comes her way," I continue. "She never backs down from the things that scare her. I used to think I didn't have to be like that. That she was supposed to be good at the things that were hard for me, and I was supposed to do the same for her. But the whole time, I should've been following her example. That's one of the first things we learn in baseball. Watch the other players. See what works for them, then find your own version of that. Hopefully it's not too late for me to try."

Bobby Ramos lets out a "Hell yeah!"

Everyone cracks up.

One laugh comes through louder, hanging on when the rest of the crowd has quieted.

I'd know that sound anywhere. My favorite sound. My favorite person. The one who claps first and laughs hardest. The best audience member in the world. Where Alina Dennis once stood alone, there is now Dee beside her, eyes fixed on me.

"No matter how much distance I create between us, or how much I try to ignore my own thoughts, this person is always on my mind. She told me once that I get to choose who matters to me. And I choose her." I pause to smile at the beautiful woman I love. "Dee."

Several people in the crowd gasp. A few others let out *awws*.

"Dee," I say again, met with more excitement. "I let myself be content with an average life. Then you reminded me how to make the ordinary things exceptional. Without you, I never would have tried to smuggle a cat into a baseball game or spent a single extra thought on my waitress's personal life." She laughs, urging me on as only she can. "I listened to your episode about me. All of them, actually. And I'm sorry you felt like you had to do that. I'm sorry for everything. You put yourself on the line for me, over and over, and it's only right I do the same here. Thank you for letting me have space to figure myself out, but I don't need it anymore. Because I am only half as good without you. So if you'll have me, I'd love to start living my life with you by my side. You've always been my compass, guiding me toward the future I want. When we're together, every day is an adventure. And you are the greatest part of that. Always."

Dee rushes up the side steps. She presses her hand onto my chest, feeling the wild beat of my heart. Then she grabs the microphone from me.

The DJ leans forward, riveted.

"Ben," she says into the mic. "You know very well I've made a career out of saying way too much about my personal life. And I just promised I wasn't going to do that anymore!"

The crowd gives her the laugher she deserves.

"For you, I will make an exception," she says softer, moving her free hand from my chest to my face. "Because you are an illegally handsome ray of sunshine, and I'll be damned if I let you stand up here and make a show of this without me." She turns to the crowd. "Yes, he is Name Redacted."

As they react with clapping, Dee looks at me with that perfect face of hers, heart-shaped and filled with fire.

"I love you," I tell her, pressing my hand over the mic so only she can hear me.

I love you too, she mouths.

She gets up on her tiptoes, but I don't let her kiss me. Because this time, there will be no question of who started it. I wrap my arm around her waist and dip her, then lean down and kiss her with everything I've got. She meets my pressure in the way only she can, delicate with me when I anticipate passion. She always gives me the exact thing I don't realize I need until I have it.

When we right ourselves, the DJ takes the microphone from

Dee's hand. "How about that?" he says. "Let's give it up for these two!"

We step off the platform together, hand in hand, greeted by the loud applause of our former classmates. As we fold into their warm welcome, Dee keeps a hold on me. I stop us in the thick of things, pressed against the people who used to surround us every day at school. Just like old times, we slip into our own version of the world, where for a moment, no one else matters but us. I place both hands on the small of her back and pull her close to me. We start swaying to the beat of the slow song the DJ's put on for this moment.

"The family who took Abe called me yesterday," I say. "Turns out, the real Piddles showed up at their door. Abe was an imposter."

Dee's eyes light up even more than I expect, filling with the tears I know embarrass her. She can't help it, though. The hope shines through. *"Our cat."*

"That's right. And lucky for us, before they realized, they chipped our boy and got all his shots up to date. He's waiting for us to come and get him."

Grinning wide, she squeezes my shoulders with her hands. "Guess they don't know their own fucking cat."

"Embarrassing."

"A downright shame." I press my lips against hers so hard we almost fall over. I start kissing her over and over. Her mouth. Her cheeks. Her nose. "I just missed you so goddamn much," I tell her. In the background, I hear the rising cheers of our classmates. But all I see is Dee.

"I missed you more," she tells me, laughing as I cover her in affection. When I stop, she rubs her thumb across my cheek. "I can't believe you're here."

"I'll always be here," I assure her. "I'm never leaving again."

She smiles. "Wait. If we have to go get Abe, does this mean we're taking another road trip?"

I tuck my hand under her chin and pull her mouth to mine, planting the gentlest kiss I can manage on her lips. Then against her soft mouth I whisper, "I was thinking this time we'd fly."

"I'll go anywhere with you," she whispers back. "Home and away."

ILLINOIS

(ONE YEAR LATER)

40

DEE

Ben Porter has just hit the game-winning home run.

His teammates rush the field to celebrate. The first to reach him is Darius Carlson, his best friend from work and an incredibly reliable right fielder. He opts for a jumping hug, smothering Ben once he lands back at home plate. Bobby Ramos, one of Ben's high school teammates and a hell of a consistent third baseman, Hulk-rips the jersey off Ben's back, revealing the plain white tee Ben has on underneath. Javi—the most surprisingly effective pitcher to ever accidentally throw a ninety-mile-per-hour fastball and then freak out and ask to be put in a different position—carries out the ceremonial Gatorade.

"You get to do the honors," he says as he hands it over to me.

Turns out, the key to getting me to enjoy baseball is to let me play. So I—the notoriously unpredictable center fielder on the worst adult amateur baseball team in the entire Chicago Metropolitan Baseball Association—dump yellow electrolyte juice all over my fiancé.

Once the cold rush passes, he turns around to see it's me who has doused him, and he sweeps me up in his arms.

"Did you see that?" he asks me, knowing full well I did. I was standing a few paces away from third base when it happened, waiting for him to hit it out of the park and send all of us home.

"See what?" I tease as I kiss him, tasting sugar water. The front of his shirt has drenched me, scenting both of us in lemon. "Now tell me why that happened."

"Because my Venus is in my third house?" he jokes as he sets me down.

I laugh. "Have I told you lately that I love you?"

"Once or twice."

We start our walk toward the dugout together. Ben stops and pulls an actual card out of his back pocket where he's written down most of his natal chart placements. Unfortunately, the Gatorade has rendered most of it illegible.

"It's okay," I say. "We can make you a new one when we get home."

He ignores me, rooting around in his back pocket for something else. A folded-up piece of paper. He turns his back to me while he opens it up. "Oh thank god," he says softly.

"What is it?"

"I put your letter in my pocket for luck," he explains, showing me the note I wrote for the time capsule when we were eighteen. "I thought it might be ruined, but the other paper protected it."

"You put that in your pocket every game?" I ask, both shocked and touched.

"I just tried it for the first time," he tells me sheepishly. "I've been bringing different things with me each week, hoping to find something that will give us good energy out on the field. This is the first object that's worked, so now I have to keep using it."

It's sweet to see him a little embarrassed by this. Even sweeter that he thinks my old note has somehow made him better at baseball.

"I'm truly humbled and honored to be a part of a new superstitious ritual for you," I say. "Maybe we should get that note laminated so we don't have to worry about Gatorade ruining it? Should I start bringing my note from you too? Should we ask the entire team to carry personal objects in their pockets so that we can finally score more runs?"

I'm kidding, but Ben considers it in earnest. "It's worth trying."

We start gathering up our equipment in the dugout. "Then I'll be sure to bring some Twizzlers to the next game."

Ben grins. "They *have* always been good luck for us."

Jade, our star catcher, yells out the postgame plans to the whole team. "Dinner at Ben and Dee's!"

Victoria, our reluctant left fielder, excuses herself by rubbing her hand over her tiny baby bump and shrugging. She has never once run toward a single ball that has come her way. For that reason alone, I will let her play right up until her doctor tells her it's unsafe. Which so far will be never, because she does not swing at any of the pitches thrown at her either. In fact, she actively backs away. She is here for the snacks and the socialization, and she's proud of that.

Ben presses his forehead to mine. "I told Darius we could," he whispers, sheepish. "I mean, I hit the game-winning ball. It's our first win in three weeks." His eyes go soft. "*Please?*"

"I haven't even said anything," I remind him.

He pulls back to make a face that tells me full well I don't need to communicate with words to get my point across. "I'll make sure everyone's out at a good time. We'll be in bed early. I promise."

He knows Javi and I are recording bright and early tomorrow.

We're still in the process of interviewing old high school class-mates. All year we've brought on people we knew well and peo-ple we hardly knew, and we have talked to them about who we used to be to each other. It's been incredibly enlightening. Once we saw how well it was going with the people from my grade, we started getting people from Javi's grade too. We've cleared up so many long-standing misconceptions that neither Javi nor I want to stop this classmate series yet. Plus Javi has started dating Derek Blake as a result of this, and I've got Ben, so we can't deny it's worked out well for us both personally and professionally. We're learning more than we ever could have imagined from these people we've known our whole lives, and it's made us truly love our work again.

Richie, our perpetually enthusiastic shortstop, comes up be-side Ben. "Please." He folds his bottom lip down. "We gotta do it up for this guy."

"Fine," I relent.

Richie high-fives me. Ben does too. It's taken a while to get the two of them back to this level of closeness, but with a lot of family therapy and some very strategically planned game nights on my part, they are almost the brothers I used to know way back when. Maybe even better, because now Ben is more hon-est with Richie about when he annoys him. Which is another victory worth celebrating—Ben not letting people walk all over him in the name of being nice. Although he's still too polite to tell his biological father about his pineapple allergy. After Ben and his mom reached out to Dr. Ward and told him the truth, Dr. Ward started sending us fruit arrangements on holidays. They always have pineapples in them. Ben calls and thanks Dr. Ward for the gift, and they have a brief, friendly conversation. Ben's not ready for anything more yet. It will take time. But the process has begun, and I'm so proud of him for continuing to try. His efforts have even inspired me. We're getting lunch with *my* dad next week.

"We need to be in bed early, though," I remind Ben. "A *promise is a promise.*"

He smiles at me. At us.

We all leave the dugout as clean as we found it. Then as a team, still in our matching green jerseys, we start our short trek to our third-floor brownstone, with the back porch Ben has converted into a full-blown enclosed catio. Abe is lounging out there when we return, soaking up the Chicago summer sun.

"Piddles!" Ben calls out.

He snaps his fingers together to draw Abe inside. We started saying Piddles as a bit. But like most things Ben and I do together, the joke became reality, and then it became habit. Lucky for me, it will never stop being funny when Ben uses the nickname with loving sincerity.

Abe trots into the living room. He nudges his head into Ben's hand, then mine, happy to have us home. Our friends follow shortly after, until our quaint, bright living room—with the orange accent wall Ben and I painted together, and the prominent dinosaur figurine we got at the Field Museum gift shop after Ben proposed to me in front of Sue the T. rex—gets filled with the sound of our laughter and conversation.

This life is so much different from the one we led a year ago, though most pieces are the same. They're just rearranged to better suit us. Ben still teaches in Indiana. The drive takes him thirty minutes most mornings. Forty on the way back. But now he *plays* baseball in the summer instead of coaching it. Even though we're the worst team in the league, he loves it. It's something for him. Not for others.

This baseball thing has changed me too. It's fun. It's hard. I don't have to worry about whether or not it will make me money, because none of us are playing to win, and I'm not the only one earning income for my household anymore. I play to hang out with my friends. To keep myself young. To stay humble.

Then at night, I get to sleep beside Ben Porter. What could be better?

We've created a life we love, no one piece all mine or all Ben's. Everything here is ours. And we intend to keep it that way forever.

ACKNOWLEDGMENTS

I wrote this book during the earlier parts of the pandemic. For several months, Dee and Ben were my very best imaginary friends, keeping me company when no one else could. I came to know them so well that it was almost impossible to actually write about them. That's how close they felt to me. And maybe it's strange, but because of that, I want to start this section by thanking myself. Good job, Bridgey. You did it! The book exists! I am proud of you!

Kerry Donovan, my fantastic editor, thank you a million times over for your truly touching feedback. You knew just what to say to help me get this book to shine. I am so lucky to work with you! I remain deeply amazed and in awe of the entire Berkley team. Mary Baker, Fareeda Bullert, Angelina Krahn, and everyone else who had a hand in bringing this book to life: You are all rock stars to me. Vi-An Nguyen, thank you for another knockout cover design! You captured Dee and Ben perfectly.

As always, I am eternally grateful to my agent, Taylor Haggerty, for making this book possible and continuing to guide me. Shout-out to Jasmine Brown and the rest of the awesome Root Literary team as well for all your incredible hard work!

Hollis, even when the pandemic limited our friendship to FaceTime and texting, our four hands stayed glued to the wheel. Time's not linear, so we are already in Maine, and we always will be. Alex, you already know the Goldfish are for you. Thank you for scouting all of LA's bowling alleys with me, and for *always* committing to the bit. Ryan E., the best roommate in the world, I look forward to every knock you place at my door, even when I'm napping. I'd be nowhere without your sweet tea, banana pudding, big heart, and good stories. Jake, my non-biological twin, no one can touch the heights of our nostalgia. We are children of District 145, forever competing in life's spelling bees together. Mia (Mimi to me), thank you for being such a constant, joyous presence in my life. May we never spend a single Thanksgiving apart. Ryan S., all your sweet voice memos are treasures, just like you. Mo, whether it's coffee or campaigning, you are a bright spot in my day. Brittany, Caeli Lu (Ray), and Vince: I feel unexplainably lucky to have had all of you in my life for nearly two decades now. We are FOURever friends.

To my writer pals, whew! I love you big-time. Emily and Austin, our friendship is no timeline anomaly. Every single day you two bowl me over with your generosity, talent, and care. This one is for the Sims and all the rabbit holes we fall down. Aminah, my dream friend, thank you so much for the ice cream deliveries and the virtual writing sprints we did when we couldn't meet up in person. Bree, Farrah, Maura, and my new online writer friends who bless me with excitement and insight: It's so cool to be a part of this community with you. I really cherish getting to grow together and getting to read the beautiful stories you write.

Much love to my parents; my sisters Liz, Raina, and Rose; my brother, John; and my nieces and nephews: Deklin, Brielle,

Caleb, Brannon, Lily, Emma, and Sophie. Rose, you're still my best reader. Thanks for the phone call with this one. I needed it.

To Jemma, my unforgettable angry cat, you were around for half of my life, and every minute, even when you were hissing, was a gift. I could never write a cat like you, because no words could do justice to your complexity. You live in the window of my heart now.

And finally, to every reader who has chosen one of my books to keep them company, I am more grateful than I can ever properly express. It is, as always, a supreme honor to have you here.

Keep reading for an excerpt from
Bridget Morrissey's novel . . .

LOVE SCENES

Available in paperback from Jove!

Week One of Production

Slumped into my sectional with cold pasta in my lap and a glass of water balanced against a pillow, I type my name into the Netflix search bar.

S-L-O-A-N-E.

F-O-R-D.

The first four seasons of my crime scene procedural *The Seeker* come up first. There I am with a dark brunette bob, wearing a lab coat and hustling around, giving everyone coy looks while cracking guarded jokes, making sure my harmless crush on Detective Colfax is only a touch better disguised than my chest, which is always slightly revealed in a V-neck.

The Seeker has filmed almost one hundred episodes. Ninety-two feature me as a clever-but-soft blood spatter analyst named Tess, best known for her ability to coldly analyze a dead body, then turn all fluttery and fumbling around her crush. Not a single one features anything I need to see right now. Getting surprisingly killed off in the third episode of the fifth season of a critically ignored drama? One my own family doesn't even bother to tune in for anymore?

That's punishment enough.

A strange crackle coming from the direction of my kitchen

startles me. At 3:43 in the morning, the television is my only source of light, softly glowing onto my tear-swollen face. Otherwise my house is pitch-dark.

For an agonizing stretch I sit frozen, ticking down my options.

1. It's an intruder coming to murder me, and my only weapons are an Apple TV remote, a lethal dose of self-pity, and a fork.

2. It's my younger sister Tyler ending our unspoken stand-off and surprising me with a visit, ready to crash in her old bedroom before our first day of shooting tomorrow.

3. It's one of the constant murmurs of this strange old place in the hills of Laurel Canyon, full of crooked nooks and squeaking floorboards. Sloped ceilings and a small stained glass window in the bathroom of all places.

It's obviously number three, I decide with a tentative exhale.

This home was meant for shared gasps at unexplained sounds. For laughter to cover the bristle of shrubbery in the backyard. But Tyler's got her own condo now. A girlfriend to live with and a rescue pup.

I've got leftover bucatini on my lap and a deep-seated fear that I'm not talented enough to ever work in this town again.

Below *The Seeker*, there's one other Sloane Ford property available to stream. And of course it's *A Little Luck*, because even Netflix is mocking me. The last thing I want to watch is Joseph Donovan's smug grin while I self-soothe with cold pasta and light crying.

A *Little Luck* was by far the worst filming experience I've ever had. Thinking of that production sends a shiver down my spine, especially considering what I'm facing tomorrow.

Which is exactly why I press play.

The film opens on the lush Irish countryside, cast against searing gray skies. In spite of myself, the sight still makes me suck back a longing breath, gulping like the Killarney breezes are once again lashing my cheeks.

The opener is an overhead tracking shot, following me on a bicycle as I wheel through town. My stunt double shot most of it. It's a seamless transition from her to me. By the time I park my bike next to the market and take off my helmet, only a trained eye would notice that my shoulders aren't quite as defined as hers. My skin a shade paler. The dyed red of my hair a touch more yellow.

The first twenty minutes are pretty stale. My work is fine—I was still doing too much with my face back then, a theater tic I've put a lot of conscious effort toward calming. Mom told me not to start with stage training. She said to do on-camera work and scene study classes outside of college and get a degree in something else. Dad told me he cut his teeth in the theater when he went to California State back in the day, and that all great actors need that kind of foundation.

As usual, I listened to the wrong parent.

A *Little Luck* drags on until—it pains me to even think it— Joseph Donovan appears. He's the stock boy at the costume store where my character is working. She's an American who has taken a year off school to find herself in Ireland. He's staying in town to save money and earn back his family's farm after they're forced to sell. It doesn't make a lot of sense, but this isn't a movie designed to require an examination of the specifics. It's all about glances. Touches. Wind through hair as lovers kiss atop a cliff.

Off-screen, you hear me say, "Excuse me, it's my first day here. I'm not sure where I'm supposed to go."

Joseph stops lifting boxes, back to the audience. His right hand lingers for a beat. Then he turns toward the camera lens—slowly, methodically—daring us to look away from the chiseled angles of his upsettingly exceptional face.

The director set up the shot so we meet Joseph by gazing up at his six-foot-three frame. His blue eyes pop against the cream of his Aran sweater. A native of Ireland himself, Joseph complained the iconic look was too on the nose. Wardrobe didn't budge. They wanted this moment. The stark contrast of Joseph's boyish features and his brooding edges. His dark blond hair combed into a subtle swish. His ocean-swept eyes touched with hints of sadness. And the brogue. It was all about the brogue melting off those lips.

Good god. It's no wonder I loathe him.

I make it a few more minutes into the movie before deciding there's no way I can watch myself kiss that bastard tonight. Smug asshole. Most unprofessional man I have ever worked with in my entire career. And goddamn brilliant on-screen in spite of it.

His career has skyrocketed since we shot this. And I'm hours away from the start of a made-up producing job handed to me by my famous family to fill the void of my most recent bout of unemployment.

I close my eyes, trying to sleep, needing to wake up in fighting form.

But Joseph Donovan's features are carved into my mind,

etched against the backs of my eyelids like the sun at high noon, burning me.

My mother greets my late arrival with an unbroken stare, arms folded across her chest and aviator sunglasses tipped down past the bridge of her nose, leaned up against the wall of Stage 15. She's wearing a baby-blue crewneck tucked into a pair of tight black jeans. Her long blond locks are in a ponytail pulled through a black ball cap, but she's left the bang pieces out to frame her face, because she hates when she looks too severe.

From this distance, she could easily pass for a twenty-five-year-old. Even up close, actually. She has the skin of someone who has had a professional aesthetician for decades, and the unmistakable glow of a person who cherishes being important to strangers. It's the hard-earned confidence that gives her age away. The no-bullshit facade of a fifty-eight-year-old woman who has seen it all and is no longer impressed by any of it. When the acting world turned on her, she picked herself up and transformed into a producer, intending to make a better life for other women in the business.

Right now she looks ready to turn on me just as effectively.

"Do you really not care about this?" she asks. Years of smoking have left an indelible mark on her voice, a sandpaper grittiness that's as iconic as her beaming smile.

"Hi, Mom. Good to see you too. Yes. Everything is okay. Thank you for worrying." It's hard not to wheeze, having done my best power walking impression to get to her, not a drop of caffeine in my system to offset my lack of sleep.

"You look tired." She pinches my skin, then gives me a perfunctory cheek kiss. "We've got a lot to cover in not a lot of time. I'm gonna be running around today, so I need you to keep eyes on everyone and make sure we're running a tight ship. You know how crucial the first few days are in establishing a tone. It starts at the top of the chain, Sloane."

"I'd hardly call myself the top of the chain here," I quip. "You made my job up."

The look she gives me makes actual goose bumps form along my arms.

"I'm sorry," I correct. "I turned off my alarm instead of hitting snooze. It was an accident that will never happen again."

"Oh, Sloaney, please don't act like you're new to this. Not now. Always set at least three backup alarms. I can't have everyone on set thinking you can get away with whatever you want just because you're my kid." She says all of this without breaking pace, dragging me along like we're doing our own Aaron Sorkin walk and talk. "At least you're dressed well."

The only helpful decision I made last night was to set this morning's outfit out on my dresser, feeling that strange kind of restless dread that made me both overplan and underprepare. Naturally I've ended up in nearly the same look as Mom, only in a different color scheme, with my shirt a muted yellow, my jeans a vivid blue, and my unplanned ball cap a heather gray. The best thing about having a long bob is being able to plant a hat on my head and have my whole style look intentionally casual, when the truth is I barely had time to brush my teeth, much less my hair.

"Twins." I gesture to our complementary ensembles, hoping to lighten the mood.

"Don't be generous," she scoffs. "I haven't been allowed to play a thirty-year-old since I was twenty-five."

This version of my mother—Kitty Porter: *boss lady*—is utterly incorrigible. I never thought I'd say it, but I miss her usual wandering 6:00 a.m. phone calls to me, talking about her cats and her yoga mat and her favorite Brené Brown quotes.

She once spent twenty full minutes detailing the way the sunlight in her office was streaming onto a picture of Tyler; our younger brother, Powell; and me. It's a black-and-white portrait shot by Annie Leibovitz, and we're all piled onto one another like puppies. Tyler was eleven and had recently chopped off all her hair but hadn't yet solved how to style it. It was a scrappy brunette mess, dangerously close to bowl cut territory. Powell was nine and cute as ever. As far as I'm concerned, he still looks the same. Like a soft butter roll just out of the oven, with his hair that same iconic blond as Mom's. And then there was fourteen-year-old me rocking the classic braces-and-bangs combo, my hair a greasy brown and ironed straight as a pin. Even the bangs.

"I won't screw up again." The tremble in my voice surprises me. She hasn't made me this nervous since I bravely admitted to her that despite her sage advice, I was going to study acting in college after all.

"Good." She does the eagle-eyed hand gesture she picked up from Robert De Niro in *Meet the Parents*. "Keep eyes on everything. And make sure Tyler's calm."

"I'm on it."

The problem is, I haven't looked at the call sheet. I don't know who the first AD or the second AD is. Or what we're shooting today.

Knowing too much hurts too much. It amplifies the ugly voice in the back of my head that reminds me that once upon a time, the leading role in this production was supposed to be mine.

I do know that the movie has a working title of *Horizons*. It's a romantic World War II drama. My stepdad wrote it. My sister's directing it alongside him. My mom's going to be acting in it for the first time in almost twenty years. She's playing a supporting role, a widow named Vera who battles an illness while also having a secret love affair with the Black woman who lives down the hall. That role will be played by my dad's other ex-wife, Melanie Davidson, mother of my youngest sister, Sarai, who just turned eleven and surprisingly does not have a part in this project. *Yet.*

It's a good old-fashioned nepotistic family circus over here.

And in another world, I would be the center of it all. The face on the poster. The top of the call sheet. The main character, a schoolteacher named Elise whose life gets upended when her old neighbor returns home from the war right as her mother's illness is progressing.

Instead I'm here as a consulting producer, and no one—not even me—has any idea what that job really entails.

When I was growing up, summertime meant moviemaking time. Tyler would take one of our parents' fancy video cameras into the backyard of whichever house we were staying at for the week, and she'd direct Powell and me through one of our many terrible homemade remakes. Who isn't a fan of two siblings playing love interests that refuse to even hug? Makes for a stunning re-creation of *Titanic*.

In spite of Powell and me begging Tyler to turn every remake into an action film where we kill each other, there was a magic to our backyard passion projects. A desire among all three of us siblings to find a way to capture a good story. We could transform the pool at Mom's Calabasas mansion into the Atlantic in 1912. We could turn the gate in front of Dad's Beverly Hills estate into the prison cell from *Chicago*.

I started visiting my parents on set when I was old enough to walk. I've watched directors yell in my mother's face for no reason. Sat in my dad's trailer while he argued with important people about call times and script changes and hairpieces. Witnessed my parents' marriage to each other dissolve before my eyes, all over on-set jealousies, box office numbers, and critical praise favoring one of them over the other. I know how terrible and toxic show business really is. I've always known.

But there's a part of me that's always wished for it to feel like it did in the backyard with my siblings. Pure and spontaneous and fun, fueled solely by the desire to create something memorable together.

We almost have that here.

Almost.

Most of the soundstage has been transformed into the entire fourth floor of a 1940s apartment building, with cameras around the apartment that Elise shares with Vera. Their living room is done up in muted reds and soft lavenders. There's just the right amount of clutter. Stacks of papers probably meant to be Elise's writings. Sewing and knitting tools strewn about. A coffee mug resting on a faded newspaper. A small window for daylight to spill through.

I wander into this half shell of a home, feeling truly awake for the first time this morning, running my finger across the coffee table as if expecting to collect dust. That's how lived-in and real this world feels, with the magical, curated quality only a good film set can bring.

Life, but bigger somehow. Safer.

The kitchen is off to the side, as narrow as a tunnel with faded checkerboard tiles on the floor. This is where the leads will have part of their big love scene. A flame of jealousy flares up inside me. It takes a village to get a great performance out of an actor. I know if I were Haven Church, I'd be really excited by all the work my family has done to help her bring Elise to life.

But I'm not Haven Church. I don't have twenty-three million followers on Instagram or an entire generation of young people who grew up watching me on my own multi-cam sitcom. I am thirty years old, my career hanging on by a fraying thread, only here because of a very embarrassing opening in my schedule that's allowed me to be completely free for the next five weeks.

"Looks magnificent, no?"

To my left stands the writer and codirector of this movie, and Mom's new husband, Guy Cicero. *New* is the wrong word, because they've been married for fifteen years, but any person after Dad will always be new. As is anyone after Mom on his side. Unspoken rules of divorce.

"It's really good," I tell him as he pulls me into a tight, sincere hug. "Thanks for letting me be a part of it after all. I'm sorry I'm late."

"Please! Of course! You know I always wanted you here with us." Guy makes a broad gesture, his arm circling the whole soundstage, stopping once he's swept past me. "It is *almost* as I pictured it all," he says, leaving me to interpret that as I please.

"It's perfect," I assure him.

"No. But it's a place for an adventure to begin." He pauses with his typical flourish. "Your sister was looking for you, by the way."

He proceeds to follow me until we find Tyler huddled in a dark corner behind the bathroom set, poring over the shot bible. Her hair is shorter, only a few centimeters past a buzz cut, and she's got on her signature slouchy black clothes, draping off all her sharper angles. She's always been so much longer and leaner than me you'd think we had one different parent between us. But she got Mom's flawless skin and Dad's angled jawline, and I got Mom's button nose and Dad's thick brows. Powell got almost nothing from Dad at all. He's Mom 2.0: blond hair, forest-green eyes, and a smile that lights up like a Christmas tree.

Tyler's the coolest of the three of us, catching the best genetics and the most interesting personality traits. Secretly soft inside with a fascinatingly serene exterior. A wicked sense of humor that appears in hushed tones, only heard if you're paying close attention. And a silly side that's even more private, coming out in moments of sheer hysteria, like when the two of us stayed up for an entire night doing impressions of our dad, making each other laugh so hard that my stomach was sore for three days afterward.

She and I haven't seen each other in person since Dad was in the hospital. Our last communication of any kind was via professional email regarding my role on set. Truthfully, the haunting memory of her signing off from that interaction by typing out *Warmly, Tyler* was the only thing with enough power to wake me up today.

We both know my taking this producing job came solely from the emotional toll of Dad's heart attack. Reality hits harder under hospital lights. You forgive before you're ready. You agree to responsibilities you don't actually want because it means being around people you love, even when they make you so upset you could scream.

I tap her on the shoulder.

"You made it," she says when she realizes it's me, letting out an audible sigh.

"Of course. Couldn't miss your directorial debut." It comes out sarcastic when I actually meant it to be earnest.

The words sit in the air, stale.

"Remind me what we're shooting today?" I ask.

"You shithead. You didn't even look at the schedule, did you?"

Admitting incompetence has always been the fastest way to even the playing field between us.

"We're doing all of Calvin and Elise's first kiss," she continues. "And the beginning of their second kissing scene."

"I always say to start with the tough stuff," Guy chimes in. "That way you're sure that what you have is going to work. *Throw the actors to the wolves.*"

He's wearing a backward newsboy cap and thin glasses with light yellow frames. A timelessly Guy Cicero ensemble. The happiest-looking half-Cuban, half-Italian man to ever wear a corduroy blazer with patches on the elbows. It's as if I can see him delivering this exact line on the set of every movie he's ever made, the actors standing before him ever changing and him staying almost exactly the same, the passage of time only evident through the creasing around his eyes.

"He wanted our first day to be the full sex scene. I was like, 'Guy, these people just met,'" Tyler adds. "We don't do movies like that anymore."

Guy throws his hands up. "I know, I know. But in a movie like this, if the sex scene doesn't work, the whole thing is a bust!"

I give him the laugh he's looking for. We can't let this be awkward. We have to be professionals here.

Except we're also family. Hard to set boundaries with each other when we've never had them before.

To pivot, I shake hands with him, and then with Tyler, who looks confused until I say, "As your resident consulting producer, thank you *so much* for this consultation. I look forward to many more."

"You're the worst," she tells me. Then she goes serious so fast it gives me emotional whiplash. "Thank you for doing this, Bub. I know this won't be easy for you. I really appreciate it."

"Of course," I say quickly, not looking to dwell. "I'm gonna go get some coffee."

It's a quiet scene by craft services. Crew members move around in all directions like ants on a hill, finalizing small details until it's time for action. My entire drive here, I told myself not to care. That no good would come from wishing things had been different.

No matter how it came about, taking this producing job was ultimately my choice. And I will commit to it like I commit to everything else in my life: headfirst while silently panicking.

"Would ya look at who it is?"

The voice stops me in my tracks, my hand midway toward reaching for a banana. I cover for the pause as best I can, desperate not to reveal even the slightest trace of nerves.

"Is that not Sloane Ford I see? Staring at the fruit bowl like it's tea leaves telling her a fortune?"

I turn around, and there he stands in a taupe button-down, sleeves rolled up to midbicep, suspenders holding up loose brown slacks. He has on circular wire-rim glasses, and his hair is combed back to show us every pore of his deceivingly cherubic face.

My hand squeezes the banana so tight that the insides start to push out of the skin.

Joseph fucking Donovan.

"Can I help you?" I ask, keeping my tone even.

He has the nerve to laugh. A piece of his newly darkened

hair dares to fall across his forehead like he's an Irish James Dean. He's trying to charm away all the bad feelings between us, using his brogue like it's got some sort of mystical power over American women.

"Funny way to greet a war hero such as myself."

I take it all in. The prosthetic burns on the tops of his hands. The trace of a fake scar above his left eyebrow. The calculated swoop of his hair. He looks every bit the part of the romantic hero. Unfortunately, no amount of costuming can cover up his incompetence.

"It wasn't meant to be a greeting." I look past him as if I can see in the distance some task that requires my immediate attention.

He follows my eye, seeing nothing, then whips around again. Smirking. "I was surprised to hear you turned down Elise."

"As if I was going to take the role with you as Calvin. Now if you'll excuse me, I have some stuff to do." I leave my squished banana inside the basket, quietly cursing myself for not pouring a cup of coffee first.

"Wait a second."

Joseph jogs up to meet me. He rests his hand on my shoulder to stop my momentum. When I turn to face him, he looks puzzled.

"I want this shoot to go well," he says.

I suppress an eye roll. "I'm sure you do."

"I'm catering lunch today," he explains, like it's meant to impress me. It *is* a nice gesture, one that always helps to establish a good tone on set, but it doesn't need to be announced.

"Okay." He cannot possibly expect me to give him credit. Not after what we've been through.

"It's coming from a small spot over on Magnolia in the Valley. They do a proper spread."

"Nice."

"It's the least I could do," he says.

"Most definitely."

"I hope you know I'm really grateful for this job."

I can't help but stare at him. Silent. Processing.

Stewing.

"Sloane, I know this'll sound like a joke, but I'm not who I used to be," he says finally. His eyes cut into me so deep I almost believe him.

Then I remember what an incredible actor he is. Emmy nominated just last year.

Nothing good comes from believing a man like Joseph Donovan.

I stumble away from him, nearly knocking over a set wall in the process.

"You forgot your banana," he calls out.

"No I didn't," I call back.

This is exactly why I should've trusted my instincts when I first said I didn't want any part in making this movie. Because here I am. Headfirst. And silently panicking.

Provvidenza Catalano 2020

Bridget Morrissey lives in Los Angeles, California, but hails from Oak Forest, Illinois. When she is not writing, she can be found coaching gymnastics or headlining concerts in her living room.

Ready to find
your next great read?

Let us help.

Visit prh.com/nextread

Penguin
Random
House